Something to Live For

Velma and Reba Rush Ellyson

PublishAmerica
Baltimore

© 2010 by Velma and Reba Rush Ellyson.
All rights reserved. No part of this book may be reproduced, stored in a retrieval system or transmitted in any form or by any means without the prior written permission of the publishers, except by a reviewer who may quote brief passages in a review to be printed in a newspaper, magazine or journal.

First printing

All characters in this book are fictitious, and any resemblance to real persons, living or dead, is coincidental.

PublishAmerica has allowed this work to remain exactly as the author intended, verbatim, without editorial input.

Hardcover 978-1-4489-6160-3
Softcover 978-1-4489-4357-9
PUBLISHED BY PUBLISHAMERICA, LLLP
www.publishamerica.com
Baltimore

Printed in the United States of America

*This book is dedicated to my Mother, Reba, who started it,
my dear friend, Maggie, who encouraged me to finish it,
my father, Hayden, who nurtured my love of history
and to all my ancestors who chose this beautiful state, West Virginia,
in which to settle so I can call it my home.*

Reba Ellyson, my Mother, started writing this book when I was in high school. I typed it for her. Years later, I found the brittle, yellow, faded pages she had started in the bottom of a box of family photographs.

1

It seemed that life had always held breathlessness for Callie Morris with a current of uncertainty like the flowing water beneath the surface of Calico Creek. She was never sure of just what she was actually remembering; what was the result of her expansive imagination. Sometimes her imagination made her clamp her teeth together until a sharp, razor-like pain brought a moment of forgetfulness. Her remembrances and imagination were somehow linked with and a part of the glistening, narrow, twisting mountain creek called Calico. Combined, they made her days and nights seem to be made of some hazy material shot through with streaks of vivid color.

The creek and its name seemed to be inseparable from her. When she had been very small, she thought she was Calico. Later the sound of it seemed to be a faraway place. Then there were the frightening times when Calico seemed to be a menacing, distorted very old woman who clutched at her. There were other times when the word was a song or a picture of a young woman with laughter in her eyes leaning over Callie and about ready to lift her up. When the world was this, she felt all safe and warm inside.

She overheard Mama, Uncle Jim and Mammy talk about a Calico. Sometimes it was with happy voices, sometimes sad.

"Remember the ball for my sixteenth birthday at Calico Place, Jim?" Mama had asked as she and Uncle Jim sat in their willow wood rockers in front of the field stone fireplace with a roaring fire lighting the room.

"How could I possibly forget, Caroline? You were definitely the bell of the ball that night."

"I just loved that lavender taffeta dress with lace and pearl trim around the neck. When I swirled around the floor the taffeta rustled. And remember, Mammy, you had fixed my hair special for that night? You'd put fresh flowers in between the braids like around a crown on my head and you made ringlets to hang down my back. Remember that Mammy?"

"Yes'em I shoo' do. Yo' was a site fo' sore eyes dat nite. I's don't think I's seen a person look mo' lak' an angel in my life." Mammy spoke from the kitchen where she was washing the supper dishes.

"Remember Mama had let me wear her special pearl necklace with matching long dangling pearl earrings. She even let me wear her pearl bracelet and matching ring. I loved them."

Uncle Jim interrupted Mama and Mammy's conversation. "What I remember was thinking I never would get my turn to dance with you that night. Every young man from miles around in Jackson County had come hoping he'd have a chance to dance with you. It was a miracle I got to dance with you that one time."

Mama threw back her head, laughed in a lilting manner and even her eyes seemed to be laughing.

"And that night I met ..." Suddenly sadness came over her face.

Uncle Jim reached across the space that separated their two rocking chairs and patted her hand.

"Callie chil, I don't sees yo' come in. Git over her an' let me git dat creek dirt off'en yo' face." With Mammy's words, Mama and Uncle Jim stopped talking.

Today was one of the times when Callie needed to think of Mama as the beautiful young woman with laughter in her eyes. Mama had been staying in her bed most of the time for the last few weeks. She would have weak spells when her whole body would shake; shake so much that it seemed the bed would collapse. Beautiful Mama would be exhausted after one of these spells. Mammy would wipe her brow with a soft wet rag. Callie would sit by her bed, hold Mama's hand or stroke Mama's graying auburn hair. Then Mammy would sing a soft song, one that a mother would sing as she cradled her baby in her arms. Eventually Mama would fall asleep.

This morning Mama had had one of her weak spells. If Callie were not careful, Mammy Jo would turn into the menacing old woman who clutched at her. In fact, Mammy had almost seemed like that evil one just a moment ago.

Mammy had hurried Callie out of the cabin door with, "Go long chil. Yo' Mama need sum quiet frum' yo'. Her heart so tiawd. Been dat' way since

8

SOMETHING TO LIVE FOR

Calico Place. Yo' jest traypinsin' heah; traypisin' there. She ain't gonna git no rest wuth' yo'heah. Go 'long now. Go to da' creek; see if you can fin' sum' creasy greens fo' supper. Yo' heah me chil? Git!"

Callie knew no reason for Mammy's impatience. She hadn't been "traypinsin' heah; traypisin' there." She'd stroked Mama's hair until Mama had fallen asleep.

"HUM, sometimes Mammy Jo treats me no better than a stray animal," she thought. "But, I just have to forget Mammy's scolding me like that. It makes me have that scared feeling down deep in my stomach." When she got that feeling she wasn't sure who she really was or sure of anything for that matter.

She stretched out on the creek bank and watched the swiftly flowing water dash madly against the rocks. It burst into countless crystal balls. Its pale green changed into a sparkling diamond spray over and over again. Gradually the rhythm of the repeated action and warmth of the sun soothed her and she felt safe. She knew who she was and where she was. Calico Creek was an old friend.

Her mind wandered to the first time she thought she remembered seeing Calico Creek. Mama was standing right by that big rock on the rise near where the cabin stands. Calico Creek made a small bend at that site. She could still hear Mama's voice.

"There is no way to blot out all that has happened. Nor is there any way of foreseeing in the future, what will come. But we do know that as long as we have each other and Callie, we will have enough to live on because we will have something to live for."

The tall man Callie called Uncle Jim had sort of smiled as Mama went on.

"Perhaps it is even better, Jim, that we do remember the past. It's much better to live in the here and now; much better to live with our mistakes and over come them than to ignore them and let them grow; grow until they become twisted, dark, cruel things that strike back at us.

"We named our creek Calico, just as we named Callie," she paused "after something that is over yet something that can never really be over. Some day Callie's children will claim her name as theirs. They will attach none of the bitterness of the source of the names. It will be the same as this mountain creek joining a river. The river will lose itself in the immensity of the ocean.

9

There the water is evaporated and comes back again someday as rain to this little mountain creek. Everywhere there's continuity that cannot be denied."

At the time Mama had said those word, Callie hadn't been sure of what they meant but she had remember the big word continuity. It had a sound that she liked as she like the sound of Calico. Later she had asked Mama what the word meant. Mama had said that it just meant that things always go on and on. Callie even thought that the word itself sounded like that now and she called it one of her marching words.

Jim was another of her marching words and that wasn't because of its sound. It was because of Uncle Jim himself. He always stood straight as a stick and his shoulders seemed to be thrown slightly to his back making his chest push forward. When he walked, it was with deliberate steps that made him appear to be marching up and down the rise; marching anywhere he went. Then too, he always held his head so high and proud that Mama called him her soldier boy.

Lately though, Uncle Jim had slowed in his walk as if he had to be careful. His manner wasn't as casual as usual and he always seemed to be in a hurry. For days he would be gone from the cabin. Callie didn't know where he went or spent his time. She did know that he took trips back across the mountains to a place called Lewisburg and to the Jackson River country. She also knew that his trips were becoming more and more frequent.

After one of his trips across the mountains, Mama and Uncle Jim would talk for hours sitting in front of the fireplace or in the summer, the rocking chairs would be moved to the front porch for these conversations.

"I stopped by to call on Judge Moore. He asked about you, Caroline, and wanted to know how you were doing. His wife died this spring and he's all alone now in that big ole house except for the servants. Even his fields seemed to be getting rundown now that he's not able to oversee them anymore. That worthless son of his, Junior, ran off with some woman from Philadelphia just when he was needed most. People around Jackson County say she's been filling his head with that nonsense about freeing slaves and…" Abruptly, Uncle Jim stopped in mid sentence.

"It's alright, Jim. I've learned to accept the pain the 'Free the Slaves' movement can cause some people. But if there are three things I've done right in my life; marrying Calvin was one, having Callie is two and freeing Mammy is three." She paused. Then with that wonderful smile lighting up her face said, "No, there are four things I've done right in my life. The fourth is being lucky enough to have been born into the right family so I'd have you as my cousin."

Callie rolled over and watched a big ant creep from under a dry brown leaf. The ant crossed a dark, wet waxy leaf. The sun struck her in the middle of her shoulder blades and made her feel warm and drowsy. The stillness of the woods and the music that Calico Creek made began to erase all of the troublesome doubts and unanswered questions that she had about the conversations she'd overheard between Mama and Uncle Jim. She watched the ant move over and under leaves until her eyes felt very heavy. She closed them.

The piercing scream awakened her. At first, she thought it was a dream. In the next instant, she knew with clarity that she had heard it. She was running up the path to the cabin; the scream had come from Mammy. Suddenly the scream came again. Callie ran faster. The scream came again and this time, it seemed to echo and reecho. Ever after that moment, she would remember her frantic rush up the path, her breathless hesitancy on the threshold when everything in the world seemed to be still and suspended. She thought she was seeing things.

Mama was lying so strangely in her bed. Somehow, she looked more like Mama's doll, Liza, she had give to Callie; looked like Liza when Callie pretended Liza was asleep. Mammy was on her knees by the bed, her turbaned head bent over on the feather tick. She was sobbing uncontrollably. Callie knew now why Mammy had said those words this morning that had been puzzling her; "traypinsin' heah; traypisin' there." She knew now why Mama had said she believed she would rest for just a little while so often. Mama was very sick. Mama slept a lot. Maybe, maybe she might even just be asleep now.

This thought was blanked out by the plea that came from Mammy, "Oh Lawd, whut us gwine a do? Whut can us'ens do in dis' wilderness. Miss Caroline gone! Mist'a Jim off on one his trips."

Mammy's voice began to gather like the steam did in the kettle over the hearth fire. Callie knew a scream was sure to come again and that it would be more than she could stand. So she tried to speak like Mama did when Mammy said it was best for a thing to be this way and Mama wanted it to be done another way.

"MAMMY! Stop that nonsense! You know very well that Mama's still here! Stop that carrying on! Stop it right now!"

Slowly Mammy turned her eyes but they looked glazed and vacant. She gave a little jump, "Lawd Miss! U's scare me! Yo' look mo' lak ole Miss Caroline evah day yo' live! Lawd hav' mercy on us, po' Miss Caroline! Oh Lawd, she gone now, po' troubled chil. She gon' an' lef' us heah. Whut's we gwine do?"

Mammy began to get ready to scream again. Callie knew she must do something. Quickly she went over to the bed, grabbed Mammy's fat shoulders and with all of her strength shook her. "Mammy, you're being silly. Look here Mammy. She's not gone. I can touch her, see?"

Carefully she touched Mama's face and could hardly keep from screaming herself. Never had she felt anything like the awful cold of Mama's face under her hand. Her heart began to race. "There is something the matter with Mama! Something's terribly, terribly wrong. Mammy, stop that howling and get something warm to put over Mamma. She's so cold. Mammy! Do you hear me?"

This time Callie shook Mammy savagely. Slowly she turned to look at Callie. All the anguish of the human heart was in that look. Callie thought Mammy's eyes had the look of the doe Uncle Jim had not quite killed with one shot and had to shoot the second time. For days Callie could shut her eyes and still see that doe. She had not been able to eat any of its meat.

Mammy gave a long sigh and said with effort, "Chil yo' Mama gone. Gon, Lord hep huh. Lord luv' my chil's soul. She's gone wheah she ain't never comin' back frum. Miss Caroline's gon' to be wid de Lord Jesus. Lord, Lord, oh blessed Jesus, luv' my po' lil' Miss Caroline."

"Mammy, do you mean my Mama's dead? Mammy! Answer me! Answer me before I cut of a branch and whip you like they say my Grandmother use to do!"

"Lord chil, don't you' dare use Ole Miss name in da' presence of da' dead." Mammy raised her joined hands for prayer and looked to the ceiling. "Lord hep us po' sinners an' hep de soul of my po' lil' Miss Caroline to git safe to you'. An' please Lord, giv' huh rest, she ben so tiawd fo' so long. She's had so much trouble on dis earth. She ben through a powerful lot ev'ah since Ole Miss done what she done."

Mammy's words allowed Callie to accept that Mama was dead; dead just like the animals Uncle Jim shot.

"Mammy! This is no time for carrying on. There're things we must do, things Mama would want done. I can't do them by myself." Callie thought her voice sounded like it belonged to someone else. The words were hollow but they seemed to bring Mammy back to reality.

"Lawd yes, chil, we has mo' to do now then evah befo'. An' we cain't do it by ourselvfs neithah. In 'de mornin' somehow we got to fine Misser Jim or go back to Ole Miss."

"Ole Miss? Do you mean Mama's Mother at Calico Place when you say Ole Miss?"

"Yes, Chil, Ole Miss yo' Mama's Mama… an' yo' Grandmother. Dat who yo' live wid' 'til we's comes heah. Yo' Mama livin' all huh life wuff Ole Miss at Calico Place almos'. Yo' wuz born dare too. Dare Miss Caroline hev' all she want an' evah thin' she should hav'. Dat is she hav' evah thing shes want frum Ole Miss 'til she meet yo' Daddy. Den when she wants him, Ole Miss say no. Fo' da fust time ev-ah Miss Caroline ax's for somethin', Ole Miss say no. Sometin' get de matter wid Miss Caroline den, nothin' or nobody can do nothin' to kee huh frum yo' Papa."

"What was the matter with my Daddy, Mammy?"

Mammy seemed not to hear. Callie knew that she had forgotten that she was even there in the room because she was so troubled about Mama. She might as well let her go on; anything was better than screaming.

"Miss Caroline say she follow dat Calvin Morris to da ends of da earth. Dat she follow him weah-evah he go. Dat she would hav' him no mattah whut Ole Miss say or do. An dat 'xactly why we's here. She sneak 'way and marry yo' Daddy ovah in Westmoreland County. Den yo' Daddy lef' Jackson Rivah 'n cum to 'dis side of da mountains. He thinks he can make it easier heah an' dey might hav' a chance at bein' happy. Evah thing might hab been alright effen we's hadn't cross da mountains. Lawdy but he wuz wrong. Ole Miss puts a spell on all us no matta where's we's go. Yo' Daddy an' Miss Caroline nevah hev a chance."

Callie heard her dog, Rim, tied by a chain behind the cabin start barking.

Bitterness showed in Mammy's face but Callie stood spellbound. Here were some answers to some of the questions that had always bothered her.

"Misser Jim, he hep' us to git ta yo' Papa. First wintah we's heah, yo' Daddy get a chill, den da fe'vaa an' die. Miss Caroline write an' ax Misser Jim den to come back an' take care ov us. Misser Jim come' lak Miss Caroline kno'ed he would. He always hers tho' he huh cousin. Lawd how Misser Jim luv' my po' lil' Miss! He take care of huh, take care all us'ens. Oh Lawd, wheah's he now? Why don' he come back fo' us? Some how we have to fin' him in dis wilderness now or ——?"

Suddenly Mammy's voice stopped in mid sentence. The flames from the fireplace outlined a huge grotesque shape standing just inside the cabin. Callie's heart began to pound with a new and heavy sharpness. Suddenly she saw that the shape moved silently into the cabin.

The next moment there were two; then three shapes turned into men. Mammy's eyes got bigger and bigger. The whites got as white as Mama's six bone china plates. From Mammy's throat, came a sound Callie knew she would hear forever. She saw a muscular arm lift, saw a big wide knife on a handle flash in the fires light. In came smashing down into the top of Mammy's head and a red gooey ooze popped out of the top of Mammy's head.

Mammy's fat squat figure seemed to spin crazily like a leaf caught in the current of Calico Creek. Stark terror clutched at Callie. A gurgling, rumble like sound came from Mammy. Old Rim began to bark franticly. Momentarily the men were distracted.

In that brief moment of time, Callie slid into the dark, safe shadows of the cabins walls. One of the men found the cabinet where food was kept and with animal greed, the others rushed to get their share. That was lucky for Callie. She gained the cabin's door. The sooty blackness of night engulfed her.

Uncertainty and fears of the day, the terror of the attack on Mammy were no longer nameless. They were very near, very real and one thought began to shape in her mind. She must put distance between herself and the dark fearful shapes that became men.

Rocks stabbed through her soft moccasins, briers clutched and tore her dress. She could think of nothing but the fear that took her very breath. With knowledge of the mountain trails, she had but one hope. If she followed Calico Creek down stream, it would lead her to lower ground on its way a larger river. Every part of her body ached. Darkness took over the world. She felt as if she had to keep running even in the dark; she fell headfirst and then tumbled down the side of the mountain. Aching from head to toe, she crawled under a bush too exhausted to think, hurting too much to go on.

Callie Morris, age fifteen, slept in the mountain vastness, a mountain wilderness know to the outside world as the Virginia territory of West Au-

SOMETHING TO LIVE FOR

gusta in 1861. It was the western most part of Virginia. Some called it the land beyond the Alleghenies. Callie Morris who had been unsure of herself before, who had so many unanswered questions, now had had everything taken from her. Her only links with safety was a man long overdue from an unexplained and unknown destination and a small mountain creek. She thought it eventually flowed into a river called Kanawha according to what she had heard Uncle Jim say.

The morning was hazy with fog. Fresh dew covered the ground. She was stiff and did not feel like herself. The air seemed thick and damp. She felt as if it had seeped in to her body; she felt like soggy half-baked pone. Her legs moved as if they were made of stone. When she made a step, millions of nails seemed to stick in the bottom of her feet. She stood and looked about her. Surely, there was some way to find Calico Creek and the cabin. She couldn't leave Mama with those dreadful men. Even if they killed her too, she had to get back to Mama and Mammy.

The fog lifted slightly and Callie could see a mountain on her left. There would be boulders on the mountain that she could use as a spy rock to see over the country. Many times she had listened to Uncle Jim tell stories of how the white man had learned to use them as the Indians had done. Without hesitation, she began to move towards the mountain. Her legs pained her and the bottom of her feet were cut and bruised. She ached all over but she kept on; she knew that everything depended on her finding Calico Creek again.

When the sun was high in the sky, she still had seen no sign of Calico Creek. She was just about to sit down at the futility of it all and give in to the river of tears that was building up inside her, when she noticed the beginning of a cliff far to the right. With new strength, Callie kept on until she stood on the very edge of the jutting rock. Almost doubting that she was actually seeing what she was seeing below her, she yelled with delight, "There it is!"

Below her was the twisting and turning ribbon that was Calico Creek. Now she cared little for the jagged-rock pain in her feet. She had direction. All she had to do was to get to that stream, follow it upstream. Eventually it would lead her to the little knoll where the cabin stood.

It was well along into late afternoon when she heard Rim barking. She started running in the direction from where his barking came. Then she saw the cabin in the distance. No smoke rose from the chimney. It looked utterly alone as if no one lived there. Callie knew though that the bodies of Mama and Mammy were there.

Uncle Jim had often played the game he called Indian warriors with Callie. Now she realized that he had really been teaching her something of value. She knew just how to creep up on the cabin as an Indian would, creep silently as she and Uncle Jim had often done when they had pretended they were about to rescue a trapped settler right out from under the Indians noses. She must go on to the cabin even if she wasn't for sure if those men were still inside or not. Now was not the time to be afraid. She had to take care of Mama and Mammy. Her heart began to race and she was almost sick at her stomach when she thought of the red ooze and Mammy's head. She took a deep breath, swallowed hard and kept on creeping towards the cabin.

At last, she could look into the window. She took a deep breath, clamped her hand over her mouth, held her breath for a few seconds and felt a little dizzy. She could hardly keep from screaming.

Uncle Jim sat with bowed head by Mama's bed holding one of her hand. She glanced around the room and saw that he had done something with Mammy. Even the blood had been cleaned from the floor. Mammy was not there.

She entered the doorway.

"Uncle Jim! Is it really you?"

"Callie! Child, where in heavens name have you been? I thought those dammed renegades had taken you with them. There is no limit to what those thieving bastards will do. For the love of God, what did they do to Caroline?"

"Nothing, Uncle Jim. Mama was already dead when they came." She paused and bit her lip to keep from screaming. "But Mammy, oh Uncle Jim, you should have seen Mammy's head."

Callie felt her stomach sort of leap and her mouth felt salty, yet bitter and warm. She swallowed quickly. Then without warning, a black velvety curtain came up from the floor, threw itself over her and pulled her to the floor with it.

The sun was coming through the west window when Callie woke. For a moment, she thought she had been dreaming all the terrible events of the past two days. A fire burned in the stone fireplace; she smelled hoecakes. Outside she heard the methodical hammering of nails being pounded into wood. She went to the door and saw Uncle Jim covered in sawdust. Under a large oak tree near the woods, she saw a fresh mound of dirt with a wooden cross tied together with raw hide.

Slowing inside her, a scream began to form. She knew what she was seeing. Uncle Jim was making a coffin box. Without being told, she knew her beautiful Mama would be placed inside with the boards nailed down tight over the top. The fresh mound of dirt was where Uncle Jim had buried Mammy. All the horror came back and she began to tremble. She could not keep her lips from quivering. Turning she saw the red splotches on the fireplace stone. It's not a dream; it's all true. Mama and Mammy are dead. No longer could she hold in the scream!

Uncle Jim dropped his hammer. Running through the door, he folded her into his strong muscular arms and stroked her hair.

"Callie, you're awake at last. Poor child, this is so hard on you. Let it out child. Scream, yell, or do what ever you have to do. Let it out child."

He swept her off her feet and carried her to one of the rocking chairs in front of the fireplace. Her body trembled. Sobs came from deep inside her body. She thought a part of her heart came with each one. He rocked her back and forth, stroked her hair and kept repeating, "Everything will be all right, Callie. I'm here. I'm here. You're safe now. Let it out. Let it out."

No more tears could come from her body. Her throat was sore from the screams she had made. She felt nothing; only numbness.

"Let's see if you can eat a few of these hoe cakes and drink some coffee now, Callie."

With that, he gently stood her on her feet. Though her hands trembled and her knees seemed made of jelly, Callie walked slowly to the table. She ate the hoecakes and swallowed the scalding coffee made from parched corn. They seemed to give her strength and awaken her from the numbness. Reality hit her like a hard punch in her gut. I can't be a child anymore. I have to be a grown up young woman. I'm facing an unknown future. What I have to do is remember all the happiness of life here with Mama, Mammy and my beloved Calico Creek so that I can live through this immediate time.

Callie Jo Morris, daughter of Calvin and Caroline Morris, threw off the robe of childhood and became a young woman at 15 years old in 1861 on this day. She had been born at a place called Calico Place over the mountains but raised in the mountains of West Augusta. From the time she could remember, she had lived here by Calico Creek in this lush mountain land with her beautiful Mama, Uncle Jim and Mammy. They were a solid family unit in a wilderness filled with rhododendrons, pink dogwood trees, mountain laurel, red bud and an abundance of wild flowers. Birds, rabbits, squirrels and elusive bears lived in the woods that fringed the cleared fields around the cabin. The fertile ground provided an abundance of vegetables and flowers that Mammy and Mama turned into delightful delicious meals. She chased fireflies in the field, turned over rocks in the creek to find baby snakes in the spring and played "catch the stick" with her dog, Rim, that Uncle Jim had brought her from across the mountain. Mammy and she picked apples and peaches, all sorts of berries from the land around the cabin. It was a wonderful idyllic life.

The methodical pounding started again. Callie turned to look at Mama's bed. There was an object wrapped in a beautiful quilt of many colors made of calico that she had seen Mammy lovingly make. Mama's doll Liza was placed near it, the doll that Mama had given her when she was little.

"Callie my love, Miss Liza says I'm too grown up for her now. She begged me to let her be your doll because you're the most beautiful, sweet little girl she has ever seen. She promises she'll always be beside you at night to help you sleep and be a good doll for you."

"Oh Mama! Really, can Liza be my doll?"

With that memory, she smiled. I can still hear Mama singing softly to Liza and me as she tucked us into a feather bed and drew the feather-filled comforter over us, "Rock a bye babies, in the tree top. When the wind blows, the cradle will rock. When the bow breaks the cradle will fall, down will come babies, cradles and all." Her voice sounded like an angels.

"There are things we must do and things you must know, Callie." She became aware that Uncle Jim was speaking to her. "In times such as these you never know when your life will be taken. We must make a journey to Calico Place. You clean up the kitchen; pack up a few things to take with you and I'll go back outside to finish my job. It will be dark soon.

"We'll leave at sun rise in the morning. I don't have time to start lamenting and give those bastards another chance; enough time to strike again."

Uncle Jim pounded on the box and lid until the sun was ready to set behind the green purplish pine trees. Callie saw him place it onto the bed of the farm wagon near the cabin. He marched purposefully through the cabin door, eyes focused on Mama's bed. Bending his tall body to the object in the calico quilt, he gently raised and cuddled it in his arms. Callie saw the

SOMETHING TO LIVE FOR

tears that trickled down his face. He turned, marched through the door and gently placed the calico quilt that held her Mama's body into the box. She could not hear what he was saying as he leaned over the box. Touching his fingers to his lips, he kissed them. Then he slowly moved his fingers to the calico quilt and gently touched it near the top. He stood erect, marched to a near-by tree where the lid stood upright against it. Picking it up, he placed it on top of the box. Callie could not bear to watch any longer.

Turning, her eyes caught sight of Liza still lying on Mama's bed. I must take her with us on the trip she thought. Liza will want to go with Mama and me.

Uncle Jim came to the door.

"There's nothing left for us to do Callie, but take your Mama back to Calico Place. Mammy's buried. I've packed a few of your Mama prized possessions and some supplies we'll need. They're in the wagon. Tomorrow before sunrise I'll hook up the team, put your things in the wagon and we'll leave for Jackson River country. Pack up some of the hard cakes if you can find any left and some jerky. If not I'll shoot some game along the way and we'll cook it over a campfire. Pack some parched corn too."

Callie did not sleep well that night even though she held Liza close to her. After the fire had long ago died in the fireplace, she sat straight up in bed. Mammy's scream awakened her. Her eyes darted across the room. She saw Uncle Jim's long body stretched out on his bed, his hands folded behind his head and saw his eyes wide open and staring up at the ceiling. I must remember what he told me, she told herself. "Everything will be all right, Callie. I'm here. I'm here. You're safe now."

The neighing of the horses woke her this time. She smelled coffee in the cabin. The first rays of orange were filtering through the cabin window. Quickly she dressed. "I'm up and dressed, Uncle Jim," she yelled.

"Get yourself some coffee and eat some jerky I left on the table. I'm almost finished with the horses and we'll be on our way. Last thing to do will be to pack up the coffee pot and put ole Rim in the wagon."

No, she thought, the last thing to do will be to take Liza to the wagon.

2

Callie kept her eyes focused on Calico Creek until it disappeared behind a large boulder as the team began to pull the wagon up a mountain pass. Rim ran happily behind the wagon only distracted by an occasional rabbit that darted out of the bushes along the road.

Although Callie could always see the mountains that surrounded the cabin, she had never really been to the top of any of them. She had always wondered what was on the other side. The Jackson River Valley she had heard Mama, Mammy and Uncle Jim talk about on occasion was on the other side of a mountain. Her imagination from what they had said led her to believe that the valley was dotted with huge homes and large fields. Calico Place was one of those large homes. Another home was occasionally mentioned. It was called Mount Morris.

As they described it, Mount Morris was a large two story white structure that sat on the top of a knoll surrounded by large Magnolia trees. She wasn't exactly sure what a magnolia tree was but apparently, it had large fragrant blooms on it in the late spring.

"Uncle Jim, is Mount Morris where my papa lived?"

"Yes, Callie."

"Will I get to see it when we get to Jackson River country?"

There was total silence except for the sounds coming from the woods and the clopping of the horse's hoofs that seemed to last forever. She saw Uncle Jim take a deep breath.

"No, Callie. You won't get to see it."

"Why?"

"It burned to the ground before you were born."

"Is that why Mama and Papa came to Calico Creek?"
"That's part of the reason, Callie."
"What are the other parts?"

Silence, total silence from Uncle Jim! Callie had learned long ago that when he had decided he wasn't going to talk any more, he didn't!

"Callie, honestly girl, I'm not sure which you do more; ask questions or see mysterious beautiful and sometimes frightening things around you. You and your inquisitive and imaginative mind! " That's what he'd said to her once.

She had started to ask him what the word inquisitive meant but had seen Mama shake her head in a slight movement that said, "No, no." "Mama must be looking down at me now and shaking her head, 'no, no'," she thought.

It was one of those perfect robin egg blue-sky days. She loved this type of sky. It challenged her to find hidden pictures made in its clouds. Just when she thought she'd found a picture, the wind would change the cloud shape, taking it away with no warning.

"Hum, wonder what I can find today," she thought.

"DINOSAUR!"

"What?"

"I see a dinosaur, Uncle Jim."

He thought a minute and then chuckled. "There you go again, Callie! You've found something in the clouds haven't you? Quick. Show it to me before it blows away."

Callie pointed to the spot where she saw it in the sky and not a moment to soon. Its tail was starting to dissolve and its head sag.

"You find a picture, Uncle Jim. Bet I can beat you finding one."

She wasn't sure if he was looking for a picture or not. She was too busy trying to find one before he did.

"Robin."

"Where, Uncle Jim?"

"Robin …egg blue. That's the color you call the sky." He tilted back his head; laughed and laughed.

"Oh, Uncle Jim!" she said with disgust. Actually, she was smiling in her heart. This was the first time she had heard him laugh so heartily in a long time.

The horses were laboring more as the incline on the road became steeper and steeper. The wagon moved slower as the pull was more of a struggle for them. Sweat began to appear on their backs. Rim wasn't running as fast as he had previously and his tongue had started hanging out of his mouth.

"It's a long story Callie about your Mama and Papa and other things. Right now, I'd best give these horses and Rim a break. Get them all some water." Uncle Jim spoke.

That said he turned the wagon down a one-lane path on the left with grass growing in the middle of wagon tracks. At the end of the path, Callie saw the most dramatic, beautiful waterfall she had ever seen. Abruptly the mountainside stopped. Hollowed out at its foot was a pool of clear blue green water. Holding her head back as far as it would go, she opened her eyes wide as she saw a rush of white water, oxidized by mixing with the air, plummet to one ledge, spread its spray, then plummet to another and another. Each time its spray widened as it leaped to the next ledge until it got to the very last ledge. There were huge rock outcroppings on each side making a spout that sent the water half way to the width of the middle of the pool at it's base. When the water hit the pool, the force of it caused sprays of water to jump up above the pool. Clumps of budding rhododendrons clung precariously on the sides of the ledges to frame this cascading waterfall. Here and there, pink dogwoods beginning to bloom shone through naked trees showing the faint green of spring that would become the leaves of summer. They were mixed among the green purplish pines. Chunks of rocks that had fallen off the mountain scattered about in and near the pool. Large green ferns grew on the pools edge.

Rim ran immediately to the pool and jumped into the cooling waters. Uncle Jim unhitched the horses wet with sweat from the hard pull up the mountain and led them to a spot where there was plenty of grass for them to eat and water. Callie could not resist the temptation to remove her moccasins, sit on a rock that had fallen off the mountain and stick her feet into the cooling water.

Uncle Jim busied himself. He pulled tin cups from a backpack and got some jerky Callie had packed. He walked to one side of the path, dipped the cups in a mountain spring and handed her one. Then he pulled some jerky from his shirt pocket and handed her a piece.

"It is so beautiful here Uncle Jim. What is this place called?"

"I don't know that it's ever been given a name, Callie; not since the Indians first discovered it long before the white man came to these hills. But you can tell from the well worn path leading off the road to it, people have known for a long time about the good spring water here."

"I think I'll call it 'three tier fountain'."

He looked at her with a question on his face.

"See how three ledges have water leaping off them just like water fountains I've seen in those books you bring me?"

Uncle Jim chuckled then. "You're just like your Mother, Callie. She always had her eyes open for beauty anywhere around her. She'd hold what she had seen in her minds eye to help her get through any bad times. You hold on to this beauty for your bad times, Callie."

His countenance changed to one of sadness once again. He fed Rim some bites of jerky.

"Think I'll go for a little walk up the mountain, Callie. You watch the horses that they don't stray."

Callie watched as Rim plunged back into the cooling water. The horses grazed contently on the grass and occasionally sipped the water at their feet. Mama would have loved it here, she thought. She drew in her breath at the thought. I have used the words, would have. Clasping her hands to her mouth, she held back the cry of anguish that was forming inside her. She could not hold back the tears that were forming in her eyes. Her tongue reached out to catch one as it cascaded down her cheek. Startled she realized it had a salty taste. Retrieving Liza from the wagon, she pulled her knees up to her chest, held Liza tightly in her arms and sobbed.

When Uncle Jim returned he hitched the horses to the wagon, picked up Rim and put him in the back of it. With a "gitty up," the horses started on their strenuous trek continuing up the mountain.

Turning to her he said, "There are happenings going on in this world that you must know about before we reach the Jackson River country." Pausing as though trying to decide just how to tell her about what she needed or should know, he continued.

"We've been living in a part of Virginia called West Augusta. People came to this side of the Alleghenies for many reasons. Many like your Mama, Papa and me came because of things that had happened in Virginia. We thought if we put the mountains between us and the old life, we could make a better life for ourselves than what we were leaving. There's been good people come and there's been bad. As a whole, the people of West Augusta are alike as far as possessions and the land are concerned.

"This land is different from low land Virginia. It's mountainous and doesn't have many places where big plantations can develop. For the most part, a man in West Augusta clears only what he can take care of himself; owns only what he needs by necessity. We mountain folks work hard to scrape out a livin' from this land. Virginia has promised us better roads, better schools, even a railroad that can connect us to the low land of Virginia. We've paid our taxes to the Commonwealth of Virginia but have seen very little in return from them.

"All these years, the big places in Virginia have grown and prospered because they have had slaves to help plant and care for the crops. They've used their taxes and ours to build fine colleges and university for their children; roads they can easily travel and even railroads to ship the cotton and other products to the big cities of the north and south; even outside the country. Now it looks as if the time is here when the small places in West Augusta will be fighting the big places in Virginia with the poor slaves caught in middle."

"But Uncle Jim, all of this has nothing to do with us."

"Well, that's what I thought at first. I thought we had moved so far into the West Augusta mountains because of your Grandmother's, my Aunt Tish's dammed unreasonableness and wrath," he paused and took a deep breath, "that we could stay here and let the big plantations and the North fight their own battles. Then on a trip to Lewisburg and Jackson River, I found out it wasn't just the big places like Calico Place spoilin' for a fight. It was the whole state of Virginia including parts of West Augusta. It's all about whether a state has the right to govern itself or the federal government can tell it what it should do. Other southern states agree with Virginia, states should have the right to govern themselves.

"That includes us even us on Calico Creek. We are either going to have to defend what is ours and our way of life, or, by God, we'll all be dancing a damm Yankee tune. Who do you think killed Mammy? Nobody but damm Yankees; killed her because I wasn't there; wanted to send me a message."

"Uncle Jim. How do you know it was damm Yankees? They didn't have on any uniforms that I saw."

It was as if he did not even hear her question.

"God knows what might have happened to Caroline. It's a blessing that she was dead. And you, child, it must be that the Lord has a special purpose cut out for you. Yes sir, the Lord spared you for a purpose and I'm going to tell you something that even Caroline didn't know."

He paused. Callie leaned closer to him. She waited with heightened interest to learn what she would know that he would not tell her Mother.

"On my trips away from the cabin, I have been doing some scouting and recruiting for the south. I've had to pick sides. Difficult as it was, my southern upbringing would not let me choose any side but the south. Many guys I went to school with at Virginia Military Institute have already put on the Confederate grey. Too many of them have explained to me how the damm Yankees are trying to take away states rights. They also tell me the Yankees are filling the heads of the slaves with the notion that they should be free men. I have to say though, that your Papa had me convinced that it was true that the slaves should be free men before…"

His voiced trailed off with that sound of sadness she'd heard before.

"Go on Uncle Jim. Finish what you were saying."

"They understand that I have my obligations to take care of you, Caroline and Mammy. I told them I would help them any way I could though, and I am."

He didn't speak for what seemed like an eternity to Callie. Then he said, "There'll be plenty of time for me to tell you the rest, Callie. We have another days ride before we get to Lewisburg. Then it's at least a day, maybe more until we get across the mountains to the James River country and Calico Place."

They rode for hours without one word spoken. Rim curled up in a ball in the back of the wagon; slept with his face on his front paws. Callie thought about all that Uncle Jim had told her so far. She was confused by the different tones in his voice. Sometimes it was soft and loving when he spoke of her Mama; sometimes harsh as when he spoke of the damm Yankees. Then there had been times when he seemed hesitant to continue on a train of thought he had started. That happened every time her Papa was mentioned. More questions popped into her head that she wanted to ask him.

Eventually they came to what appeared to be the top of the mountain. The land leveled off into a plateau. There was an occasional cleared field with a cabin tucked near it. In the distance, a dog would bark and Rim would perk up his ears and act as though he was going to jump from the wagon bed to find the other dog.

"No boy, you stay with us," Uncle Jim would yell. "You're going to find a good home on down the road."

The sun was starting to move lower in the western sky. Uncle Jim turned the wagon down another wider, more traveled one-lane path. He pulled into a cleared spot where it was obvious other wagons had camped. A ring was made of rock and there was charred wood showing it had been used for many fires.

He unharnessed the horses from the wagon and led them by their bridles to a spot near the woods where there was ample grass for their grazing and a small stream of water running from another mountain spring. He tied them by a long rope to a nearby tree. Rim had followed to lap up some water.

"Come Callie. I want to show you one of the marvels of West Augusta." He whistled then shouted, "Come on, Rim. You can go too." Rim bounced across the distance and walked by Callie's side as they started down a narrow path through the woods.

Abruptly the woods stopped. Ahead of them was a large rock ledge jutting out into a space of blue before a mountain filled in across a large expanse.

"Come Callie, take my hand. You stay, Rim."

With those words he led her carefully out onto the ledge to a rock on top. He motioned for her to sit on the rock.

"Tell me what you see, Callie."

From this rock, she could see into the blue space that was between the ledge and the other mountain across the way.

"Is that Calico Creek?" She pointed to a thin ribbon of water at the bottom of the space.

He chuckled. "No, that's much larger than a creek. In fact, it's a river. It only looks as small as a creek because you're so high above it. It's called the New River and what you're looking into is the New River Gorge."

"Really?"

"Yes, and it's a very strange river because it doesn't flow south like most rivers. Starting in the Carolinas, it flows north to West Augusta. It's said to be older than the Nile River your Mama talked about when she read 'the Book'."

He sighed at the memory of Caroline reading at her services from 'the Book' and took a deep breath.

"This rock you're sitting on is called the Lover's Leap rock. When the Cherokee and Shawnee Indians lived here years ago, a Cherokee girl fell in love with a Shawnee brave. Her father did not like him; forbid her to see him. They would sneak away and meet on this rock. One night they were seen by a another brave. Her father learned where they were. He brought along other braves with the intent to kill her lover. When the couple heard the drums beating they knew what was about to happen. They locked arms together and jumped into the canyon from this rock."

"That's terrible, Uncle Jim."

"It would be if it were true." He chuckled. "But it's just a made up story although there have been many other couples who have almost had to jump from a rock like this to be together."

He grew silent.

She watched the way the clouds cast shadows on the side of the mountain across the gorge. Trees turned different shades of green as the shadow of the clouds moved along the mountainside. An occasional hawk circled in the airflow that swept up the mountainside from the gorge floor. The sun was moving lower in the sky. Uncle Jim just gazed deep in thought at nothing.

"Let's go back to the wagon now. I'm going to get a fire started. You and Rim can watch the fire while I go find us something for supper."

She heard two shots in the distant woods. Then he appeared holding two dead squirrels by their tails. With rapid speed, he skinned and gutted them. He roasted them over a fire. Slowly turning the squirrels over the open fire, he said, "Tomorrow, Callie, we will stay at an Inn I know outside of Lewisburg. Before we get there we'll have to go across Big Sewell Mountain and a couple of smaller mountains."

Uncle Jim brought rolled up blankets from the wagon. He spread them over a bed of pine needles. That night they slept under the stars. Rim snuggled up against Callie. Liza was snuggled beside Caroline's coffin.

Warming sunrays hitting her face awakened her. Callie smelled parched corn coffee. She jolted to an upright sitting position. Where am I? Mama? Mammy? Where are they?

After rubbing her eyes in the palms of her hands, she pulled them from her face and looked about her. She saw Rim, then the wagon with its precious cargo. Shaking her head to clear her thoughts, she struggled to place the scene she saw around her.

"You're awake sleepy head!" Uncle Jim speaking from behind the horses where he was straightening the harness. "Get yourself a cup of coffee and some jerky. We'll be on our way soon to Lewisburg."

She took a deep breath and stretched her arms and back. Soon they were on the main trail again.

"There's so much that you should know, Callie, and so little time to tell it before we reach the Inn where we'll stay tonight. In all your sorrow, it may be hard for you to realize that these are hard times everywhere for every one. A man never knows who his enemy is or from which direction he'll come. War is likely to be declared any minute and then it'll be neighbor against neighbor; right against wrong.

"On my trips from Calico Creek I've sometimes delivered messages between commanders of the southern forces in the Lewisburg area and some in Jackson River country. Those messages may have been what those men at the cabin were trying to find. For sure, they were trying to find me to find out what I know. I'm not sure that they have given up. A damm Yankee sticks to a task like a leach. They're still likely to be around somewhere close."

Her heart came up in her throat as a flood of memories came back to her; Mama lying cold on her bed, Mammy and the red ooze from her head, running through the dark to get away from that awful scene. She bit her lower lip to keep from screaming.

Uncle Jim reached over and patted her hand as she had often seen him pat Mamas.

"Tonight after dark, I must leave the Inn to take a message to a commander in Organ Cave."

"A commander lives in a cave? Why?"

"Because there are big things planned to start happening soon. That's the best place he could find where he could hide and get what he needs to make gun powder."

"Is it far from the Inn?"

"Not really. I cross the Greenbrier River and ride a little further. It's very important when we get to the Inn that you don't ask any questions of anyone."

She hesitated a moment and they asked, "May I ask you now what the other reasons were that Mama and Papa came to Calico Creek?"

He was quiet for a while collecting his thoughts as to how much to tell her and what her fragile emotional state could accept at this time.

"Your Mama ran away to marry your Papa against the wishes of your Grandmother Hill. Aunt Tish was VERY unhappy that her only child would have anything to do with 'po white trash' as she called the Morris'. Actually, they weren't poor at all. They owned more land than your Grandmother; had more slaves and wealth. She called them 'white trash' because they had picked the side of the Yankees when it looked like the struggle was beginning. They were one of the first plantation owners to free their slaves and then went around the country trying to talk others into doing the same. They had treated their people so fairly when they were slaves. they remained with the Morris's even after they were freed."

"Is this what Mammy meant when she said Mama had had so much trouble in her life?"

"The Morris's loved Caroline," he paused. "Everyone loved Caroline. When your Mama walked into a room. it was if a giant bolt of sunshine entered. Her laugh was infectious. There wasn't a prettier girl anywhere. She was the most popular girl with both the girls and boys in Jackson River country.

"The Morris's welcomed her into their home and were thrilled that she'd chosen to marry their son. She and your Papa were very happy. Then that awful night came." He dropped his head and swallowed.

"Go on Uncle Jim."

"To this day no one knows what is or isn't the truth. Some say it was southern boys, dressed in Yankee uniforms, sent to shut up the Morris' from preaching to the slaves about freedom. Some say it was ... this is hard to tell you, Callie. Some say your Grandmother sent men to start a fire. Whoever it was, they did a good job.

"Your Mama and Papa were lucky to have gotten out of the house alive. His folks weren't so lucky. It burned to the ground. People think your Papa's sister may have escaped. In the confusion of the fire, no one can remember actually seeing her leave the house."

Callie was silent for a while thinking about what her next question should be ask of him.

"Where did Mama and Papa stay after the fire?"

"That was the problem. They didn't have anywhere to go. For a while, they lived with some of the former slaves on the plantation. Then your Mama found out that you were coming into the world. That's when your Mama and Papa came up with a plan.

"Your Papa had heard about the land of West Augusta where all men in most parts were free regardless of their color of their skin. He'd heard that there, a man worked with his own sweat to clear the land and provide for his family. He didn't depend on slaves to do it for him. Your Papa believed that was the way it should be. So did your Mama. He decided that he would go to West Augusta, stake out some land, clear it, build a cabin and then send for your Mama ...and you."

"But what would Mama and I do while he was doing that?"

"That was where the hard part of the plan came in for Caroline. She would have to beg Aunt Tish to let her come home, swear that your Papa had run off, left her all alone and she had no where to live."

"And..."

"Aunt Tish was horrible to her when she moved back to Calico Place. Her friends would come by to visit and Aunt Tish wouldn't let them see her. She hid all your Mama's pretty dresses and made her wear the same one for weeks. Only Mammy was allowed to speak to your Mama and then only to deliver messages from her mother. Aunt Tish would not speak to your Mama in person."

He was silent for a long time. Then he took a deep breath and continued.

"When Aunt Tish found out that you were going to be born, her treatment of your mother became more harsh. She locked your Mama in her room. Mammy could only go to the room three times a day. She was forbidden to say one word to your Mama. Aunt Tish refused to speak to her again even through Mammy. When it came time for you to be born, Aunt Tish sent Mammy to help."

Tears started forming in his eyes and he swallowed hard to hold them inside.

"Your Grandmother never saw you, held you, or rocked you to sleep. Only your sweet Mama and Mammy, when she could stay in the room long enough, would do those things for you."

"It must have been awful for Mama and me."

"Not really, you were the one bright spot in Caroline's life. She loved you so much. She would sing to you for hours and hours, fuss with your hair, tell you stories.

"Somehow she had also confided to Mammy the plan for you and your Mama to meet your Papa in West Augusta. When Aunt Tish came to visit with my Mother one day, Mammy manage to sneak away, come to our house and find me. She told me of the plan and asked me if I'd take you and your Mama to find your Papa when the word came that he was ready. Mammy pleaded with me to take her too. Of course I said I would do anything to help Caroline…and you."

They rode in silence for a while as the wagon passed seams of black exposed in the side of the mountain pass. As they descended Big Sewell Mountain, the topography of the land started to change. Now there were formations of limestone appearing among the naked trees of the mountains. From a distance, some looked like the castles she had read about in the books Uncle Jim brought her or the stories her Mama read to her. The wagon would passed by open mouths in the limestone leading to caves deep in the hillside.

Further, the mountains became less rugged than the one they had climbed to get to where she saw the New River Gorge. The mountains weren't as tall, were further apart and more rounded. Land at the foot of these mountains rolled away from them for greater distances than any she had seen before. There were indentations in the surface of the ground that Uncle Jim said were sinkholes.

"Uncle Jim, how did you know when it was time to come and get Mama, Mammy and me?"

He chucked at that question. "Your Mama and Papa weren't the only people who could make secret plans. Mammy and I made our own. I had one of the older fellows on our plantation pretend that he was courting Mammy. It didn't seem strange to anyone that he'd be riding back and forth after his work was done to see her. This went on for months until the night he came back with the message that your Papa was ready."

"How did Mammy know that Papa was ready?"

"The south isn't the only side sending messages back and forth across the mountains. The north sends them too. Your Papa had one of the messengers secretly take the message to Mammy.

"The next day I took my Mother to visit with Aunt Tish. Mammy and I met to make our final plan."

"But what if Grandmother Hill found out?"

He lowered his head and shook it. "She did. I don't know how but she did. That was the bad part. I had a carriage waiting behind the barn. After dark, I had snuck up to the second floor where you and your Mama were. Caroline had packed two satchels for the trip. Mammy had taken the satchels out of the room earlier that day. We made it down the darkened staircase without any problems."

He paused, shook his head and a frown appeared on his face.

"But when we turned the corner to enter the hall that led to the back porch, your Grandmother was standing there with her whip. She made its leather crack in the air.

"Her voice was as angry as the rattle on a rattlesnake about the strike as she cried out, 'I tell you here and now you turncoat. I'll never call you a nephew of mine again, Jim. And as for you Miss Caroline, you can run away to that po' white trash you call a husband to that God forsaken land but you will not, I repeat, YOU WILL NOT, take my grandbaby into the mess you have made for yourself!'

"Angrily she threw down the whip," Uncle Jim continued, "lunged at you with hands open like claws to rip you from Caroline's arms. Your Mama screamed. Then ebony arms came out from behind Aunt Tish, wrapped them around her waist and lifted her into the air. I took you from your Mama's arms, yelled to her to run as fast as she could and not to look back.

"As I ran down the path to the barn, I turned to see a face to go with the arms that were holding your Grandmother screaming and kicking, her feet flailing the air. It was the face of Mammy's fellow."

"But where was Mammy?"

"Mammy was waiting with the wagon behind the barn. She had already placed the satchels in the back. Your Mama ran to her open arms. Mammy kept stroking her hair and whispering, 'Hush chile. We's be on ours way now.' Then she handed Liza to your Mother and said, 'Miz Caroline gwine take care Liza. I'se take care Miss Callie. We's best be goin'.' I handed you to Mammy, we all climbed in the wagon and we were off to West Augusta."

It was Callie's turn to be silent. She was remembering all the times Mammy had told her little bits and pieces of the puzzle and could now understand how they all fit together; conversations that she'd overheard between Uncle Jim and her Mama. The puzzle was finally beginning to make sense.

Uncle Jim stopped the wagon on top of a mountain where the trees parted exposing a vast valley below. Pointing to it he said, "That's what is called the beautiful Greenbrier Valley you see below, Callie. It's really like the land near the Jackson River country; people live in homes like the homes there. In fact, this part of West Augusta is more like the rest of Virginia than like the other parts of West Augusta.

"We're going to climb down off this mountain, cross those fields filled with sink holes for about six miles and then we'll be at the Inn where we'll be spending the night."

With those words. he gently took her by the shoulders and turned her to face him.

"Callie, it is very important that you remember. You CAN NOT ask any questions of me or anyone; react to any comment made or anything you may hear or see. You must not tell a single soul of the talks we've had on our trip to here. Your life and my life are depending on this. Do you understand me, Callie?

"The country is like a tinderbox about ready to explode. Anything could happen at any minute. Promise me, Callie, you will not talk to or question any one in the Inn no matter what you see or hear. Promise me if I ask you to do something, you will do it immediately without questions." The seriousness in his eyes frightened her.

That week the tinderbox had exploded. All the haggling about slaves, states rights, all the fiery speeches and newspaper articles were abruptly hushed. Guns opened fire at Fort Sumter, April 13, 1861. Overnight everyone had to make up their minds. One was either with the South or one was going to wear the Federal blue. A telegraph operator tapped the Sumter message to Washington, tapped it over the wire to a Georgian mansion in Columbia, South Carolina. The message was carried into a beautiful rose garden in North Carolina. A sweaty black boy, with eyes rolling to heaven, blurted it out after having ridden the fastest horse Judge Bane had all the way from Monte Hall to the big house of Charles Bane near Charlottesville, Virginia. The telegraphed words finally reached the red clay roads over the blue sky tipped Alleghenies to the mountain vastness of West Augusta.

This was it. The die was cast. You might fight your neighbor or you might even fight your brother. The whole country seemed to be divided in its opinion. There was one thing for certain, you were going to fight.

A stagecoach lumbered to a stop. The driver's coat was covered in red clay dust and his team of horses looked like lathered satin. He jumped to the ground and brought the news to the Garman Inn near the town of Lewisburg late on the evening of April 15, 1861.

"Look at those blue-grey mountains, Uncle Jim."

His eyes followed the direction her hand was pointing. Off in the distance, across a wide expanse of fields with sinkholes he saw a mountain of the Alleghenies behind smaller hills terminating in the Greenbrier Valley plateau. He pulled the team to a stop, jumped off the wagon and lifted her down. Rim ran excitedly to explore this new territory.

"That is the last big mountain we'll cross in West Augusta to get to Calico Place."

"Will the blue-grey color still be there when we get in that mountain, Uncle Jim?"

He chuckled, "No. It's the air and the sunrays that make it look blue-grey. When we get in it, it will have the same colors as the mountains we've traveled through."

"Remember the song Mama use to sing?" she asked.

She didn't wait for his answer. Immediately she started singing, "In the blue ridge mountains of Virginia, on the trail of the lonesome pines. I'll be going back to old Virginia, to the girl that I left behind."

Turning slowly to him, she said, "That's what we're doing, isn't Uncle Jim. We're going back to old Virginia …but we're …" Sadness filled her eyes.

Uncle Jim wrapped his arm around her shoulder and led her to the wagon. He didn't comment on her last remark.

"Come on Rim." He shouted. "It's time for you to see your new home."

"Gitty up!"

They started descending the mountain. Limestone out-cropping was broken with layers of other colors, the rusty sand color of the sandstone, darker grey that would become shale.

From the wagon that had been following the Kanawha-Staunton Turnpike, Callie saw something that looked like a huge red clay cabin.

"Uncle Jim, what is that red building that I see that looks like it could be a cabin but it's too big for a cabin?"

"That's a big house made of red brick. That's the Garman Inn where we're staying tonight. A lot of the big places on this side of the mountains are made of brick."

"It's so big to be a house."

"Well, if you think it's big; just wait until you see your Grandmother's house. The Garman Inn can't even hold a candle to Calico Place for bigness or grandeur."

"But where do they get the red bricks to build the houses?"

"They make them. There's red clay in the soil here and in other parts of Virginia."

The road went down the hill and made a little bend to the right. Uncle Jim stopped the wagon before what Callie thought at first had to be an open room with big white columns going to the rafters.

"What ya gawkin' at gal? Ain't ya' never seen a porch before?" A thin faced man in a doorman's suit of blue with a lot of gold braid on the sleeves and at the shoulders spoke from beside a door.

Callie hesitated, opened her mouth to speak but didn't remembering Uncle Jim's words to her earlier that day.

Just then, Uncle Jim spoke from behind the wagon, "Watch your manners, sir. I'll thank you to speak with some courtesy to my relative."

"Relative, huh! That's what all you Southern men say. She ain't no more your relative than she is mine. If she weren't so spindly, you might have competition, bud."

"I'm warning you for the last time to keep your vile mouth shut or I'll smash it shut for you. This box contains her dead Mother's body. This is no time for an argument. Come along, Callie."

Callie followed Uncle Jim through a wide door with glass panels all around it. As she stepped over the threshold, she heard the man shout, "Damm arrogant rebel!" Then he said in a snide voice that only he and Callie could hear, "Well gentleman Jim Hill, you and your relative are in for a BIG surprise!"

Callie began to tremble but Uncle Jim seemed not to hear his comment. Excitement filled the room they had entered. Someone was shouting, "You can be damm certain that this here is going to be a war! It's going to touch all of us. Nothing left for us to do but fight our way through to the end of it."

"You'll be fightin' sooner than you expect to be. John here heard the Federals are sending a war ship up the James…"

"Yep! Heard that over at Lexington the other day; said it was a ship of war called the Pawnee with 10,000 Federal troops aboard and orders to plunder and take whatever they wanted from Virginia."

"Why those dammed blue coated devils! We'll tar and feather ever last man jack among 'em! Maybe we better get started on the bastards who are snoopin' around here. How about fixin' their…"

"Wait a minute friend," spoke the man whom Uncle Jim had asked about lodging. "I run a place that's neutral here; not for the south but not for the north either. I'll tolerate no trouble making here! Sammy, show that gentleman to the door."

Callie gasped as the biggest black man she had ever seen, grabbed the man by his shoulders and lifted him off his feet. With giant steps, he carried the man through the door. The scene made her think of the Giant in the Jack and the Bean Stalk story. He wore gold hoop earrings in his ears. His had a queer sort of smile that made Callie afraid until she saw that he couldn't help it. There were dreadful scars around his mouth that made him seem to be smiling all the time.

Callie had stood as if her moccasins were glued to the floor all this time. Returning from the doorway, the black giant came back and stood silently near the Innkeeper.

"Take Mr. Hill and Miss Callie up to the west corner room, Sammy, the one that has the little room adjoining the big one. Do anything that's required of you. They have had great sorrow in the last few days and we must show them every courtesy."

The giant bowed a stiff sort of bow then motioned for them to follow. Callie thought, "He must be a mute."

She was thrilled with the tiny room Sammy motioned would be hers. Carefully he carried her satchel in and placed it on the bed. Then making motions that she guessed meant he was going back to the wagon, he disappeared. When he returned, he brought the doll Liza and handed it to her. He must have sensed her loneliness. She knew he was her friend.

The warm, candle-lit room and the soft feather bed made the horror of Mama and Mammy's deaths seem almost unreal. Uncle Jim had had Mama's coffin put in a tight, windowless shed that the innkeeper used for storage. He had asked that Rim sleep there too. She was beginning to feel safe. Of all the things in the world she wanted most, it was the feeling of being safe. If only she could lose forever that feeling everything was slipping away from underneath her without her being able to do anything about it.

She guessed right now she was worse off than she had ever been in her life. Mama was dead and she had no one but Uncle Jim. Somehow, she just couldn't believe she could count on a Grandmother who had been so cruel to her own daughter, Caroline. That man in the room downstairs had said that the war was going to affect everyone. Uncle Jim would probably go off fighting.

Then Callie thought of Calico Creek and three tier waterfalls. They were things that were real to hold onto. I'll be old enough and brave enough when we get back, she thought, to take care of myself at Calico Creek.

She began to become drowsy and closed her eyes. She lay down on the feather tick bed with Liza. Suddenly her shoulders were shaking. She heard Uncle Jim's voice in her ear.

In a low whisper he said, "Listen Callie, I'm going on to Organ Cave tonight. The commander there must get the message I have for him and know about the battle at Fort Sumter. I'll tell you all about it in the morning. Get up and latch the door after me. Then go back to bed and I'll be back before you are even awake in the morning. Don't cry; everything is going to work out alright. Take Liza back to bed with you. Here, I'll put her in bed right now."

Before she could ask any questions, he was out the door and gone. Quickly she threw the latch back into place and jumped into bed with Liza. Whatever happened, whatever it would mean to her, she was not going to worry about it tonight. Tomorrow she would act even more grown up and settle things in her mind. Tonight she was going to hold onto that feeling of the safety of this room, the memories of Calico Creek, the three-tier waterfalls and hold onto Liza.

"Liza," she whispered softly to the doll, "I'll be holding onto you every night from now it. It's just you and me now, Liza, now that Mama and Mammy's are gone and Uncle Jim will be off fighting in a war."

The room was dark when she woke to a persistent, yet light tapping on the door from the other room. Instantly she was out of bed and across the room to the door.

"Uncle Jim?"

"Yes, it's me."

Callie threw the latch softly and Uncle Jim was in the room. His coat and shoes were covered with a thick coat of dust. Even his eyebrows were coated with it. Wrinkles around his eyes seemed to be deeper. She knew without asking that he hadn't slept all night. Even though he seemed dead tired, there was urgency and something desperate in his manner.

"You will need to dress quickly. Callie. We have to be on our way before the other guests are up. Many lives depend on us getting through to Calico Place today. I'm taking no chances. Where is Liza? Quick, undress her and bring her to me. Hurry Callie! while I write some messages down."

Callie thought he must be crazy from his tiredness. However, she did as she was told and undressed her. Liza looked mad when her soft cotton body was exposed and she wore nothing but the china shoes that came half way up to her knees.

Uncle Jim had been writing on small pieces of paper. Then he took Liza and with his pin knife, split the seam on the underneath side of Liza's left leg. He pulled out the sawdust; put the tightly folded papers in the leg. Carefully he put the sawdust over the paper. From the tabletop, he picked up a needle with thread and sewed up the seam.

Callie was fascinated.

"Uncle Jim, why did …?"

He raised his pointing finger to his mouth. "Shhhhhhhhhhh!"

Then he rose, took her shoulders into his huge hands and looked her straight in the eyes.

"Listen to me Callie as you have never listened before and don't forget what I'm saying." His voice was very low and tense. "Those papers have very important messages for your Grandmother. I can not explain everything now. I want to be on the road by sunrise.

"Bring me your satchel and then go to your room. Lock the latch behind you. I'll come get you when the wagon is ready."

3

The sky had only a hint of the orange of a rising sun. A fog had settled overnight in the Greenbrier Valley. Uncle Jim gave the horses a sharp crack of the whip. The team jolted forward in the harness and were off and running.

Callie turned to look at the shed where Mama had spent the night. She saw the man called Sammy with the gold hoop earrings gently stroking the top of Rim's head as the wagon pulled away from the shed.

"Sammy's a good man Callie. He'll take good care of Rim; probably spoil him rotten."

Rim seemed happy to be standing next to Sammy. He was wagging his tail and looking into Sammy eyes. They had bonded.

"Goodbye my good and faithful friend," she said silently to Rim as she waved her hand to both of them. "I'll miss you terribly but right now, I have more than enough to do just to take care of myself."

The Greenbrier Valley was framed by the foothills of the Alleghenies. Callie realized it was actually a plateau. The wagon descended down towards a river that she could see in the distance.

As he approached the river Uncle Jim said, "I think this is far enough away from town to stop." He turned down a path that led to the river.

"What river is this Uncle Jim?"

"The Greenbrier River. After we stop to talk, we'll cross it and be on our way."

He turned to her and said, "I've been watching and listening for people following us but don't believe any are. I will tell you now what happened last night and about Liza.

"Somehow I have a feeling that the Yankees know I slipped out of the Inn last night. They may have suspected I was carrying a message to Organ Cave. They may have discovered Organ Cave by now and know there are Confederate soldiers living in it. I may have been followed."

His eyes turned dark as he continued. "They will want the information they think I'll be carrying from Organ Cave and will stop at nothing to get it. That is why Liza is carrying it. They will never suspect a doll. If anything happens to me, be sure that when you are alone with your Grandmother at Calico Place, you tell her where the message is hidden and give her Liza immediately."

He jerked his head up and with great confidence said, "It takes more than damm Yankees to outsmart a Hill of Virginia. We'll outsmart the whole damm Yankee army or die in the attempt to do so; the sneaking, dirty bastards!"

They were less than ten miles from Lewisburg when Callie noticed a row of two story white cottages set in the woods. There was a larger building.

Pointing to the buildings, she asked, "What is that Uncle Jim?"

"That Callie is the Old White and the private cottages of very wealthy plantation owners." He replied.

"But why on earth would anybody build all that out here in the middle of nowhere?"

He explained to her that on the grounds of the Old White there was a spring that people believed had all sorts of healing powers. They came to drink the water from the spring in hope that they would have better health. It was also much cooler in the mountains in the hot summer than on the plantations in the low land.

The road continued through open lonely stretches with the never-ending hazards of the Alleghenies in the distance looming like a sentinel. Often they passed gentle meadows with peaceful cattle grazing. At the end of a tree-lined lane there would be a white columned porch with green shuttered long windows that could just barely be seen from the dirt lane leading to it. Then the road would run through miles of rhododendron, red bud bushes, dogwood and trees with tiny green leaves. Callie noticed that everything was in fuller bloom than they had been at three tier waterfalls. The air even seemed warmer.

"Remember the blue mountain you saw yesterday? We're about to start climbing it."

Uncle Jim had been right. It didn't look blue at all now. Except for the flowering trees and bushes in fuller bloom, it looked just like the mountain they had climbed to get to the waterfall.

They were climbing a steep, narrower mountain road with towering cliffs in the distance. Sometimes the cliffs were so close that Callie could almost reach from the wagon and touch them.

"We'll stop here to get some spring water."

"Uncle Jim. Who was at Organ Cave last night? What is it like inside a cave like that?"

"The Commander and some of his troops were inside. Other soldiers were posted at the entry to guard it. They use torches to light the inside of the cave. I could hear men working deep inside the cave filtering the saltpeter in hoppers. There are large hangings from the ceiling that look like icicles. The funny thing is there are also these same icicle hangings except they're upside down and growing up from the floor."

"You're kidding me. Nothing can grow up from the floor."

He chuckled. "Sure they can, Callie. The water drops from the ceiling of the cave to the floor. In the water, there is dissolved limestone from the ceiling. It drops, the water evaporates and the new limestone deposits on the floor. It takes thousands and thousands of years for this to happen. There's one drop, the water evaporates and the limestone dries. Then another drop on top of that and the limestone dries on top of the first limestone that dried. It goes on and on and on. With each drop, the icicle begins to get bigger and bigger growing towards the ceiling.

"Well then how do the ones from the ceiling happen?" she asked.

"It's basically the same way except the ones from the ceiling start forming around a little bump of limestone on the ceiling. Water carrying limestone collects around the bump and evaporates. The limestone dries that was in the water and makes the bump get longer. Then more water collects around the longer bump, and on and on and on."

"But what made the cave in the first place?" shaking her head, she inquired.

"Millions and millions of years ago the place where the limestone is now was an ocean. Dead sea creatures dropped to bottom of the ocean, their bodies decayed and turned into limestone from the pressure of the ocean above."

"Now I can't believe that, Uncle Jim! Look at these mountains. How on earth could an ocean have been here?"

He chuckled. "These mountains weren't always here, Callie. In fact, they were pushed up from the ocean. Think about putting your hands on either side of a towel lying on a table. What would happen if you started pushing on both ends of the towel towards the middle at the same time?"

She thought for a minute, spread her hands apart and pretended she was pushing a towel from either side. "The towel would push up in the middle."

He pointed to a rock cliff across a stream on the other side of the road. "Look at those rocks over there. Do you see how there is a layers of grey limestone, then a layer that is the color of sand, other layers of other colors? Look at how the layers are not lying straight to the ground but tilted up from one end."

"Whew, Mother Nature sure gave a hard push on one to get that big ole mountain to stand up on one side like that."

Again he laughed. Callie was so glad to hear him laughing at her comments. It had been so long since she had known him to be this carefree that he would even allow himself the pleasure of a chuckle and he had laughed yesterday at her sky picture. "It probably has to do with all this talk about a war that's been going on for a long time that he told me about," she thought.

His laughter reminded her of the times when she would pretend to be asleep in the cabin. Uncle Jim, Mama and Mammy would be sitting in their chairs around the fireplace. She couldn't always hear what they were saying but they would break out in a burst of laughter. One of them would say, "Shhhhhhhhh, we're going to wake up Callie."

Mama's laugh was always the best. It would sound like a hundred crickets chirping or birds singing at the same time. Mammy's was a deep laugh that started in the bottom of her stomach and rolled out of her mouth. Uncle Jim's was more controlled. It came in spurts and was very deep in tone. "OH PLEASE. Don't stop." she would silently plead from her pretended sleep. "I love to hear you laughing."

"We might as well grab a bite to eat while we're here. I'll check to see if there's any water nearby for the horses.," as he led them to a near-by stream.

After lunch, they continued on winding their way up the mountain on the road that followed the stream. The rhododendrons and pink dogwood trees were blooming even more and red bud bushes were bursting with a brilliant color that made them look iridescent.

"Uncle Jim, what made Organ Cave?"

"Water is a very powerful carver of caves. Once it can find an opening to get down into those layers it starts working on the softest layers of rock it can find. It will wash away all the sand in the sand stone first for instance, because sandstone is softer than limestone. The limestone is hard enough that it can still hold up what is above it even with the layer of sandstone gone. The space left when the sandstone is gone, is a cave. That's also what causes the sink holes we saw in the Greenbrier Valley."

"I wondered what caused those sink holes. Uncle Jim, what is salt peter?"

He chuckled again. "You're not going to like the answer to that question, Callie. Remember when I pointed out those strange looking creatures flying in the air that night that the moon was really bright at Calico Creek. The bats, remember? Well, Callie, some caves have many, many bats living in them. On the floor below where all these bats hang on the ceiling is their… ah … dried droppings."

"That's disgusting! Why would anyone be interested in dried bat droppings?"

"Actually it's very valuable. It's important for us to use to make powder for our rifles fire." His mood changed. "I guess we'll be fighting over who gets the saltpeter from Organ Cave one of these days, the south or the north."

The wagon stopped again.

"There she is Callie. The good ole Jackson River Valley. We've almost made it. God I hope…"

His eyes wandered down the steep road with a dangerous drop on the left side of the wagon. Down the hill about two hundred feet, where it went between two huge boulders. Scraggly white pine grew in the crevices of the rocks. Green, waxy rhododendron formed a curtain around their base.

Callie felt a slow warning begin to stir in her yet there was no apparent reason for the feeling. The scene was one of beauty; contrasts of lights and darks. Low-lying foothills were encircling the peaceful valley and river. Blue, purple mountains again appeared beyond the valley. Maybe she was just imaging things. She sat up straight.

"Uncle Jim?" It was half a question, half a statement of fear. Looking at him, she knew the answer. He too had sensed whatever the warning feeling was about too.

With extreme seriousness in his voice, he said, "Callie, remember that if anything happens to me, you are to take the wagon on to Calico Place as fast as you can. Don't stop or talk to anyone. Keep on this road. The Calico Place lane will be the first one that turns off to the left. Lord God, Callie, you must remember. Now pray that we get through."

The wagon neared the boulders. As it came close to them, Uncle Jim's whip lashed out and the horses bolted forward. A shot rang out; dirt and rocks flew up just in front of the horses. A man jumped from the side of the boulder where he had been hiding in a clump of rhododendron. He grabbed the reins and brought the wagon to a sudden halt.

Liza fell to the dashboard. Quickly Callie grabbed for her and held her tight. Liza's black china eyes looked scared. Everything happened at once. Now there were half a dozen men in the road.

A big man pulled Uncle Jim from the wagon.

"Git his gun boys. Murray, search him. He's bound to be carryin' it. Ain't had no time ta give it ta nobody. Know he went straight ta his room when he got back."

"Nutin' here, Capt'n. Nutin' in any of his pockets. Must have it some place in the wagon. Gawd Almighty. What's that box in the back?"

Until then, Uncle Jim had stood silently.

"Surely even a soldier of the North recognizes a coffin box. Surely, you have respect for the dead. That box contains the body of my cousin, Mrs. Caroline Hill Morris. I'm taking her back to Jackson River country for burial."

"Sez you reb. Sez you. We ain't taking no chances and we ain't takin' no Rebs word for nutin'. Split those planks boys. Let's have a look see."

A nauseating odor came from the box as the planks were loosened. Callie began to fear that the black smothering velvet curtain was going to get her again. This time she fought it. She would not; she could not faint.

"Lord God, Capt'n. 'It's a cadaver alright. An' sure stinkin' like bloody hell. 'Tain't been disturbed for a day or so."

"Cain't tell for sure by lookin', Murray. Run your hand down round the sides and underneath the edges."

"O.K. Capt'n. Jes' ain't nothin' here."

The man addressed as "Capt'n" turned to Uncle Jim who stood as if he no longer cared or was alive.

"Where is it, Reb? Don't you want to live anymore? Ya ought to know we mean business. We need that information, Reb. And we're gonna to have it."

He walked closer to Uncle Jim.

"Not talkin' huh? Maybe this will help."

He slapped Uncle Jim's face, first on one side and then on the other until his head wobbled. A dark purple red color came into it. Still Uncle Jim stood silently. Without warning, the man kicked him in the stomach. Uncle Jim fell backwards.

"Why you dirty ..."

"AH HA. Reb gonna to talk is he? Reb don't like rough treatment. Reb's one ov those southern gentlemen. Alright Reb, give us the information we know you're carryin' and you can go. Tell us now or jes' hand over the little ole piece of paper where you wrote it."

Uncle Jim bit his lips and Callie saw a streak of bright red begin to trickle down his chin. In the brief look he gave her, she saw that his eyes were the steely grey that Mama always called the fighting Hill eyes. She knew that the men were not going to get anything out of him. It was going to be up to her and Liza to carrying out his goal. "If I can only get the wagon away from them," she thought.

"Alright, Reb. We've waited long enough. Not talkin'? We'll do somethin' else then. Pull him over against the rock boys and stand him up. Get your guns ready. Reb'll be ready and willin' to talk after he faces our guns."

Callie's heart began to pound and doubled up in its leaps.

"Oh Lord, please don't let them shoot him right before my eyes. I can't stand anymore, not after Mama and Mammy. Lord I just can't stand it," she prayed silently.

"Reb, I give you this one last chance." The leaders voice made Callie think of a rattlesnake that had been coiled and ready to strike at her. The poisonous venom it held was as cold and deadly as the sound of his words now.

"Hand over the information Reb, or as the Lord as my witness, you're a dead man."

Silence. The leader's face grew red. The men watched. Callie tensed.

"For the last time REB? Where is it? I will not fool with you anymore."

Uncle Jim stood as if he hadn't heard or cared.

"OK boys. Let him have it!"

Sharp sounds of rifle fire deafened Callie. Uncle Jim grabbed his stomach, shuttered and fell forward as his knees buckled out from under him. In that instant, the horses reared. Callie had the presence of mind to grab the reins. Liza fell to the bottom of the wagon. Then they were racing down the road.

"Gawd Almight! Look at that team go, Capt'n. The girl is getting' away! Want us to try an' stop her?"

"Let her go boys. She can't do no harm. Let her take the corpse to that plantation. Even the enemy has a right to bury the dead."

4

The first road that turned off to the left was a white sandy one winding between red banks dotted on either side with tall, dark pine trees. They were so even that Callie knew someone had to have set them out; someone with the eye of an artist that knew the colors of the lane, banks and trees would someday be a picture. It turned, straightened and curved again.

Then at the end of a long straight stretch appeared another picture. Calico Place was different from the other houses she had seen on the road. Huge, graceful, feathery maples sheltered a rambling red, two story house with straight double windows and white square columns going up to the roof at the entry. A small balcony supported by a wrought iron grill frame that came out of the second story at the entry with what looked to be double windows. It was centered above a massive entry.

"My goodness. I bet that balcony is only for looks. It's like the one in the Romeo and Juliet book, Liza." Liza sat beside Callie in the passenger space.

The entry door had double doors, taller than a normal door with a transit above them. It stopped just below the wrought iron grill frame of the balcony. On either side of the double doors and transit, were wide glass panels from the floor of the porch to match the height of the transit. These glass sidepieces and the transit were beveled glass. With the sun beginning to set in the west, its rays struck the beveled glass and made them sparkle like a trillion diamonds.

Massive solid black walnut double doors, wider than a usual door, had large brass rings for door knockers. Below the doorknockers were brass doorknobs.

"Those doors and those sparkling diamond side pieces have to be as wide as one end of our cabin on Calico Creek." Callie told Liza.

Steps as wide as the entry door and made of limestone stopped at a flag stone path. It led to a white sand circle that connected it to the white sandy road. Inside the circle, neatly trimmed boxwoods made a second circle. Inside the second circle was a magnificent three-tiered statue. It reminded Callie of the three-tiered waterfall.

The columns did not stop to frame only the main entry as they had at the Garman Inn. On either side of the entry, they continued along the front of the porch to a roof that separated the first and second floor. Turning the corner they continued down each side as far as the eye could see. In between each column were doublewide widows that went from porch floor to the ceiling. Beveled glass was also in the top part of each window.

"Now I remember. I heard Uncle Jim and Mama discussing how people thought their taxes were based on how many doors they had in their houses. This house was built with what looks like windows but they open like doors.

"What was it Mammy had said, They's live on da' rite an' party on da' left; party all thru da' nite." She was speaking to Liza.

Mama had told her once that her bedroom was on the second floor to the left of the entry and her Grandmother's was on the right. From those windows, they could see a guest coach turn onto the last straight stretch of lane leading to the house. She had also said that her mother loved to be waiting at the top of the staircase when the huge entry doors opened. Then she would swoop down the stairs like a bird in flight to greet the guests.

Oh. I've forgotten about Mama, she thought. Callie yelled "Gitty up."

Soon she was walking up the flagstone path and limestone steps with Liza in her arms. She could see the intricate design in the beveled glass. The bright ring knockers looked like Mama's gold ring. Callie lifted one.

Instantly, as if he had been standing just inside waiting for her to knock, an ebony color older man opened the door.

Yes'em?"

"Is my Grandmother at home?"

"Is yo' Grandmother home?" Amazement spread over the ebony face. "Whut yo' mean, Miss? "Dis is where Miss Leticia Hill liv'." His eyes wandered to the wagon with its long box. "We ain't buyin' nuthin' now, Miss."

"I don't expect you too. I am Callie Morris and I have my Mama's body out there in the wagon. I'll thank you to stop your chatter and tell my Grandmother that we are here."

"Lawd a mercy!" He scurried off just like a startled woods rabbit and left the door wide open.

Callie had never seen anything as beautiful before as the entry hall. It had shining floors that seemed to go on forever. The bottom of a creamy white staircase, as wide as the two entry doors, was centered in the middle. It continued until it reached the second floor level. On either side of the staircase at the top, there was a hall space. On either side the width of the entry were creamy white spindles in a railing. The entry was open from the floor to the ceiling of the second floor. Hanging from a large brass ball at the ceiling was an elaborate chandelier with countless crystal spears. The spears hung from rings. At each level as it dropped toward the floor, the ring became wider and had more spears. The last ring had to be bigger than the opening to the fireplace at Callie Creek.

Callie stood fascinated. She heard a very light step in the distance. A small, very straight person was coming down the hall.

The woman standing in front of her seemed to have no definite age. She stood erect and proud as if she had been right all of her life and was determined to be the same for the rest of it. Her severe black dress was broken by fine, frothy white lace at the neck and wrists. Black jet earrings sparkled from her ears like evil lights. Her sharp, angular face was highlighted by piercing eyes fringed with heavy black lashes. These eyes looked at Callie as if she were a piece of furniture or a sack of flour she might be buying. A tiny, black lace cap sat coquettishly on the back of gleaming white hair arranged in a braided cornet style. The cap and the styling of the hair gave her head the appearance of a crown. She carried a black whip in her right hand.

Callie looked again into the piercing eyes. She thought, "If she's my Grandmother, she could be pretty if she would just smile and let her eyes laugh."

Her heart skipped a beat. The eyes had that same deadly quality that the enemy leader had had when he talked to Uncle Jim. "She hates me already. She's an ugly, old mean woman. She looks at me as if I am nothing. She doesn't see me, not really. What will I do if she won't help me with poor Mama?" thought Callie.

"Henry tells me that you claim to be my Granddaughter; that you have your Mother's body in that wagon out there. Speak, Miss, since you have created this disturbance, let's have it settled." The words were spoken forcefully and unemotionally.

"That is true, Mam."

"What have you to prove you are who you say you are?" the woman's cold voice bellowed.

Callie thrust Liza forward. "Surely you remember Mama's doll, Liza. Mama said her Papa brought it back from South Carolina when he visited his brother there who was sick."

"Yes, it appears to be the same doll. But how do I know you have not stolen it?"

"Mam, Mama's cousin, Jim Hill, asked me to tell you something about Liza when we were alone." Callie's eyes glanced at Henry.

With a flick of wrist on a raised arm directed at Henry, he left. Her Grandmothers hand tightened its grip on the whip.

Callie looked to either side of the woman. She also turned to see if anyone was behind her.

"Mam, in the left leg of Liza you'll find messages Uncle Jim said to give to you immediately. You'll know his writing, won't you? We were attacked up at the top of the mountain you can see from here and …"

Callie swallowed hard.

"…the men shot and killed him."

"Give me the doll!"

Her hands reached for Liza. Callie remembered the clutching claws of the old woman who had disturbed her thoughts on Calico Creek. They were the same claw like fingers she had seen in dreams. It's true what Uncle Jim had told me. This woman had reached that way for me this way when I was little and lived here.

Without another word, her Grandmother took Liza, turned and went into the third door opening off the hall on the right of the staircase. The hall ran towards the back of the house.

"There must be a dozen doors," thought Callie. She counted. "One, two, three, four." A fifth door was on the wall joining the hall that went across the back of the house.

A very tall, light bronze woman in a grey striped dress and white apron was standing silently in front of the fifth door. Her black hair was braided, wrapped around her head similar to her Grandmothers. What caught Callie's eyes were the huge golden hoops earrings was wearing.

"I know I've seen earrings like those before, but where?" Callie wondered.

The woman's large eyes never wavered from Callie. All at once, Callie felt as though the black smothering velvety curtain was going to come up from the floor again. She did not want to faint now. Quickly she sat down on the shining floor.

The bronze statue came to life. "Miss! Git up! Dat's no place fo' a Hill ta sit. I kin see you' is one. Yo' da very pitcher ov Miss Caroline befo' she hav' so much trouble. If'in Madam looks at nothin' but yo' eyes she sees theys be Hill eyes. Heah, take dis' chair. What's be yo' name, Miss?"

"Callie."

"Callie? I kin hear Miss Caroline now shoutin' at Madam she gonna name her baby fo' its Daddy an' Calico Place. I'se guess Callie be part Calvin 'nd part Calico. Miss Caroline say nothin' Madam say or do mak' heh change heh mind. I'se kin still see Madam stormin' ov da' parlor withou' a word when Miss Caroline sez' dat. I knowed it be all ovah fo' Miss Caroline. I knowed she's gonna hav' ta' leave heah sum time. She an' Madam both set in dare ways. Won't giv' a inch. An' we be knowin' nothin' but trouble since yo' Mama say dem words."

"Angel, stop that idle chatter! Tell Henry to see if the girl has anything in the wagon that's worth bringing into the house. Then take her up to Miss Caroline's room. See that she has a bath and …" that same cold voice said from the third open door.

Suddenly she turned and faced Callie at the entry door. Her eyes became a hate filled steely grey. "Get her out of that horrible garb. She looks like white trash eaten up by lice and vermin. When AND if she can be made presentable, bring her back to the library.

"And tell Henry to put those flea bag horses in the far field. I don't want any of my friends to see such animals on this property. After he takes that pitiful coffin off the wagon, he can burn the wagon or push it in the river too. I want it out of my sight!"

She continued barking orders. "Tell him after he gets those flea bag horses and that wagon out of my sight, he's to get the carriage ready to take me for a ride."

"That's my Grandmother?" Callie thought. "She called me lice covered white trash and meant it! She's cruel. She hates me. I hate her too. Oh Mama! What will I do?"

Callie's mind reacted but her body seemed numb and as if it belonged to someone else. Never in her life had she been so tired. "Oh Lord, Mama's dead and I could just about die myself. I'll never be able to stay here with that evil woman even if she is my Grandmother," she said to herself.

"Cum 'long, Miss Callie. Thin's gonna git betta ifen yo' hav' good bath." The words were softly spoken with a persuasive quality in them. "'An' sum new clothes ain't gonna hurt none. I's knows where yo' Mama's pretty brown calico dress at. Yo' Mama jest luved ta' wear it. An' it jest 'bout fit yo'." Seeing that Callie seemed to be held in a daze, the voice became more insistent, "Cum now!"

Callie followed like a robot. Some how all of the things that had happened seemed to have tumbled together and now they were like a big mountain she and Uncle Jim had crossed. Even if she tried her best, she could not stop the flashes of Mama lying cold on her bed, Mammy's head covered in red ooze and Uncle Jim falling to the ground. The feeling of being safe, secure and warm was totally gone. There seemed to be a cold liquid that was beginning to slowly flow through her veins. As it moved with the beats of her heart, she felt its coldness spreading throughout every part of her body.

The room to which Angel led her was the front one with two wide windows looking out at a view of the driveway and the lane leading to it. It was papered in a pattern of yellow roses on a cream-colored background. A cherry highboy, dressing table, four-poster bed, a slipper chair covered in green velvet, a large full-length mirror, pictures and small mementoes filled the room. It looked as if a girl had just stepped out of it, had just left and gone downstairs. Callie had a sense that she had been in this room before though the only time it could have been was when she was a mere baby.

Sounds started coming to her. Mammy's frightened shriek became a shrill sound that made her shut her eyes tight and clamp her hands over her ears hard. She heard the clop, clop pounding of the horses hoofs as they raced down the mountain leaving Uncle Jim dead by the boulder. The black velvety smothering curtain began to surround her. Hold on Callie! She told herself.

Angel threw open the huge wardrobe door. Inside, there were dresses of every imaginable hue.

"Miss Caroline's things ben kept jest likes she leff 'em. Mollie an' me do 'em up case she cum back. I'se gonna make ovah fo' yo'." As Angel talked, she was busy opening drawers, laying items of clothing on the bed. Callie watched her as if in a dream.

SOMETHING TO LIVE FOR

Angel pulled a cord by the bed. Immediately a younger servant girl came into the room. Two servant boys appeared behind her carrying a big wooden tub between them. They left the room and returned with wooden buckets full of steaming water. The girl began filling it with the water; the boys left to get more. Angel sprinkled something into it, took a long wooden paddle and began stirring. White foam started forming in the water and the smell of roses filled the room. This ritual was repeated until the wooden tub had white foam almost to the top.

Callie felt some of the tiredness leaving as she slipped into the tub and the foamy white suds loosened the grime from her body. At Angel's command, she ducked her head under the foam to loosen the grime even in her hair. The younger girl poured pitchers of lukewarm water over her hair. Angel massaged her head and then gently dried it with huge towels. Her whole body, even her hair, smelled of roses. She felt some of the tight bands around her forehead begin to weaken.

Finally, she stood before the full-length mirror. Angel slipped a white lace edged undergarment over her head; next came the brown calico dress. It had pale cream lace outlining the neckline with a large pale cream ribbon bow centered on the neckline in the front. Long streamers of the same pale cream ribbon fell almost to the waist. Lace was on the bottom of the short sleeves.

"Putt dis' pretty in da middle da bow, Miss Callie." Angel handed her an oval broach with a woman's face carved in a butterscotch background. The woman wore a gold necklace placed in the middle of her necklace and in it was a diamond. All around the outside of the broach were cream-colored pearls.

Angel reached into the box where she had found the broach and pulled out matching earrings. "Put dee's on yo' ears."

They were an almost perfect match to the large cameo broach. The women in the earrings had been carved to look at each other from either side of Callie's face. Smaller cream-colored pearls surrounded even the earrings. The only detail missing was the necklace and diamond on the broach.

"I's gonna do sumthin' wuth yo' hair."

Callie sat at the dressing table and Angel began brushing her hair. For the first time Callie saw that, her hair was a deep auburn with golden highlights. The sun light streaming through the window made the highlights look like golden threads. Angel brushed her hair over and over again.

Instead of the two braids, she had been use to wearing; Angel braided part of Callie's hair and made a circular crown on top of her head. Then she twisted the remaining strands strand after stands on a long stick object, held her hair on it for a few seconds. When the hair sprang free, cascades of curls fell down her back, around her shoulders and made a burnish copper frame for her face.

A light tapping was heard at the door. The young girl answered the door and returned with Liza. "Mister Henry say ta tells yo' Madam say she done wuth dis thing."

THING? The Old Devil called Liza a THING? Callie's eyes started to fill with tears.

"Yo' be da' softness of Miss Caroline an' the heady wine strength of Madam. Yo' ben threw so much but yo' heart still cry fo' Liza. An' yo' as pretty as yo' Mama. Yo'll play da' very devil wiff lots ov dem boys 'round da James, Miss Callie. Get up an' see fo' yo'self."

Callie looked into the mirror. The girl she saw there had a slender, willowy body with soft feminine curves just beginning to show. Her mouth might be a little too large for some peoples taste in beauty but it made her face appealing because of its sensuality. For the first time, Callie saw herself as she really was. Callie Morris, fifteen, parents dead, future uncertain, suffering from shock. The beginnings of a young woman were showing in the mirror and a strong feminine nature would be surfacing.

The library was filled with shadows when Callie and Angel finally entered it. Her Grandmother looked very small and old as she sat in a chair by the window.

"Miss Callie's ready, Madam."

"Good!"

Grandmother looked her over but made no comment.

"Sammy has been proving somewhat difficult about cutting the grave stone; talking nonsense about voodoo and spells. Botheration! I will have to give him the medicine he needs to make him forget such talk."

As she talked she picked up a whip from the windowsill. Its whine cut the air as she made it snap sharply. Even Angel seemed to cringe at the sound.

"You fix her up like this at the crack of dawn tomorrow, Angel. We have to take care of some business, tomorrow."

"Yes Madam."

"She can go back up to the room and get out of those clothes. I don't want her messing them up before tomorrow. Then take some food up to her.

"Tell Henry to bring around the carriage in about ten minutes."

Grandmother raised her arm, flipped her wrist toward the door with her usual jester for removing anyone from her presence.

Callie saw the black leather carriage leaving the lane pulled by a matching black horse. Henry sat in the driver's seat wearing his special uniform used only when he took the Madam calling on her neighbors. Her Grandmother sat in the middle of the back seat. She was dressed totally in black and had a tight snug fitting hat, trimmed in black lace held on by black ribbon wrapped over her head and tied under her chin. She sat upright and very still. Callie could only see the back of her head and had no idea what face she was wearing.

Angel tapped softly on the door. "Miss Callie, I'se brung yo' supper."

Callie smelled the blend of all sorts of delightful aromas enter the room. She had not had a hot cooked meal forever it seemed. Her mouth started to water. "I had no idea I was so hungry, Angel."

Angel placed the tray on the dressing table and turned to leave.

"Oh please, Angel, stay with me while I eat. I don't want to be here in this room all by myself eating. And I'd like you to stay until I fall asleep."

"I'se can't Miss Callie. Madam don't want none us folks eatin' or talkin' ta nobody she don't say 'rite. She go 'nd crack dat whip hard cross my back if'n I'se don't do lik' she say. Sures I do, she fine out. I'se get Mr. Whip ta' morrow."

Angel turned and left the room.

The carriage stopped after about two miles on the edge of the woods.

"Go ahead, Henry, make your call."

With that command, Henry cupped his hands around his mouth and made the sound of a hoot owl. After a few minutes, the sound of a hoot owl was heard coming from a distance. He cupped his hands around his mouth again and this time he repeated the sound of a hoot owl three times. Two sounds of the hoot owl answered.

They waited until a man appeared out of the woods carrying a rifle. "Evenin' Miss Hill. You got some messages for me?"

She reached into her black leather glove and pulled small notes from inside. "Jim Hill sent these to give to the General. The war is starting. It's important you get these to General Lee as soon as possible."

"Yes Mam. I'll do that as soon as I get my horse and follow you home to be sure you make it alright."

"That won't be necessary. My driver is taking me on to Mrs. Martha Hill's house. There is other news I must tell her."

"Good night to you then, Mam."

Martha and Letchia Hill were sister-in laws. They had married the twin Hill brothers of the Jackson River country in Charleston, South Carolina. Land belonging to the Hill brother's father was divided in half with each brother receiving an equal share. The third younger brother was given gold as his part of the inheritance. Traditionally the oldest boy in the family inherited the entire family plantation to keep it in one large parcel.

The elder Mr. Hill would laugh and say, "Guess I'll have to split the land up. Mother isn't sure which one came first; besides you can't tell them apart anyway."

The twins had met Martha Springer and Letchia Worthington on a visit with their younger brother in Charleston, South Carolina. As was traditional in the South, young women from wealthy families were given a "coming out" party when they turned sixteen. One big ball was held each year to present them to society.

Having become one of Charleston's leading citizens, their younger brother had invited his older brothers to attend the party. It was important to have as many eligible bachelors to attend as possible. In reality, the purpose of the ball was match making.

The Federal Building's second floor in Charleston was decorated with magnolias and assorted flowers from the local gardens on the night of the ball. A string quartet sat in one corner on fragile looking gold gilt chairs. The windows were open to allow a breeze to filter into the room from the Charleston harbor. All the girl's parents had tried to outdo each other in providing their daughters with the most elaborate dresses to be made or imported from overseas. The young men donned their finest formal attire.

"Miss Martha Springer, may I present my older brother, James Hill of Jackson River, Virginia."

SOMETHING TO LIVE FOR

Taking one of her gloved hands in his, his grey eyes met hers; he bowed and kissed the top of the glove. It was love at first sight for both of them. They danced only with each other the entire night.

Before the night was over, James Hill had asked her father's permission to call on her the next day. They were married within six months and he took his bride back to the home he had built on a knoll over-looking the James River.

Theirs was a very happy marriage. He called her "Darly-one." She never lost the flutter in her heart when she would see him coming down the lane from a trip. It was said that they would often pretend they heard a string quartet. He would take her in his arms and swirl her around any room. This could happen in the morning, evening, anytime of day and for no apparent reason. Their eyes never parted as she gazed up at her tall, grey-eyed husband, the love of her life.

When their only child, a son, was born, they named him James Springer Hill. Everyone called him Jim to distinguish him from his father.

Mrs. Martha Springer Hill became a virtual recluse when the love of her life died suddenly ten years ago. She never wore any color but the black of mourning from the day the accident that took him. A lock of his hair was placed in a locket she wore constantly around her neck. Her hand would clutch it tightly; she would close her eyes and swirl around a room to a string quartet only she heard playing for her in her mind. Only Jim could persuade her to leave the home occasionally on the James River where she had come as a young bride and go for a ride to visit with Letchia.

John Hill met Miss Letchia Worthington at the same ball in Charleston, South Carolina. He had proposed marriage within a year of the ball and brought his new bride back to the home he had built. Theirs was not a happy marriage.

Edward Worthington, Letchia's father, had obtained his wealth in the shipping business. He had acquired a fleet of ships that sailed the Caribbean in search of spices, and it was rumored, human cargo as well.

It was on a trip when he was Captain of one of the ships that human cargo did return with him; Letchia's mother. The people of Charleston could not quite figure out exactly what nationality she was because she had blue eyes but her hair was jet black. Her skin appeared to be suntanned year round even though the women of the time took great care to protect their skin from the sun with parasols or by staying in their homes when the sun was high in the sky. They could accept that her speech pattern would be different coming from a foreign land but tongues wagged behind closed doors about who her parents could have been.

With his acquired wealth from the shipping business, Mr. Worthington built one of the finest houses on the waterfront of Charleston harbor for his new bride. He filled it with furnishing brought from England. He dressed her in the finest dresses money could buy. The jewels he bestowed on her that would have made a queen happy.

Nothing could please her. People would hear the two of them screaming at each other all night long on a hot summer's eve when the windows were open. There were days when no one would see her. The servants gossiped among themselves that he drank too much. She demanded more and more from him to be happy; threw temper tantrums. The servants said there were times when they would see bruises on her body. Some said she even practiced voodoo.

Even the birth of their daughter, Letchia, did not stop any of this behavior. In fact, her temper tantrums increased because he started focusing all his attention on his daughter. Nothing was too good for little Miss Letchia.

Money talks. Even with all of the gossip, the excesses given to Miss Letchia, their only child, the Worthington's were accepted into Charleston's high society. People had to admit Miss Letchia was a beautiful young girl.

The young men of Charleston who had been taken in by her beauty were driven away by her temper. John Hill knew nothing of the behavior of her family or her temper tantrums. He was completely taken in by her beauty. Fearing that she would never find a husband, she decided to set her sights on him. She did not love him. He was only her escape from a future as a spinster.

"Miss Martha, Miss Letchia here ta see yo'."

Letchia was led into the parlor where Martha was sitting in a chair, clutching her locket and staring into the fire in the fireplace. No one heard the conversation between the two women. What they did hear was a scream that sounded like a wild animal caught in a steel trap. Then they saw Miss Letchia exit the room.

She motioned to the servant who had led her to Martha. "You have work to do at the crack of dawn. Mr. Jim Hill was shot to death in the pass at the two boulders before you reach on the crest of the mountain on the road leading to West Augusta. Take some men and go get his body. Have some men build a coffin while you are gone. Have some men dig his grave by his father. We'll bury him tomorrow after I bury Caroline."

That was it; no sign of emotion. She left the house and climbed into the carriage.

Callie watched and listened until well after dark for her Grandmother's carriage to return. It never did before she finally accepted the heaviness of her eyes, gathered Liza in her arms and fell asleep.

5

The next morning Angel dressed Callie in the brown dress, with the cameo jewelry and fixed her hair as she had the night before. Breakfast was sent to her room. She was told to remain there until her Grandmother sent for her.

Callie went to her window and looked to see if a carriage had been drawn to the front of her house. Her gaze stopped at the statute and the circular boxwood hedge.

"What was it Mama and Mammy told me about that circle, Liza?"

"Now I remember. I had asked Mama why the name of the place where we had lived was Calico Place. Mama, Mammy and I were stringing beans in the kitchen for supper."

"Well dear," Mama started, "when my Papa and your Uncle Jim decided to build his house on land his father had given him, he studied pictures and books of different kinds of gardens. He was very fond of flowers or any plant that he could grow and he had a green thumb."

"Green thumb, Mama?" I had asked. "She either didn't hear my question or ignored it, Liza."

"The gardens he picked out for his new home were to be styled after the flower gardens of English palaces; different flowers of different heights blended together in a profusion of color. While the men worked on building the house, the women planted the flowers to a design that he had made."

Mammy spoke up. "Yes'em that how it wuz. Me 'nd sum women we's plantin', waterin' 'dem flowers. An' it turns out a beautiful site when 'dem flowers starts ta bloom. Master John, he be up there ons da' porch on da' second floor workin' on it 'nd I'se yells up ta' him, ' whut it looks like frum up dare, Master John?'"

"He looks down 'nd he say, 'lik' a calico quilt made all kinds ov colors. Mammy, dat's it! I'se gwine'a calls 'dis place Calico Place."

"Oh Mama, I hope I can see the flowers that look like a calico quilt some day."

Mammy got an angry look on her face.

"The flowers aren't there any more, Callie. My Mother changed them," Mama said softly.

"'Dat Old Devil, she says Master John spins too much time in 'dem flowers; says it not a proper look in front da' house. He go on trip; she throws one her fits. Says all dem flowers ta gets pulled 'nd burned jest ta spite Master John. She sure a Old Devil, dat one."

"Mammy, please go out to the well and get some water. We need to start it boiling for these beans." That was Mama's way of saying, "This is the end of this conversation."

Callie heard a gentle knock at the door.

"Madam say you'se cum now, Miss Callie."

"Well Liza," she said as she swallowed hard to hold back tears. "It's time for you and I to go and say good bye to Mama."

Her Grandmother was standing at the foot of the stairs. "Turn around, girl. Let me see if you look presentable enough to take out in public. "WHAT IS THAT?" a claw hand came out and snatched Liza from her. "Henry, get this thing taken back up to her room. She needs to start acting her age. Get in the carriage, Miss. We have to bury your Mother. Then we'll go to Ms. Martha's and bury that turncoat son of her that sided with your Mother."

"THING! Liza is a thing?" Callie screamed inside.

Callie was being driven in a double carriage down the white sand lane again. Her grandmother sat in the seat in front of her. Neither had spoken a word before or after the carriage left the house. A sharp turn to the right, up a little hill there appeared a small grey stone chapel. A low fieldstone wall surrounded a plot with a wrought iron gate. Tall green-black pines whispered over the curious shaped gravestones.

"I wonder if I'll get to see Grandfather John's tombstone," Callie thought. "I remember when I asked what had happened to Grandfather John that Mama had said he died a year after his twin brother, James, died. Mama had said after James died, he seldom ate, lost weight, never smiled and grew weaker as the days went by. That winter when the fever came his body had been so weak his heart just stopped."

Mammy had spoken then and said, "He's die ov'a a broken heart. His heart break 'cause he lose his folks, Master James 'nd…" Mammy lowered her head, "'cause he ain't been happy since 'da day he's bring 'dat Old Devil home. Shes makes his life a misery. Only thing he be happy 'bout was yo', Miss Caroline 'nd he's luv yo' wuth all da' heart lef' in him." Tears had filled Mammy's eyes.

Callie heard the crunchy sound and felt her feet walking on a sponge of layers and layers of pine needles giving way beneath her feet. It was a cloudless day. An eerie scene unfolded before her eyes as the sun rays were touching a raw yawning hole with a pile of red clay on one side. Her Mama's grave! Her Mama! There in the pine box that lay in the shadows of the pines.

Numbed with heartbreak and utterly weariness, Callie followed her Grandmother's upright, unforgiving figure to the side of the open grave. This couldn't be happening. It was a nightmare. She must wake herself! She struggled but she was awake. This was no dream; it was happening. They were going to bury Mama. All the warmth, laughing and loving that was Mama; who had always been so pretty even in her drab homespun. Mama, the woman that Uncle Jim had loved and followed, shared a life of wilderness hardship with on Calico Creek. OH GOD, this can't be the end!

They were at the grave now and as they stopped, a little group of slaves who had been half hidden by the low overhanging branches, made shadows where they stood silently as if to form a protective circle around the older man seated on the ground. Slowly as if all the weight of the world was on his shoulders, the man raised a powerful arm. His hand held a stone chisel.

With sudden awareness, Callie knew that he was cutting her Mama's gravestone. The finality of it all made each beat of her heart a pulsing ache that tore at the very center of her being. Mama, who always provided laughter, a sense of safety and a presence that always made Callie know she was loved and was wanted. "God! What will I do? How can I stay here?" she said silently as she looked up to the sky.

Sharp, unfeeling, unemotional, harsh words broke in on her grief. "Henry, have the box lowered. Then get the boys to work and fill up the hole quickly."

NO GOOD BYES for Mama! No sorrow at this parting that was forever. No regrets or tears for all the times and words that might have been. She might just as well have said, "Bury my dog, Henry, the beast is dead and therefore of no use to me."

"Oh Dear God in Heaven," Callie prayed silently. "We had services for Hoppy. Mama should have a service. Uncle Jim had said that the little rabbit he had found in the field might not be able to live. We had all had tried to make Hoppy live. Mama would try to get Hoppy to lick the warm milk from her finger; Mammy would cover him up in his box that Uncle Jim had made for him and place it near the fireplace so he would be warm. One morning, he was cold and stiff.

"Remember, Lord, Uncle Jim had dug a tiny grave for the box and made a cross tied in raw hide. Mama had read from "the Book." Mammy had sung, 'Jesus loves da' little child'ens ... an' bunnies, an' birds dat fly.' Oh Lord," she pleaded, "We need to have a service for Mama."

Callie could not remember ever having been to a church. They had lived to far away from one on Calico Creek. Uncle Jim, Mammy, Mama and she had gone to a little cove on Calico Creek and had what Mama called services. They had sung, Mama had read from "the Book" and prayed. Mammy mumbled an affirmative to almost every word she heard.

Mama had read a lot from "the Book." Callie had no idea of the proper words of the burial ritual were but now some of the words that Mama had read a lot came back to her. She couldn't remember the exact words but they said something about, "Let not your heart be troubled. Ye who believe in God believe also in me. In my Fathers house are many mansions. I go to prepare a place for you; that where I am, there may ye also be." Sodden, heavy lumps of red clay fell with an everlasting, hollow thud sound on the rough pine coffin box.

"Faster, boys! Get to work and stop piddling around. Cover up that hole quickly. We have another task to finish."

"She is NOT HUMAN," Callie thought. "She's burying her only child, her only daughter and all she can say is 'faster boys'! Oh Mama, I can't stand it. I can't hold on any longer. Mama you can not leave me with her. Uncle Jim is gone; Mammy is gone. Forgive me Liza."

From the innermost part of her, Callie felt a sudden and a over powering strength. Before anyone could stop her, Callie jumped into the open grave.

"Lawd a mercy!"

"Look whut she done!"

"Ah'm leavin' dis heah place!"

"Oh Lawd! Oh Lawd"

"Hav' mercy on yo' chillin's Lawd!"

"Get that silly girl out of the grave, Henry! Such carryings on! No stamina at all. This is what happens when the good blood of the Hills and Worthington's mixed with the watered down, poor white trash blood of the Morris'. Get her out of there! DO YOU HEAR ME!"

The men stood motionless. The whites rolled back in their bulging, terrified eyes.

"This will help you remember to do what I ask!"

The whine of the whip cut the air, over and over again. Thin cotton shirts split and angry welts appeared on every black back it touched. A huge form jumped into the grave and lifted Callie to other waiting hands. She was stood up on her feet. A violent, uncontrollable trembling took possession of Callie. A small, ringed hand struck her face a stinging blow.

"That is no fitting conduct for any young lady, Miss. I will tolerate no more such behavior on Calico Place. Straighten up now or you will feel the music of the whip just as these boys have!"

With unleashed fury, blind with animal ferocity, Callie had but one thought: to smash the words right back into her Grandmother's hateful face. With all the strength she had, she struck her Grandmother. The blow turned her Grandmother's face to one side and it almost touched her shoulder. Callie lunged at her Grandmother and felt pleasure as her fingernails tore down the other side of her face through the soft flesh. She would tear the Old Devil to pieces! If the Old Devil had no feeling for Mama, she, Callie, would give her something to feel. She would tear her until she wouldn't be able to use that whip on anyone every again.

"HENRY! GET HER OFF ME! HENRY! DO YOU HEAR ME?!"

"Hep me boys. Dis' no way to do at a grave. De' Lawd won't stand fo' no sech carryin' on lak' dis. We's sho' be in a heap ov trouble den'. No Sah, He ain't nevah gonna stan' fo' dis! Pull 'em apart."

"Get the rope from the carriage, Henry. Tie her hands and arms down to her sides. She's not herself. She's insane; crazy. Crazy or not, she shall stand and watch what finally happens to all who disobey. She shall see this business finished. I shall have that satisfaction. She will be taught her lesson right here and now!"

Callie felt the rope bite into the flesh of her wrists and arms. Several hand slaps on her face by her Grandmother made her head wobble crazily like a flower on a broken stem. She heard the thuds of the clay as the men worked faster now. She saw the evil, cruel gleam of satisfaction on her Grandmother's face.

Now she felt absolutely nothing. She, Callie Morris was no longer here. She felt nothing! Nothingness seemed to be felt in any inch of her body. There was no world around her. It was wonderful! Nothing, nothing, nothing was the sound that the red clay made hitting the coffin now. In a soundless meaningless, in a singsong ditty heard only in her head, she made her words repeat, "Nothing, nothing, ha ha ha. Nothing, nothing, ha ha ha!"

"Her mind has snapped, Henry. Take her back to the house. Angel you go with her." Her Grandmother pointed to a large field hand, "You go with them and stand outside the door in case Angel needs you to help her."

"And Henry, tell Nate to bring the single carriage for me. I still have to go and bury that turncoat Jim Hill. But I will not take that ..." she pointed her finger at Callie, "thing with me to disgrace the Hill name!"

Angle slept that night on the floor by Callie's bed. She had undressed Callie as one would a doll. Callie seemed not to be present in her body. Liza was tucked in her arms but Callie did not even seem to respond to Liza.

Angel tried to get Callie to eat some of the breakfast sent up from the kitchen. It was useless.

"Madam say git hers dressed. Dey go back to da' grave yard." announced the girl who brought the tray from the kitchen.

Nothing! It was wonderful that morning to stand beside her Grandmother and on command, read the words on the new gravestone in the little chapel cemetery. It gave Callie great satisfaction to know that the Old Devil had not won after all. Callie felt absolutely nothing.

Like the meaningless singsong ditty, she made all words repeat their rhyme. The harsh words her Grandmother commanded her to read meant nothing. "Caroline Hill Morris. (nothing nothing nothing). Forgotten as she forgot. (nothing nothing nothing,)" Callie chanted the words she saw on the stone aloud. The others she repeated silently in her mind over and over again.

They were stark, cruel words from an embittered old woman, words whose letters meant nothing to the trembling hand that carved them into the stone. They were simply a pattern of symbols that had been given him by the Madam. Even as meaningless as they were to him because he could not read, he knew that they were an accumulation of hatred that ruled Ole Miss' actions by the look on her face when she gave the symbols to him. It was bitter, alive hatred getting a fresh start. It would get a hold on the life of the young Miss called Callie, a young Miss who must have a voodoo charm working on her. She had started going crazy right before his eyes.

Callie became a living ghostly figure that merely moved and existed in her prison that was the upstairs front bedroom of Calico Place. This living ghost would stare and stare at the yellow roses in the wallpaper for days without moving. Eventually they became huge, fat, greasy bugs in Callie's mind. Their unseeing eyes were bulging and protruding.

Downstairs in the kitchen, Angel heard one of the most frightening screams she had ever heard. She ran to the hall door, opened it and stepped into the hall.

"Where did 'da cum' frum?" she yelled. Then she heard it again and again. "Oh Lawd, It's comin' frum Miss Callie's room." She ran frantically up the stairs.

"Miss Callie! Miss Callie! Whut wrong, baby?"

Angel rushed to Callie and took her into her arms.

Callie was sobbing uncontrollably taking short jerky breaths. Her whole body was trembling.

Angel started stroking her hair and moved her towards the slipper chair. "Ther' ther' Miss Callie, Angel got yo' now. Ain't nothin' gonna bother yo' long as Angel got yo.'"

Callie was sitting in her lap and Angel cradled her in her arms. She rocked her body back and forth. She sang softly to her, "Rocka bye baby in the tree top, when the wind blows, the cradle will rock. When the bough breaks, the cradle will fall. Down will come baby, cradle and all."

Angel felt that Callie was calm enough now that she could put her in bed. She pulled down the bed sheets and lowered her body to the bed. Covering her with the soft feather comforter, she raised a corner of it and placed Liza next to Callie.

"DON"T GO!" Callie sat straight up in bed. "DON"T GO. They come again!"

"Who come, baby? Ain't nobody come up da stairs ta' here."

In panting breaths, Callie said "No! No! There!" and she pointed to the window.

"Miss Callie. No one kin git in yo' window. It be too far off 'en da' ground."

"No! No!" Callie's voice was filled with fear. "Bugs! Bugs!" and she pointed to the window again.

In Callie's tormented mind, the bugs had crawled into the open grave in the chapel cemetery and lifted her Mama's dead body out of her grave. Then they carried them to the house, up the front wall and into her bedroom through the window.

There were other times when the bugs brought poor ole Mammy's pulpy red blob of a head into the room. Even after the windows had been nailed shut and wrought iron grids placed inside them, the bugs came. To Callie, they were becoming smarter and smarter. They seemed to know it was Mama's body affecting her the most. They brought it more and more. At its sight, she screamed and screamed. She could not stop even though she knew the screaming pleased them and Old Devil.

Finally, Old Devil sent for Big Tim, a field hand, to come and hold Callie while others tied her with ropes. The spells became so bad that the ropes could no longer hold her. After one of her bad spells, she would be quiet and calm. Angel would soothe her, call her "my baby," rock her and sing to her for hours at a time. Angel even persuaded her to eat a little from the tray carried from the kitchen occasionally.

No matter what Angel did, the bugs always came back. They snuck in at night. They came when anyone knocked on the door. They came with the evening's shadows and on the sounds that came over the fields that surrounded Calico Place. The bugs were sure always to come back.

Callie's hair became dull. It began to fall out even though Angel brushed and brushed it. Her eyes became vague and expressionless; her movements were lifeless and uncertain. She seemed to be losing all muscular coordination. Her speech was halting and senseless.

Weeks passed bringing no change. The slaves began to stay away from the big house. They said that there was a spell on it. They huddled together or stayed in their cabins after dark. Whispers leaked out that young Miss had seen her Mama's body carried down the hill by the bugs. Old Jane said she dreamed Miss Caroline came back to Calico Place and was working a voodoo charm on it because Madam had treated her so mean.

One night Nate was passing the place where the chapel road turned up the hill. He said he saw Miss Caroline's ghost. He knew for sure that it was

Miss Caroline because she waved to him just as she had done when she had lived at Calico Place.

Even the silly halfwit Amanda claimed that a bleeding red head would roll down the Chapel Hill when the moon was just right.

Old Miss said nothing. Her step was as sure and quick as it had always been. She was up at all hours. Sometimes she was seen on her mount, Salleebay, riding like a young blade out to see three girls in one night. Other times she spent hours behind the closed library doors with Judge Moore and Colonel Swathmore. At other times she would have Alexander, the stable groom, saddle Salleebay in the middle of the night and leave to carry a message to a distant plantation.

The plantation slaves knew that something was happening all over Jackson River country. White folks were planning something together. They could only guess at the strange happenings and grew more and more afraid.

6

The mountain vastness known as West Augusta in 1861 was a land of contrasts. Majestic, towering mountain ranges seemed to run endlessly from north to south only broken here and there by an almost unnoticeable gap or break. Earlier travelers had used these in their treks westward.

Once beyond the mountain ranges, one could expect anything in topography. There were steep mountains rimmed at the bottom with a creek of crystal clear water. Narrower rivers rushed through rock canyon walls, rivers with waterfalls, rivers with sluggish soil carrying water. All except a few flowed into the great Ohio River. Dense black-purplish green tinted virgin forests hid impenetrable, jagged cliffs. Interlocking arms of the tall trees canopied soft, leafy, moist Indian trails. A few rutted, rocky turnpikes led from east to west over which couriers carried important messages and stages labored to carry a few passengers.

Scattered, isolated mountain cabins and large meadow grass farms dotted the landscape. There were neighbors siding with the Federal stars and stripes. Yet others were holding their heads proudly at the mention of the name of Jeff Davis and saying, "Yes suh, sure as I'm standin' here, it's startin'. I'm ready to take on those damm Yankees."

In 1861, West Augusta was like a little key in a huge lock. One turns right, one was in southern territory; one turns left, one was in northern territory. Both sides knew its importance; both knew it would be a primary target. Its control might be the vital deciding factor in the war. Both sides knew that they must control the great valley through which the Kanawha River flowed on its way to the Ohio. They knew that the turnpike from Charleston to Lewisburg was really the east-west travel route with an important junction at Charleston that led directly north. If the Confederates were to hold Richmond and the Federals succeeded in keeping the established seat of government at Washington, then the break in the tide of the war might come in West Augusta by way of the Kanawha Valley and the Greenbrier Valley. Important, decisive battles would be fought in the mountains that surrounded the valley and along the Kanawha—Staunton turnpike.

Northern troops were forming along the Ohio and Pennsylvania borders. Overnight while tents of the Federals had mushroomed all over the island in the Ohio River near Wheeling, men from West Augusta were following trails, turnpikes and rivers to enlist with the Union Forces. Tall, rifle-toting men on their own wiry horses that were use to the steep, twisting, treacherous trails were following trails with names such as Saturday and Devil Hole. These were men from settlement's named Shepherdstown, Bulltown; men who drilled tirelessly and could shoot straight without apparent aim.

In the southeastern part of West Augusta, the mountain crown jewel of Virginia, their counter parts were kissing small, delicate women goodbye, giving a wave of their hand, a rousing Rebel yell on their lips or singing the lilting song about The Bonny Blue Flag. They were off to meet and "lick the damm yanks anywhere, anytime." Gay as cavaliers on their thoroughbred horses, they congregated at Cross Lanes, Gauley and Sewell Mountain. Every stage and traveler was stopped. These men on the Rebel side thought for sure the Federals would come by way of the Ohio, up the Kanawha Valley and over the turnpike to Lewisburg. Then it was a simple trip to Wytheville, Richmond and the Shenandoah Valley. They knew they had to make up in courage and bravado what they lacked in an army of strength and equipment.

If this mountain area was the crown jewel of Virginia, then Lewisburg was the huge diamond sitting at the top of the crown. The Indians had known the area near and surrounding it for its bountiful game, pure river and streams carrying fish, cool summers and healing springs near it. With the establishment of Fort Savannah and a frontier jail, the Indians and rough necks had been driven further west. The air of civility shrouded the town. Wealthy plantation owners began building large brick homes as a mountain retreat to escape the summer heat of the lowland plantations and to partake of the healing spring water. With the arrival of the wealthy plantation owners, came all of the traditions of the south's social life. Lavish parties were held in the homes or at the nearby mountain resort, The Old White. Social classes developed with the plantation owners and their servants, whom they brought with them to this mountain retreat, being considered at the top of the social ladder. In Lewisburg, it wasn't what one knew, it was whom one knew. The family name was important. Substantial wealth was also a great social asset.

The Old Stone Church had been constructed in 1796 of the native limestone of the area. There was a balcony inside where the servants sat during the services while their owners listened to the messages from the pulpit on the main floor.

Lewisburg was in every sense, a southern town. To its north and west, others had migrated determined to carve a better living for their families by their own sweat and blood. They were descendents of Irish, Scotch, Welch, and English whose forefathers had come to this young nation seeking the same for their families.

Great events were happening fast now. Northern factories were producing needed equipment and supplies at a record pace. Command of all southern armies had been taken over by General Robert E. Lee. Delegates from West Augusta had disagreed with others at Richmond over the right of Virginia to succeed from the Union. The men of this western part of Virginia held their own convention in Wheeling. Dissatisfied with the lack of attention and resources provided to West Augusta by the legislators in Richmond was long standing. A rumor was that they planned to form a new state. Everyone knew that parts of West Augusta would fight for the Union cause; parts for the southern cause. West Augusta had become a clearly divided territory.

Every day the Jackson River country steadily prepared for active participation in the war. Mrs. Hill and the other plantation owners recruited "po' white trash," men from the little mountain creeks, to fight for the south. Plantation gallants riding their thoroughbred steeds were determined to defeat the damm Yankees or die in the attempt. Calico Place became a meeting place.

Zeb Stuart, Commander of all southern cavalry, was a dinner guest one evening in early June at Calico Place. He was shown the enormous barns, stables and the orchard enclosing a meadow. Proudly Mrs. Hill told him a whole company of cavalry could be hidden in that meadow.

It was no surprise when one day early in June, the Thirty-First Calvary rode singing into Calico Place. Paths were made through and between the apple and peach trees. Grey tents were staked in this little hideaway. Beautiful thoroughbreds nickered in Calico Place's stables. Always one could hear some sound of confident men preparing for battle. The fever of the fight to come was rising with each days passing.

Scouting parties were sent from the Thirty-First across the mountains to Lewisburg. An infantry regiment passed Calico Place on its way to Organ Cave to work to retrieve the saltpeter. Centers of information were established through out the countryside. Columns of singing, excited hard riding cavalrymen dressed in butternut colored uniforms stirred up the dust along Jackson River roads. There was lots of activity everywhere. Socially brilliant balls and simple farewell parties were held. A time came when there wasn't a cabin, a home or a plantation in the whole Jackson River country that wasn't connected directly in some way with the war.

Strange and startling rumors spread like wild fire. The damm Yankees were moving men and supplies down the Ohio River, up the Kanawha River and into Charleston. A rumor said that the two commanding Confederate generals in the Kanawha Valley could not agree on battle tactics. There was even talk that General Robert E. Lee would have to have a personal face to face talking with these men if the south could ever expect to hold on to it's foothold in West Augusta. Each rumor grew in intensity of horror at the disposition of the Confederate troop's plight in West Augusta.

Meanwhile, in the upstairs front bedroom at Calico Place, one morning the sun touched the golden hoops in Angel's ears and twinkled before dull eyes. A hesitant hand went out to touch one. A halting hoarse voice in blurred syllables said something that sounded like, "Pretty. Big mans."

"Whut did yo' say baby?" There was urgency in Angel's voice. "Whut man? Where? Where yo' sees man wiff hoops lik' deze?"

Eyes that seemed not to comprehend looked into Angels. A little foolish giggle came from Callie's throat. Then she said the words again, "Pretty. Big mans." They were spoken as if she had learned them from memory.

Angle was sure of the words now. "For da luv' of God, baby, tells Angel where yo' see da' man wiff hoops lik' deze. He mights be my brother."

No amount of persuasion or pleading could get anything more from Callie. Angel began to cry. At the sight of her tears, Callie began to twist her fingers in her hair and pull at her clothes. Her mouth started to work but no sounds came from it. Angel knew that she had to distract her attention or Callie would have one of her spells.

SOMETHING TO LIVE FOR

"How yo' lik' ta take walk wiff Angel? We's fine 'nother pretty."

Callie had become fond of anything that was bright or shiny. No matter if it was a pebble, a bird's feather, a piece of glass or a flower, she called them her "pretties." They became her one and only interest.

"I go."

The two of them went for a walk on that day sometime in early June of 1861. That walk would change their lives forever.

Angel was not aware that they had turned from the Calico Place lane and were now going down a winding path half hidden in the tall meadow grass. She walked steadily on but her mind was at the big house in the sleepy bayou country of Louisiana. A little girl was clinging to the grey cotton skirt of her tall octoroon mother. Her mother who held her head proudly and stood erect; she looked like a lovely bronze statue. She stood before the small bitter woman with the twisted body sitting in a wheel chair. Angel's mother saw the bony hands that gave the woman the nick name of "cat claw" in kitchen gossip.

Angel had even seen a young slave held by both arms and around the waist as "cat claw" raked her long finger nails down the girls face and throat. "Cat claw" was the woman that the Master never loved but she had the power to make him do whatever she wanted just as she was doing now. He stood silently behind her chair.

"I've put up with a lot of things, Maurice; a lot of things from the day I married you. I knew you were nothing but a family name, a perfumed dandy with no real red blood and guts in you. I knew to expect your extravagances and your infidelity. I knew we would live on my father's money and his money alone. But ...," the voice continued. It had lost its complaining tone. Now it was filled with an ominous warning quality. Slaves feared that voice; "Cat claw" was going to strike again.

"I tell you, Maurice, I will NOT tolerate this woman and your girl child half-breed under my roof. I'll see that the whole place is burned to the ground! I'll go back to New Orleans to my father's house. But before I go, I'll have black Martha fix you. You know what that means! She'll do exactly as I tell her. You have your choice between my doing that or getting rid of that heathen woman and her half breed. AND AT ONCE!"

With that command, she wheeled herself with lightning speed from the room. Angel's mother stood silently. The Master looked out the window for a long time, turned, but did not look directly at her mother with eyes glued to the floor.

"God Margo. What will I do?" Master had said.

Angel's mother hadn't answered. There wasn't any need for her to answer. She already knew what he would do. Even Angel, as young as she was knew. They and her big ebony half brother would be sold.

Angel hadn't known what to expect next. Her Mother would have gold loops pierced through the ears of her half brother and her. She had them soldered so they could never come out. "Yo always kno's each other by deze hoops," she had said.

It was a miserable trip in the back of the farm wagon. Angel, her mother and brother were packed in it like a can of sardines as the team slowly made its way through pine groves, past tobacco and cotton fields with huge plantation homes. They had been sold to the slave traders in New Orleans and were on their wave to Richmond, Va. Slaves along the way working in the fields would briefly stop their work and bow their heads in silent prayer as the wagon passed. "Oh Lawd, hep' them po' souls find a good Master. Amen."

After what seemed like an eternity to Angel, she, her half brother and her Mother arrived in the city of Richmond. The sights and sounds of the square where they were to be sold were terrifying to her. She heard women screaming, "NO! LAWD NO! don't takes my baby frum me."

She heard the hiss of leather racing through the air to cut the back of strong ebony back. "Move on boy! It's your turn on the block!"

Her half brother was sold first. His Master grabbed him by the arm and hustled him into a waiting wagon. Angel glanced at the wagon as it started moving to see her brother place his hand on his ear and fondle the gold hoop. She touched the one in her ear as well. She was remembering that her Mother had told them always to remember that this would be their way of identifying each other some day.

A man dressed in the finery of a plantation owner looked at Angel's Mother.

"This is a fine lookin' house servant here, boys! That kid of hers shows promise too. Put them on the block together, boys."

"Sold. To the gentleman from Calico Place."

Angel had remembered that scene every time the gold loops flashed in a mirror, winked at her from her reflection in a window. They had only been a reflective memory for over thirty years. They were only a link that had meant nothing really until this half crazy little Miss, in her mixed up rambling mind, had associated them with a pair she had seen somewhere.

Whether she had actually seen them or it was just her imagination, Angel did not know. From this day on she would stay with young Miss until she had the answer, no matter what happened. Her duty to Madam could never equal the measure of the hurt she felt for her lost brother, this desire to know what had happened to him. No, somehow, someway she must find the answer. Their mother had so wanted them to be close to each other.

7

"Pretty." Callie was pointing to a woman who sat beside one of the several wagons talking with two other women. They were almost hidden in a grove of maples on the left of the orchard and the little meadow where the soldier's tents were staked. Angel knew what the wagons meant. She knew they were the soldiers "camp women." Her folks always called a thing by its name and every slave on Calico Place knew about the women who followed the army to do the bidding of the soldiers that only a woman could do.

One was a mixed blood like Angel; one, Angel recognized as one that the slaves said came from one of the finest families of James River who was "teched" in her head. The other woman, the one that Callie had pointed to, had hair like soft, silk, spun gold. It was said that she spoke with a voice filled with sweet honey but had a long knife hidden in her skirt. She was the cook for the officer's camp women. Much blood had graced the blade of this knife when men thought she was one of the "other women."

Callie running ahead suddenly stopped stupefied in front of the woman. Her mouth was gapping and pulling to one side in an idiotic grimace that Callie used whenever she was unsure of herself.

"My God! What's the matter with this girl? I've been stared at before, but never like this! Gives me the creeps. What's wrong with her? Who the devil is she?"

"Tis' Miz Callie Morris, Mam. Her grandmov' be Miz Leticia Hill 'nd owns Calico Place."

"Callie Morris? Her grandmother owns Calico Place? Good Lord! It can't be. You can't be Calvin Morris' daughter, can you? What was your mother's name, girl?" There was urgency in her voice.

Cloudy grey eyes looked into deep blue ones. A hesitant hand went out to touch the woman's hair. It rippled like gold over the woman's shoulders. The question might as well never have been asked.

"Pretty! Pretty!"

"What's the matter, girl? I asked you a question. Can't you hear?"

"Miz Callie's ain't bin well, Mam. Times she ain't herselv. Her mother be Miz Caroline Hill ov Calico Place."

"For heavens sake, you don't say. Here, let me see you honey." The voice became gentle and was softly persuasive as if it were wrapped up in the softness of fur. "If you are who you are, then you're my niece, my only brother's little baby girl that I never even got to see before that old devil Miss Hill ran them off from Calico Place."

The words meant nothing to Callie bewitched with the feel and color of the radiant hair. To Angel, they were the same as gunpowder thrown into an open fireplace. They were a definite link with all the bad things that had happened at Calico Place. She knew that Madam would never approve of this acquaintance, especially if the woman was who she said she was, Emmy Morris. In Madam's opinion, the Morris' were at the bottom of the list of all "po" white trash. They might have lived on a plantation as fine as Calico Place, but they had the audacity to free their slaves and join a movement that called for every plantation owner to do the same.

"Here honey, come here to your Aunt Emmy. What have they done to you? Calvin and Caroline's child should never be like this. Here, look at Emmy's rings. Pretty aren't they?"

A small hand was extended. Its fingers seemed covered with the twinkling lights of stones. "See. Pretty. Come on let's be friends. I'm your own Papa's sister, your own Aunt Emmy. Leave us now girls." she pointed to the other two women sitting by her side. "I want to talk to my niece."

"Emmy? Emmy? Emmy? Papa's Emmy?" Callie spoke the words in the same rhythmic pattern that she had said, "Nothing Nothing Ha Ha Ha" in the past.

Angel could hardly believe Callie had spoken. The words were enunciated clearly, as any normal person would have said them. There was no slurring of the syllables; no slurring as if her tongue was so thick it could not move to make a proper sound. The vague, cloudy look was gone from her eyes too. There had been interest in her tone of voice as if knowing who Emmy was really mattered.

"Yes, your Aunt Emmy; your Aunt Emmy that your Grandmother Hill calls 'po' white trash. But you listen to me; honey, she and her kind have about had their day." The tone had changed now, became heavy with dramatic seriousness.

"This war is going to change things about. Your Grandmother's South, with its powder puff, china-doll ladies who really are as common as the rest of us will be a thing of the past. They love, eat, fight and hunger for the same things as we do. The south's gallant, handsome sports, who at nighttime, or for that matter any chance they get, are just any other man in his animal wants. Yes sir! The dammed plantations that give a decent living only to a few on the backs of slaves while the rest of the people are left with the leavings, that's all going to be changed. Honey, a person's only hope is to be on the winning side with as much gold or jewelry as they can have. This fake money that everyone deals with in the south will not be worth a hill of beans when the end comes.

"It's time for blood kin to stick together. Your Mama's blood kin don't seem to be helping you much. They've hurt you to the very depth of your soul, I can see that. All that's the matter with you is sickness of the heart. You've lost everything you had and have not been given anything to replace it. Here, if you'll sit here by Aunt Emmy, she'll let you try on any of her rings. Come now, pick the one you want."

Shyly, all the fog gone from her eyes, all the fear that lurked at the back of them eased. Carefully, but sure of herself, Callie edged closer to her Aunt Emmy. She was being offered a pretty.

"She best not, Mam." Angel's voice was respectful but authoritative.

"Hold your tongue. What harm can one of my rings do on one of her fingers? A little warmth, a little color and beauty might do her a lot of good, might even erase some of the things that have happened to her. I'll bet there have been plenty. I know how that old devil treated Calvin and Caroline. A little love, a little sparkle might just make her a human being once more. Don't you want her to get well?"

Angel nodded in the affirmative. Her thoughts reverted back to her gold loops. "'Course Mam. I'se wish wiff all mys heart young Miss be well. I'se tried 'nd tried an' da' spells always cum back on her." She wished it more than ever now because today Callie had said something that was very important to Angel; something that she would give her very soul to know the answer that words could bring.

One ring was a deep, pure red gem that was spreading a warm glow around the icy steel feeling that Callie had carried in her heart since the evening they buried Mama. Maybe this woman even knew how to make it melt, as simple as that! If it melted, she knew the horrible bugs would have to go too. Callie looked and listened to the woman with new interest.

"Listen honey, there's two things that I have learned the hard way that might help you. You're almost grown. If you were looking right, I bet you might even have some beaus, have some fun. That'd take your mind off your troubles. Anyway, you like to hear me talk, don't you? The frightened look is gone from your eyes. Want Emmy to tell you about those two things?"

Callie nodded her head in the affirmative.

"Well there's two things that mean everything to a woman; two things that she has to watch out for. There isn't anyone else of the face of God's green earth that will help her with them except herself. One is how she looks. The other is to remember that no matter how hard times get, she will have enough to live on if she has something to live for.

"A woman can't get along without either of them. If she lets herself worry about how she's going to live on nothing she'll get as lean as a razor back hog. Men won't even take a second look at her. They'll hunt for a soft, rounded woman every time. It's their nature. She'll fret until she hears the sound of dirt hitting the lid of her coffin. Looking good and knowing you can make it through anything if you have something to live for are the only two things a woman must know."

Sunlight caught and held the many lights of the gem. Emmy's voice was soothingly confident. Callie listened. What she was saying was beginning to make sense to Angel. She knew from bitter experience that what she said was true. They sat spellbound, held by the sincerity of the voice.

"You watch out for these two things, honey. Let me tell you right now that there's no man worth losing your looks over and no man's worth his salt if he can't either stake you with the gold you need to live on or has the backbone to stand up and work to get it for you. I'll bet when you get a little flesh on you, get rid of that scary look, there'll be plenty of young men hanging around. You will be able to take your pick. Things will look different then, honey. Even your Grandmother won't matter so much. Why I could dress you up and you'd be a sight for sore eyes. Tell you what, the next time you come to see me that's what I'll do. You'd like that wouldn't you?"

"Well bless my buttons! Look what we got here. A couple of nice new girlies."

A man came bolting around the side of the tent. "Where'd you all come from?" His hand went out to touch Angel's face but quick as a rattler striking, a ring hand slapped his face sharply.

"Take your hands off her, Morgan." Emmy commanded.

"Alright Emmy, just trying to be sociable. I'd like to speak to you inside for a moment, please."

"Sorry honey, I'll have to go now. How about coming back to see me real soon?" Emmy was speaking to Callie.

"Yes. Come back." Callie took Angels hand and turned in the direction of the dirt path.

In West Augusta, the political winds of change were blowing strong. Virginia had succeeded from the Union. The delegates from this mountain territory who had so vigorously debated against succession took matters into their own hands. They met in Wheeling's Federal Custom House and declared that the group they'd organized represented the "Restored Government of Virginia," restored as a Union loyal territory. West Augusta, this "Restored Government of Virginia," was the only true Virginia.

Elsewhere in the territory, the men of the Blue and Grey engaged in battles to win the strategic locations that would be necessary for either side if they were to be victorious in the struggle.

In the Kanawha Valley, the Confederate forces crossed the Gauley River to attack the Union forces west of Charleston at Cross Lanes. Taken by surprise, the Union soldiers were routed and they returned to Ohio. The two successful feuding Confederate generals then left and moved northeast to Carnifex Ferry to take up a defensive position there.

General Robert E. Lee traveled to West Augusta to try to settle the dispute between the two generals from the Kanawha Valley now at Carnifex Ferry and to coordinate the use of the forces there. He was entertained lavishly in Lewisburg.

All the way back to Calico Place they both knew that they would go back to see Emmy again. Aunt Emmy had penetrated the hazy, crazed fog that had enveloped Callie. She had given Callie the first spark of interest in anything other than pretties she had experienced for months. In doing this for Callie, Aunt Emmy had given new hope to Angel. If the young Miss became well, then together they might find the man who wore the golden hoops in his ears.

That evening Callie sat by her window, heard the sounds from the soldier's camp and knew that under the maples in the little grove near there was a wagon and a woman who said she was Aunt Emmy. If she really was Aunt Emmy, tonight she had someone of her very own close by. Even the thought of her Grandmother wasn't as bad.

"Perhaps if I do everything the Old Devil asks me to do, stay away from her, ask no questions and think about other things when I am near her, I can get through the days. Grandmother can't bother me too much! I hate her! I wish these dark spells like I have or voodoo or some evil power would get to her. Of course, I know they won't. But if I can make it through the days, every time she takes Salleebay on one of her long rides, I can slip out of the house, go to the wagon and see Aunt Emmy." Callie thought. "I guess I've just been afraid of being alone for too long."

She glanced from the window and a yellow rose caught her attention. A sense of defiance filled her. She stared directly at it. Her gaze did not leave the rose until the light from outside the window had turned to night. Feeling warmth in her body she climbed into bed and thought, "That's all they were and have ever been. A rose painted on beige paper." Callie slept the first peaceful sleep she had had in months.

For days tensions had held Calico Place in a tenacious grip. Horses lathered in white frothy sweat had brought secretive emissaries to see Madam. Soldiers in the orchard camp worked with earnest precision, quietly without the usual joking and laughter. Thoroughly each part of the harness was checked, each rifle was readied until everything was in perfect working order. Men moved as if they were listening to a resolute, commanding drum that said, "Hurry, Hurry the time is near."

Callie slipped away again and again back to the wagons in the little grove. At first, Angel had gone with her to see Aunt Emmy. Recently, Callie had felt the strength to make the journey by her self.

Aunt Emmy had seemed withdraw lately; was quite as if her mind was on other matters. Callie returned to visit her anyway. There was no doubt in Callie's mind. Aunt Emmy was beginning to make the spells seem like they had only been a part of a bad dream.

Then one morning the Thirty-First was gone. It was as if they had been whisked away off the face of the earth by a ghostly hand. A scattered bit of equipment lay here and there but everything of importance was gone. Even the women and their wagons had disappeared.

"Angel, where did they go? Where is Aunt Emmy? Will she be back?" Callie asked in panic.

"Hush Miss Callie, don't yo' go lettin' Madam heah yo' mention dat name. Don't git yo'self all worked up. Things been happenin' over past da mountains. Charles say they's big battles takin' place an' uprisin's."

"You mean they've gone to fight the Yankees? Will they come back when it's over?" Callie asked.

"No bidy knows if'in they's will or not. Madam don't seem ta be worryin' none an' I'se 'spect she has her reasons."

"If they don't come back, how will I find Aunt Emmy?"

"Now Miss Callie, I'se told yo' 'fore. Don't be lettin' Madam hear dat name. Yo' gonna get us both in a heap ov trouble. Sides, why don't yo' take a nap lik' a good little chile? Mebbe by tomorra' we's know somethin' 'bout all da answers to whut' troublin' yo'. Yo' be Angel's nice chile now 'nd ketch yo' some shut eye lak' I'se ax yo'. Angel promise, she's cum tell yo' da very minute Angel hears anytin' at all."

Early the next morning there was plenty to tell. Detachments of the Thirty-First came tearing hell bent for leather up the lane. The defiant Rebel yell filled the morning air.

Callie was at the window. Her eyes were wide with excitement and wonderment. She realized that she was gloriously and vibrantly among the living now. Like a melody played on the spinet over and over again, she heard an inner voice singing, "She's comin' back, she's comin' back. Thank God in heaven, Aunt Emmy's comin' back."

The whole world was marvelous and her elation lasted the whole day. Even the sight of the long, dusty columns of Union prisoners, some with clumsily dressed wounds still dripping red blood that made little brown period marks in the white sand, did not disturb her. Utterly weary men carrying their rifles as if they were fishing poles, going to the stream to fish, didn't bother her. All that mattered was that Aunt Emmy would be coming soon. She could hardly wait to see her again.

What she waited for came with the first evening shadows. A coach with gay prancing horses brought Aunt Emmy and the two other women. The kitchen wagons followed behind. Callie thought she had never seen anything as exciting. She was warmed just remembering the sound of Aunt Emmy's gay lilting laughter. Everything was going to be alright. She had someone who belonged to her nearby. Tomorrow afternoon she would go to see her.

"Miss Callie! Miss Callie, wake up! There's thin's fo' yo' ta do. Yo' can't be sleepin' yo' head off. Wake up Miss Callie. Dun't yo' wants ta hear whut's happenin'?"

Angel's voice hammered into the warm, cozy drowsiness that held her. Angel's hands were insistent on her shoulders. Groggy but happily Callie had heard every word but didn't care whether she answered or not.

"Miss Callie! Fo' da last time, dun't yo' care 'bout whut's ben happenin? If'n I'se hadn't told yo' I'd wake yo' soon I's hear somethin', I'se wouldn't be foolin' 'way my time wiff yo'. Efen yo' don't hit da floor dis minute, I'se a foolin' wid yo' no mo'."

"Alright, Angel. Alright. What do you want me to do? Here I stand shivering and shaking in your presence."

"Lawdy Miss, jes' yo' listen whil's I'se tells yo' den yo's no whuts ta do. Madam plannin' a victory ball heah ta'nite at Calico Place. 'An she ben up since befo' sun up seein' 'bout da fixin's. Da whole Jackson River country done ben invited; an' all da officers at camp. Been no ball lak' dis since Miss Caroline go 'way. Git up now. I'se got to fix ovah one her party dress fo' yo'. 'Cause yo' sure gonna be swingin' 'round dat ole ball room ta'nite jes' lak Miss Caroline use ta do."

Calico Place was shrouded in the soft blue grey of day just before a sunset. Chandeliers were ablaze and every piece of furniture and silver had been polished to gleaming mirror brightness. Servant girls were dressed their best black uniform and wore starched white aprons and lace edged caps. The men were practicing their low bow. A four-piece string orchestra was setting up in the ballroom.

That evening haunting, liquid music filled the room. Women with dainty wasp waists swirled around the ballroom floor with their golden, black or auburn curls trailing behind them. Lace, lavalieres and dazzling earrings framed their faces. Men in grey uniforms with natty shell jackets, wreaths embroidered on their collars, circled the ladies around the dance floor. Flashing smiles and dimpled cheeks flirted to the love songs.

Callie loved every minute of it. She was being passed from one officer to another. She was throwing her head back in laughter; was as light on her feet as she was in her heart. Madam was watching; gave the first sign of pleased satisfaction with her Granddaughter. Callie was vivaciously alive. She was oblivious even to the passing time.

Then a hoarse, fear-filled cry entered the room. People stood motionless.

"Capt'n Norris! Capt'n Norris. Suh! The Yanks have sneaked in on us. They have overpowered the guards! They were on us before we knowed it."

There was a pause, a gasp and then a rushing torrent of words. "There is a whole darn division of them. They're beatin' up on everything in the whole blasted camp."

Abruptly the music stopped. Women stared fixedly at nothing at all, women with their hero's hands holding their mouths to stifle any scream. Frozen human statues were standing all over the ballroom. A rush of men started for the doors and windows. Sharp cracks of pistols and carbines fired from everywhere and at closer and closer range. The eerie high sound of a horse dying in agony and the rasping, shocked cry of the mortally wounded filled the room. Smoke and dust began to filter through the windows making a hazy curtain all over the ballroom. Sounds of the clash and clang of men in hand to hand combat filled the room. Guests made a frantic pell-mell rush to the outside. Mounting alarm and fear created a state of hysteria.

"Mis' Hill! Mis' Hill! Dey's settin' fire to da' house. Lawd a Mercy! It's ketchin'."

"Look ovah by da' window. Oh Lawd Miss Hill. It's got da' curtains."

Acrid smoke was coming from everywhere. Crackle, pop, swoosh and hiss, the sound of wood and fabric leaping into the fires golden mouth. Calico Place's wood had been dried in the warmth of Virginia suns for many years. Its lush velvet and brocade drapes were eagerly lapping up the flames. The tinder-box of Calico Place became a huge, grotesque nightmare burning red and gold from the inside.

"Miss Callie! Miss Callie! Cum chile! Cum baby! Git out dare fas'. Heah. Follow me…"

Callie and Angel were running down the lane with the shooting sparks from the fire chasing them. The fire's glare was lighting up the tall pines. Gasping for breath, Angel stopped.

"Dis here far 'nuff. We's safe 'nuff heah."

Small, black scurrying figures at the big house were futilely trying to save some of Calico Place from the flaming red tongues. A thin, erect figure was speeding across the porch and into the wide yawning black mouth of the entrance hall. Callie knew even before she heard the warning shouts to the woman that it was her Grandmother.

Suddenly a deafening crash of heavy timber gave way. It must have been the stairway. Two men followed her Grandmother into that black furnace. They returned alone.

Callie screamed in anguish, "Liza was in there!"

In the excitement of Calico Place burning, there had been no time to watch the progress of the fighting. Listening for the signs of war, there were none. The furor was past. Occasionally there was a short, brisk command given. Small groups of soldiers were quietly, methodically searching the grounds with fixed bayonets.

Callie and Angel crouched in the semi-darkness and saw that the soldiers were not wearing the same color uniforms as those who had been camped in the meadow or at the ball. These wore dark blue uniforms. The dying flames that flared up; highlighted the U.S. on their buttons. Then there was a flash of polished spurs on leather boots of the man on horse. Yankee Calvary! Yankee Calvary scouting the grounds meant just one thing, the Thirty-First had fled.

"Quick Miss Callie! We's cain't stay heh. They'll fin' us sho' as shootin'! Les' go an' see efen yo' Aunt Emmy is still heah."

Never had Angel looked as beautiful to Callie as she did now with her tawny, golden skin glowing in the soft flame light. Her warm brown eyes were pleading with Callie to come with her to safety. Quietly and persistently Angel continued, " Theah's nothin' fo' eithah of us at Calico Place, Miss Callie. Madam done gone; gone ta meets her maker. We's jes' go ta fin' yo' Aunt Emmy an' get her to hep us."

A straw to cling to; maybe Emmy would help them. Anyway, there wasn't anything else to do.

"Did you hear about the awful fight at Carnifex Ferry?" The regular Wednesday afternoon ladies tea group was meeting in Lewisburg.

"Wasn't it just horrible? Our poor boys sent on the run like that."

"Yes, after all that handsome General Lee did to get those two generals to work together to fight to beat those damm Yankees." Sarah informed the group.

"Wasn't he handsome? General Lee I mean. I just love the sight of his grey hair and beard with the grey of his uniform. And that horse of his, Traveler, suits him perfect."

"What I hear is the one general is blaming the other general for not doing his part in the fight and that's why they had to flee in the dark of the night."

"Honestly, if those two don't ever learn to get along together, we will hear this story over and over again!" Sarah predicted.

The truth of what had happened at Carnifex Ferry was three brigades of Union forces with heavy artillery had marched there from the north central part of West Augusta or the "Restored Government of Virginia," as it was now known. With the dissention between the two Confederate generals, with the strength of the artillery that they faced, the Confederate forces only choice was to retreat in the dark of the night. The "damm Yankees" won this battle. Carnifex Ferry was now in Union hands.

8

Hiding in the shadows of the trees, running bent over in the open places, Callie and Angel reached the half-hidden path in the meadow. Their first glimpse told them something was wrong. All the wagons were different except Aunt Emmys. Light was streaming from it. Two sentries were posted outside.

"Halt! Or we'll shoot!"

"What is it Billings?"

"Christ all Mighty! A young gal an' a light skinned woman!"

"Maybe that the ones who slipped away. Better take them to the Capt'n."

Inside the wagon, Emmy sat straight and proud by a little cherry desk. In front of her, two Union officers stood half bent over with their backs to the wagon's opening.

"Capt'n Murdock, Sir! These two women, Sir, were coming to the wagon. They come sneakin' through the grass. Don't know what for. We thought you'd best ask them, Sir."

Like a flash, Emmy was out of the chair and down the wagon steps.

"Thank God! Thank God you're safe, honey. I've been so worried!" She threw her arms around Callie.

"Wait a minute, Miss Morris. Who are these women?"

"This, Captain Archer is Miss Callie Morris, my niece. The other woman is one of the servants from Calico Place."

"Beg yo' pardon, Suh. I'se Miss Callie's personal maid."

Angel quickly grasped the opportunity of tying herself to Callie. Now that Callie was herself once again, Angel believed more strongly that ever that Callie had really seen her half brother some place before coming to Calico Place.

"Is your niece visiting you, Miss Morris? Or who is responsible for her?"

"She been livin' wuth her Gran'mother, Miss Letchia Hill, at Calico Place, Suh. An' Miss Callie's Mama jes' died dis spring. She bin at Calico Place evah since. Miss Morris, Miss Callie's Papa's sistah, Suh."

"Well, that may all be true but someone will have to assume the responsibility for her now. We can't turn her loose in the countryside. This is one devil of a mess for a young woman to be running around in with just a servant with her."

In a voice as soft as silk or velvet honey, Emmy began to speak. "Captain Archer, would it not further the plans we have been discussing by adding respectability to them if I take care of my young niece? I'm certain everyone would accept, without question, the fact of an Aunt is taking care of her orphaned niece."

"Does Aunt Emmy mean I can stay with her?"

No one paid any attention to Callie's question and doubt remained in the Captain's voice.

"Well..."

"Since we will be leaving soon, it would really look better if I said we were crossing the mountains to find a safe haven for myself and my orphaned niece. It will create a more sympathetic story. People will not doubt a story of an Aunt and her niece with their one remaining, faithful servant trying to get away from the 'damm Yankees' who had left them homeless."

"Perhaps you're right, Miss Morris. At least the girl and her servant may remain with you until further notice." Abruptly both officers left the wagon.

"Aunt Emmy, did he really mean that I can stay with you? Do you really want me to stay?"

"Yes, honey, I know your Grandmother died at Calico Place tonight. As far as I know, I'm your nearest kin now. Even 'po' white trash', as your Grandmother called me, knows how to take care of their own. Besides," a crafty calculating gleam came into Emmy's eyes. "Remember when I told you it was going to be smart to be on the winning side? There's never been a doubt in my mind now which side will win this fight. Little Emmy's been spyin' for the winnin' side all along in Confederate camps and she's gonna keep on spying for the winnin' side."

It was Wednesday again in Lewisburg; teatime.

"Have you heard what those damm Yankees are callin' General Lee?" Sarah asked.

"No. What?"

"You shouldn't even repeat it, Sarah. That just makes it spread more!"

"Well, June told Helen that her cousin in Charleston overheard some Yankees talkin'. That they were laughin' and callin' our boys all sorts of vile names; talkin' about them runnin' like scared rabbits to Meadow Buff after the Carnifex Ferry battle." She stopped to sip her tea.

"OH GO ON SARAH! You know you have us sittin' on the edge of our chairs! What are they callin' General Lee?"

Sarah continued after slowing placing her china teacup and saucer on the drum table beside her, picking up a cookie from the tray offered her by a house servant. She started to raise the cookie to her mouth.

"DON'T YOU DARE take time to eat that cookie, Sarah. WHAT are the Yankees callin' General Lee?"

"Well, you know the whole mess at Carnifex Ferry wasn't his fault. He had come to talk to those two generals about their behavior and getting' along together, remember?"

"SARAH!"

"Well, just because he went back to Richmond..."

"SARAH!" several voices joined in shouting her name this time.

Realizing she had played out her little performance as far as it would go, she said, "Those damn Yankees have started callin' him 'GRANNY' Lee."

Every woman in the room except Sarah gasped in disgust. Sarah, with a satisfied smile in her heart for her performance, took a bite from the cookie.

It was all the house servant could do to keep from dropping the tray of cookies and bursting into boisterous laughter.

"Angel, will you walk over to the grave yard with me today? I would like to see Mama's grave."

"Yes 'em. I'se be heppy ta."

"That's a good idea. Captain Murdock and Captain Archer are coming to talk to me about the final plans." Emmy interjected.

They found the hill that led to the grey stone chapel.

"Angel, why does Aunt Emmy call those men Captain? They don't wear uniforms."

"I'se got mys suspects butt you'se best ax Miss Emmy."

There was the low fieldstone wall with the wrought iron gate. The tall-black pines still stood guard over the gravestones.

Callie could not hold back the tears when she saw the gravestone at the head of her mother's grave. Angel wrapped her arms around her.

"You'se jest let it all out, girl. Let it all out."

Memories flooded Callie's mind. Uncle Jim had told her the same thing, "Let it out girl." There were the clutching claws grabbing at her, Mammy's red head, Mama lying cold on her bed, Uncle Jim dropping to the ground after the bullets ripped open his stomach.

"Let it out, girl. You'se got to cry all dat hurts in ta dis' earth. You'se Mama an' me here's. You'se safe."

Captain Archer was speaking. "The plan starts tomorrow Emmy. Junior Moore has come down from Philadelphia to take his invalid father, Judge Moore, back to Philadelphia with him. He is telling the servants that he has learned you are homeless after the defeat of the Thirty-First with whom you were traveling and has agreed to allow you, Miss Callie and Angel to stay at the Moore House until you can get your possessions and decide where you are going. You are to have use of any of the carriages and servants. You will go there tomorrow.

"You are to ask for Jefferson to take you in the carriage anytime you need to go back to your home place. He is a trusted friend and loyal to the Union. He will tell no one of your trips or their purpose."

"I understand," Emmy replied. "When will I leave, I mean when will we leave the Moore house for my next assignment."

"After you have retrieved all of the items you want from your folk's land, ask Jefferson to get word to me that you are ready to go to Richmond."

"Is Richmond where my next assignment will be?"

"No, your next assignment will be in Lewisburg in West Augusta."

She had heard Callie talk about West Augusta. It sounded like an enchanted land with the beauty of a profusion of flowers growing everywhere, mountain streams that sparkled like diamonds, skies that held mysterious pictures and something called three tier waterfalls.

"Callie is from West Augusta, Captain Archer. In fact, I think I even recall her saying that she came through Lewisburg on her trip to Jackson River."

"That's even better. She will be able to converse with the locals about West Augusta and that will really help in your being accepted into the 'society' of the town."

"Why are we going to Richmond first?"

"Our people in Lewisburg say there is a house for sale that is in the perfect location for our people to be able to come and go unseen, deliver messages to you and receive your messages. You will need to purchase furnishings for the house and the latest fashions for you and Miss Callie.

"The people that it will be important for you to socialize with to obtain information are the 'elite' of Lewisburg. You will fit right in with your upbringing and Miss Callie with her beauty will attract the young men who will tell her anything you need to know to win her affections." He chuckled at the thought of the young blades trying to use all their southern gentlemanly charms to obtain Miss Callie's favors with Aunt Emmy and her knife in the picture.

"How will I get all the furnishings to Lewisburg? How will we get there? To Richmond?"

"When I receive the word from Jefferson that you are ready to go to Richmond, I will send one of our trusted Union men to come with a confiscated carriage, dressed in the confiscated finery of a servant to take you to Richmond.

"In Richmond you will stay at Morson's Row in one of the town houses on Governor Street. Arrangements have been made for you to be there while the present renters are in Europe shopping for furniture for their new home."

"I assume then that it's furnished?" Emmy asked.

"Yes, you will be the cousin of the owner's wife who is just spending time shopping in Richmond for a couple of weeks."

"But what about the furniture and clothes I buy?"

"With each purchase, you will inform the shop owner that you want the items packed for transporting by wagon. I will send the necessary wagons when the time comes. Again, trusted Union men, dressed as servants, will pick up your purchases and bring them to you. Each day you will tell Jefferson what you have purchased and he will get the word to me so I will know how many wagons to send.

"However, you will need to take at least a week's worth of fashionable attire for you and Miss Callie with you on the trip. It wouldn't hurt to also buy Angel a couple of servant outfits to take with you and more for your stay in Lewisburg."

"Two weeks, Captain Archer? You expect me to get all this done and be on my way to Lewisburg in two weeks?" Emmy took a deep breath and shook her head.

Captain Archer chuckled. "I can't imagine there's any red blooded southern girl who wouldn't give her eye tooth to be able to go on a two weeks shopping spree at the government's expense! I bet you'll have enough purchases to fill five wagons!"

"Mama, it was awful at Calico Place. I think I had a nervous breakdown. If it hadn't been for Aunt Emmy and Angel, I might still be in the vegetable state I was in from grieving for the loss of you, Mammy and Uncle Jim. And Grandmother …"

She had started to tell her Mama about the treatment she had received from Grandmother when she remembered the fire; Grandmother's death.

"I wonder if there is a marker for Grandmother, Angel."

"Here ' tis Miss Callie."

Callie walked to where Angel was pointing at a stone on the other side of her Grandfather's gravestone. It simply had carved on it in letters "L W H."

"How was your trip to visit your Mother's grave, Callie?" Emmy was asking Callie the question. She was looking at Angel's face to see if it indicated to her whether she could continue with additional questions along this vein.

"It's exactly what I needed to do, Aunt Emmy. I told Mama all about my nervous break down; how you and Angel helped me through it." She chuckled. "I even told her I wasn't a little girl any more; that I am now a young woman."

"Good!" Emmy said with much relief in her heart.

"Now it's my turn to ask you about your afternoon, Aunt Emmy. And why do you call those men Captain when they are not wearing any uniforms?"

Aunt Emmy looked outside, closed the door and became as serious as Uncle Jim was before they had gotten to the Garman Inn.

"Callie and Angel. You MUST NEVER mention this again or tell a single soul what I am going to tell you. It is a matter of life or death for all of us."

Aunt Emmy went on to explain that she had seen who burned down her family's home the night of the dreadful fire. It was local southern boys dressed as Yankees. From that night to this day she had been spying for the Union, with different Confederate units and sending messages to the "damm Yankees." "As Calvin and your Mama probably told you, my folks were always on the Yankees side. I just let the Confederates think I was mad because the 'damm Yankees' had burned down Morris Hill."

She was still spying for the 'damm Yankees' and Captain's Archer and Murdock had brought her information on her new assignment and where they would be going. They were actually Union soldiers disguised as farmers.

"Both of you must right now promise me on the Holy book, if I had one, that you will not tell a single soul what I have told you."

"I promise."

Angel nodded her head in the affirmative.

"Where are we going Aunt Emmy?" Callie asked.

"Tomorrow we will go to Judge Moore's house. After I finish some work I must do at my folks place, a carriage will be sent to take us to Richmond."

"Richmond? Isn't that where President Jeff Davis has his house? Do you think we'll get to meet him, Aunt Emmy?"

"We won't have time, Callie. We will have exactly two weeks to purchase furnishings for our new home, lots of fancy dresses for you and me and pretty uniforms for Angel. Then we're all off for our new home."

"That sounds like lots of fun, Aunt Emmy." Callie's face lit up at the prospect of shopping for two weeks. "But where will our new home be Aunt Emmy?"

"Lewisburg in West Augusta."

"Angel," Callie shouted with glee. "Did you hear that, Angel? West Augusta! I'm going home to West Augusta!"

Callie took Angel's hands and the two of them began spinning around the small room. Aunt Emmy laughed at the sight.

In West Augusta a Union Brigadier General marched his troops south from Cheat Mountain in the north to Camp Bartow on the Greenbrier River. His goal was to reconnoiter the Confederate's position, use his artillery to drive the Confederates from their position and secure Camp Bartow for the Union. A sporadic fight ensued but he was never able to turn the enemy's right flank. Forty men of the Union died; forty men of the South. In all respects, the battle was a draw. The Union soldiers withdrew and returned to Cheat Mountain.

"What are we going to do at your folks, Aunt Emmy? Uncle Jim told me about the fire that burned down the big house." She grew solemn. "And, he told me about Papa's Mama and Papa being killed in the fire."

"Did he also tell you that my folks were one of the first plantation owners to free their slaves? That they tried to talk other plantation owners into freeing their slaves as well?"

"Yes Mam, he did."

"Well, my father was a very wise man. Long before the fighting started, long before the rumblings of war even happened, my Daddy sensed that it would happen. He decided to convert all the profits he made from selling cattle, raising cotton and tobacco, any money he made in any way into gold. 'You watch. The South will not accept that it is only right and God's will that we free the slaves. The South will fight it to the bitter end and probably even decide it wants to be a nation of its own. It will print up its own money and tell us all we have to use its money, not the Union money. I'll have no parts of any of it!'"

"And he showed your Papa and me, Callie, where he was burying all the gold. 'Someday you kids may need to use this gold. Don't you dare tell anyone where it is but when the day comes that you need it, it's yours.'"

"We're going on a treasure hunt then Aunt Emmy?"

Emmy laughed. "We sure are Callie. I know already where the treasure is buried. Rightfully, half of it is yours because you should have your Papa's part of the gold. I'll hold it for you until you need it just like the good earth and my Papa's wisdom has been holding it for us. And we're going to spend some of it to buy us a fine house in Lewisburg!"

"Did you hear that someone is coming from over the mountains to buy the old Smithson house north of town beyond the fair grounds?"

"I did, Sarah, and my girl tells me there's no question but that that place is haunted."

"HAUNTED?"

"That's absolutely right." Sarah replied. "Ole Miss Smithson was said to be as crazy as a loon. She had six children but only the one boy lived to manhood."

"And I heard he never married because he was afraid he'd pass on his Mama's craziness to his children," another lady informed the group.

"Right again." Sarah said with satisfaction in her voice that she was the one who knew everything about everyone in town and was the only one who could verify if a statement was right or wrong. "You know there are still questions about how some of her children died. Some say it was at her own hands."

"And they're all buried in that family plot with the iron fence around it."

"Right again. I guess you've all heard the story about the child that ate some blackberries off the vine growing through the fence and ..." Sarah paused to sip her tea and take a bite of cookie.

"And?"

"Well, according to my girl who told me about it," she sipped her tea again. Now that she had their undivided attention, she continued. "According to my girl who told me, the child that ate the blackberries that were growing on the grave of one of her children," sip, sip, another slow sip for effect "died."

"That's horrible!"

"Not only that, but ... May I have another cookie from your tray, please?"

"GO ON SARAH!"

"Mysterious lights have been seen in the house at all times at night. It's said that..."

Turning to the hostess she said, "My dear, I think this is the most delightful cookie I have ever eaten. You must let me have the recipe for it so I can have my girl make some. Is it apple sauce I taste in it?"

A chorus of voices shouted, "GO ON SARAH!"

"Well, it's said that the light is made from the candle that ole Miss Smithson's ghost carries through the house looking for the children."

"Aunt Emmy, I have never had as much fun in my whole life!" Callie gave her a big hug. "I don't know which dress I want to wear first. They're all so pretty! Thank you!"

"You can thank me, dear, but you also have to thank the Union."

"I'se knows I'se ain't evah had seven u'forms ta pick frum ta wear! One fo' each day of da week. An' new ones too! Ain't hand me downs lik' I'se use ta." Angel smiled. "I'se gonna fix yo' hair all pretty ta' wear wuth dem dresses ta, Miss Callie."

"Oh and Aunt Emmy, I just love the brass bed you picked out for my bedroom. And the marble top dresser with brass knobs; the chest on chest, all the beautiful things you picked out!" Callie gave Emmy a hug.

Emmy laughed. "I picked out? I could read that pout on your face if I suggested something you didn't like. Now you two get to bed. Jefferson will be here in the morning to drive us to Lewisburg."

"Lewisburg in West Augusta! Oh Aunt Emmy I don't think I'll sleep a wink tonight. I'M GOING HOME TO WEST AUGUSTA!" Callie hugged herself as if she were hugging one of the green purplish trees she loved.

Jefferson handed Aunt Emmy a note as she stepped into the carriage.

"Dis frum Captain Archer. He say yo'se ta read befo' we's gets ta Lewisburg. He say tells yo'se whut ta do when we's get there, Miss Emmy."

Aunt Emma read his note carefully.

You are to stay at the Inn on Washington Street until your furniture and other purchases arrive by wagon.

You are to contact Mr. Jonathan Henson, a lawyer on Court Street. He will assist you in the purchase of the Smithson property north of town.

You, Callie and Angel are to attend the Old Stone Presbyterian Church for Sunday services. You and Callie will sit down stairs. There is a balcony where Jefferson and Angel will sit.

Most important you MUST remember the name Sarah McKinney. She rules the town's social life and she is the one who determines if a person is accepted or not. By all means, if she approaches you, be polite but not pushy. She must invite you into her social group and that may take time.

Sarah McKinney has a son named George. Callie should be able to obtain valuable information from him.

When you have a message that you wish someone to pick up, at midnight, walk back and forth in front of the side widows in the bedroom facing west with a lit candle. You will hear two taps on the kitchen door followed by five taps. Our men who have come to get the message will make those taps.

After you have read this note and are certain you will remember its contents, destroy it. GOOD LUCK MISS EMMY. GOD BLESS YOU!

"In the blue ridge mountains of Virginia, on the trail of the lonesome pine, I'll be going back to West Augusta, to the loves that I left behind." Callie burst into song.

"Callie, that's not the way that song goes!" Aunt Emmy told her.

"I know Aunt Emmy, but it's the way I want to sing it. Look ahead at those blue mountains. See how they come one after another lapping over each other. Just wait until we get into those mountains! You will smell the freshest air you have ever smelled in your whole life. Your head will twist off trying to see all the pretty flowers. We HAVE to have Jefferson stop at some springs I know. The water is the best you will ever taste in your life!

I'll just HAVE to have time to take off my shoes and put my feet in the cool water of a mountain stream. OH AUNT EMMY, everything I ever loved in my whole life before I met you and Angel is in West Augusta!"

9

"Aunt Emmy, Angel look! There's a carpet of gold under that tree!" Callie was pointing to a large oak tree in front of a two-story brick house with round white columns standing from the porch floor to the roof.

Jefferson drove the carriage into the town of Lewisburg, Virginia in October. They had passed through mountains that looked like a calico quilt with the blend of fall leaves. There were the oak trees with their orange and gold leaves, red leafed maple trees, trees with leaves of brilliant yellow and varying shades of fading green. The purplish green of the pine trees scattered among this array of color seemed more intense.

The town was a blaze of color as well. Stately oaks and maples framed streets and walks leading to beautiful two story brick homes with manicured lawns. Flower beds with scattered flowers still blooming, were trying desperately to hold on through the last warm days of fall.

"Can't you just feel winter coming?" one of the women asked at the Wednesday afternoon ladies tea.

"Oh my dear, did I tell you about seeing the wooly worms sunning themselves on the rocks along my flower bed this week?" Sarah asked.

"No."

"I have never seen so many black ones this early. You know how they're usually that rich brown color in the center with black on either end." Sarah sipped her tea.

"I've always thought they kind of look like teddy bears," a woman spoke up from the cut velvet green and gold settee.

"I suppose that's true," Sarah answered, "but I saw almost as many solid black ones as the 'teddy bear' ones."

"You know what that means. Solid black; we're in for a bad winter." Another woman spoke.

"I just hope it holds off long enough for us to have our Thanksgiving dinners, Christmas ball and New Years Eve parties." Sarah stated.

"I hope those people who are buying the Smithson place get moved in before winter comes. Has anyone heard anything more about them?" someone asked.

Sarah immediately took command of the floor. "Yes, I have. Mr. Gumm, who owns the Inn on Washington Street, has a boy workin' for him that is sweet on one of my girls. The boy's been tellin' my girl everythin' he's been hearin' about them. Then she's been tellin' me."

She continued, "Have any of you ever seen the rooms in the Inn? They're really quite nice. Each one of them has…"

"Sarah," a voice interpreted, "tell us what you've heard about the people buying the Smithson place!"

"Well, the boy overheard the woman tellin' Mr. Gumm that the 'damm Yankees' had burned her family home and with her Mother and Father in it. She is homeless." Dramatically Sarah had emphasized damm Yankees and homeless.

"OH NO!"

"But that's not the end of it! Those 'damm Yankees' even burned her orphaned niece's Grandmother's house and her Grandmother was in it! Now her niece is homeless too."

"THOSE POOR DEARS! This is awful." A chorus of voices said.

"Mr. Gumm told Mr. McKinney," all southern women referred to their husbands as Mr. this, or Mr. that, "The woman is the sister of Mr. Jim Hill from Jackson River country." Sarah continued.

She paused and looked directly into the face of the woman sitting across from her. "Rebecca, don't you entertain Mr. Hill in your home on occasion?"

Rebecca's heart stopped and she prayed her face would not turn scarlet red. She wondered how on earth Sarah had found out that Jim Hill would stop by to see her on his trips across the mountains when her husband was busy at his store.

"Yes. Mr. Hill does business with Mr. Henry. There are times when he is unable to find Mr. Henry and needs to place a special order with me before continuing his trip."

Silently Rebecca prayed, "I hope that satisfies Sarah's curiosity and I don't have to answer more of her prying questions."

"Well I guess you've heard that Mr. Hill was killed by damm Yankees when he was taking his niece's…"

THUD, THUD, THUD! Rebecca's heart started pounding in her chest. She felt she was going to faint. She saw Sarah's mouth moving and staring at her but wasn't hearing a word she was saying. Rebecca bit her lower lip inside her mouth hard enough to bring blood, pushed her thumbnail into her next finger until it caused severe pain. Stopping the fainting and thinking clearly again, she told herself, "Keep your face emotionless, sip your tea so you can lower your eyes and pay careful attention to what Sarah is saying. Does she know something about our affair or is she just fishing for information? HOLD YOURSELF TOGETHER! NOW REBECCA!"

"What else could the poor girls Aunt do but take in her brother's daughter, his only child, and take care of her? I believe Mr. Gumm told Mr. Henry the girl's name is Callie. She is even bringing the girl's personal servant with them." Sarah continued.

"Mr. Henson, my name is Emmy Morris." She extended her gloved hand to him. "May I introduce my niece, Miss Callie Morris."

"How do you do, Miss Morris. It is my pleasure to meet you." He replied bowing slightly and nodding his head in her direction. "It's a pleasure to meet you as well, Miss Callie. Please, both of you have a seat. What may I do for you, Miss Emmy Morris?"

"I have come to Lewisburg to purchase the Smithson property."

"I have heard that inquires were being made about that property by a lady from Virginia. Hopefully, you were told the circumstances of the property sale."

"You mean that the only surviving member of the Smithson family died without leaving heirs? Yes, I was told and even that ridiculous story about the house being haunted." Aunt Emmy responded.

"Have you seen the property?"

"I am having my boy drive us there after this appointment. I am prepared to pay you in gold the amount that is requested by the executor of the estate." Emmy said calmly.

"Please draw up the necessary paper work to complete the transaction. Oh yes, and be certain to include both the names Emmy and Callie Morris on the deed. When do you think you can have the papers completed? Furniture I've purchased should be arriving from Richmond along with other purchases some time next week."

"Perhaps by this Friday, the day after tomorrow, I will have them completed. Where are you staying?"

He knew where she was staying. The whole town knew about the carriage with the two women and a servant arriving Monday at the Inn on Washington Street. Within two hours of their arrival, probably earlier, the whole town knew who they were and why they were there. He had even been told that the aunt and her niece were very pretty. He certainly agreed with that statement seeing them in person.

"At the Inn on Washington Street," Emmy replied.

"Very well, I will send someone to the Inn tomorrow to inform you if I will have the papers ready Friday to be signed."

Lewisburg, chartered in 1782, county seat of Greenbrier County, was on the far eastern side of a fertile limestone region. It was the last semblance of a civilization for travelers from the east before they journeyed on the Kanawha-Staunton Turnpike to Charleston. This narrow, rock-rutted trail led to the Kanawha Valley, gateway to the Ohio River country to the west, Shenandoah Valley and Roanoke to the east. The Lewisburg & Huttonsville Turnpike bisected the Kanawha Turnpike in Lewisburg leading north and south. The road continued south to Bluefield and Wytheville. The town spread in an attractive way over limestone acres with a large depression or sink hole in the very center. Stagecoaches met each other at the grey, cut stone Inn opposite the courthouse causing an excitement as travelers going east and west met travelers going north or south.

The one hundred or so miles of almost unbroken wilderness to Charleston had always been hazardous in normal times. Now it was even more hazardous. It was declared open territory by both Union and Confederate troops. It was a known risk to take to travel it; no one could be sure whether a stage or rider would get over the Kanawha-Stanton Turnpike alive for many reasons.

Most of the town's elite residents considered Lewisburg to be southern territory. They were loyal to the southern cause and were very outspoken about where their royalty laid. It teemed and seethed like smoldering coal with uncertainty for the other population of the surrounding area. The local organized fighting unit, the Greenbrier Rifles, was made up of sharp shooters and sons of the elite. It had already left for Camp Scary. Everyone in town and those on surrounding farms knew Lewisburg was becoming a tinderbox. If the Federalist gained control of the Kanawha Valley, the war would be carried to Virginia by way of the turnpike. The town was certain to see front line fighting.

There were Yankees hidden everywhere in the area everyone suspected. The feeling was that something was about to happen; it made men anxious eyed. It was common knowledge that all the young blood that could fight had already gone. If the Federalist should come to town, it was wide open in its defenselessness. All the "ifs" had the town on edge.

People also worried about the rumor that the two generals in the Kanawha Valley were still not agreeing on the strategy to fight a battle. They continued to disagree on how to carry out the dispatches from General Lee's headquarters and their disagreements were getting worse. General Lee himself had come to Lewisburg once to try to straighten out the mess. The fear was that if General Lee tried to come again to solve the problem, the Yankees would ambush his whole army somewhere and no telling what would happen. Their fears did not materialize. General Lee sent another General to access the situation and try to solve it.

Even more disturbing was the rumor that some of the Yankees had stolen guns stored in the cave in the back of the courthouse across from Fort Savannah. According to the rumor, the guns had been secretly given to the slaves in the area. It was all an effort of the 'damm' Yankees to enlist the help of the slaves when the trouble came, some said. Town folk felt better if they left a light burning some place in the house at night and kept a gun handy by the bed. Everyone was sure now that they could smell trouble and that it wasn't far off.

There were distractions though, moments and hours of forgetfulness. Social custom and hospitality held its head high believing the south could not be anything but victorious. Old southern traditions had to be continued. Planning by the women for social events took months. They didn't even mind when their husbands went off deer hunting, met at the lounges in the Inn's or whatever it was their husbands did.

Jefferson drove the carriage north from town past the fairgrounds. A short distance from there, he stopped the carriage and pointed. "There 'tis, Miss Emmy."

Emmy saw a two story white house with a porch running the entire length of the house sitting on a knoll that faced east towards the low land of Virginia they had left. It had square white columns from porch floor to roof placed at spaced intervals the entire length of the porch. Large twin chimneys were on either and of the house. A white picket fence appeared to enclose a yard in front of house and large golden oak trees lined the fence. A lane wound from the bottom of the knoll and disappeared at the top.

"Oh it's beautiful Aunt Emmy! Look at those trees! I bet there's a carpet of gold under each one." Callie's voice was filled with happiness as she looked at the house on the Smithson property. "Hurry Jefferson, I want to go up and see it all!"

The lane turned at the top of the knoll and went directly in front of the porch entry. There the lane widened in order to hold two carriages. One carriage could stop allowing its passengers to discharge onto a flagstone walkway leading to the house while another other carriage could pass on the other side. As the carriage got closer to the house, it became apparent that the house was actually made of brick. It was painted white. Callie saw that the steps leading to the porch were made of flagstone as well as the porch.

"Look Aunt Emmy." Callie pointed at the ceiling of the porch. It's painted blue like the sky."

"Of course it is, Dear. That's done to confuse the bees into thinking it is the sky. Then they won't try to build their hives there." Aunt Emmy explained.

"That works fo' hornets 'an wasps too. We's got them heah too." Jefferson spoke as he handed Miss Emmy a key.

"Dis key fo' da front door, Miss Emmy. I'se pick' it up whiles yo' wuz talkin' ta da lawyer."

The large door with beveled side panels opened into a central entry hall. An opening on the left entered a large room with beautiful hardwood floors. At the end of the wall seen from the entry was a large limestone fireplace with a solid black walnut mantel. It had large windows on either side. Those windows and the ones that were spaced between each column on the porch side allowed sunlight to flood the room.

"Look at this Angel." Callie had run into the room that would be the living room. "I will have to get up every morning to watch the sun rise over those mountains I see in the distance. When the sun rises behind a mountain, it is spectacular here in West Augusta.

"First the sun lights the sky behind the mountain with a soft glow as if it is saying, 'Get ready, here I come.' Then as the sky becomes lighter, the sun starts slowly peaking its head up behind the mountain and all around the sky starts filling with soft blended shades of yellows, orange and pink. After it finally climbs to the top of the mountain, the whole sky is filled with wonderful warming sunlight."

Jefferson had closed the front door and Aunt Emmy was gazing into the large room on the opposite side of the entry. Callie ran over to her.

"This is the dining room, Callie. Look how it has a large fireplace and windows to match the ones in the living room." Aunt Emmy was speaking.

"I bet that door leads directly into the kitchen." She continued.

White chair railing was on all walls. The room had been painted two shades of rose with the darker color at the bottom broken by the chair railing separating the lighter rose at the top.

"Deze da stairs go ta' da' bedrooms?" Angel was asking. On the hall side of the dining room wall, stairs climbed the wall terminating at a second floor hallway.

"Let's go see." Callie raced up the stairs followed by Angel.

Aunt Emmy had continued through the door in the dining room into a large kitchen. There was a door leading to a back porch and yard. Another door opened into a pantry and a third door opened into a hall leading to rooms behind the central entry hall. There were several smaller rooms along this back hall and a large one behind the living room wall. Opening this door, Emmy saw that it was the library.

Turning to Jefferson, she said. "Captain Simmons certainly did a good job describing these rooms to me. All the furniture I bought in Richmond will fit perfectly. The china I picked will coordinate on the dining room table. Thank heavens I bought enough pairs of those sheers to use on all those windows in the living and dining rooms."

"Aunt Emmy, come up here and pick out the bedroom you want." Callie was yelling from the banister on the second floor. "Then I'll pick out the one I want."

Emmy knew exactly which bedroom she wanted. It was the one on the end above the library with the two windows facing west.

She made a pretense of choosing her bedroom. Opening each door she walked in to survey the space. In fact she had even turned right at the top of the stairs in order to gradually get to the west end one.

"Well look at this Callie. This end bedroom has a large fireplace in it." She said.

"Oh these are smaller." Emmy said of the second and the third bedrooms as she surveyed it.

Opening the door into the room that would be hers, Emmy commented. "This one has a fireplace just like the one on the other end of the hall."

She walked to one of the windows that faced towards Lewisburg, looked out and said, "I'll take this one, Callie. That way, I can see who our guests are that are coming in the carriages up the lane. You take the big room at the other end of the hall. Is that alright dear?" She made no sign that she had even observed the two windows facing west.

"I love it, Aunt Emmy!"

"Your bedroom will be the one next to Callie on the far end, Angel."

Angel's face turned to one of shock. "But Mam, I'se ta sleep in one ov'a dem little rooms side da kitchen down stairs," she protested.

"Oh forget that nonsense, Angel. In our house, you will sleep up here on the second floor in one of the nice rooms with us! Of course, if Callie has friends sleep overnight or we have guests, you will have to sleep downstairs while they are here."

Angel was thrilled. She had never imagined in her wildest dreams that she would ever have a larger room traditionally reserved for guest use in the South. Rushing through the door of the room that was beside Callie's, she stood starry-eyed gazing around the room.

"Oh Lawd in heb'en aboves," she said turning her eyes to the ceiling, "You'se jest gots ta tell Mama ta look down heah an' see dis."

Thursday morning Emmy had Jefferson drive them around town in the morning, stopping to look at all the stores, homes and finding the Old Stone Church. Eyes peered out from behind sheer clad windows in the homes to get a glimpse of the new women in town, assess their attire and looks. The men walking on the streets with their wives on their arms, made a pretense of stopping to gaze at an object in the store window to take a good look at the new arrivals reflected in the glass of the window. They were looking to see if the women were as pretty as other men had said. Their wives, holding onto their arms, were also observing the reflections to see if the new women in town had any fashion sense at all.

That afternoon there was a soft knocking on Emmy's door. An inn servant handed her a note and said, "Mam. Master Gumm says I'se ta gives dis ta yo."

"Thank you very much," she said as she took the folded note from him. She turned, closed the door and read the note.

Written on the paper were the words, "Dear Miss Morris, I have completed the paper work necessary for you to purchase the Smithson property. If you will be so kind as to come to my office at 10:00 AM tomorrow, Friday, I will be pleased to assist you and your niece in this matter. Sincerely, Jonathan Henson."

"Callie," she said. "We must be ready to leave for Mr. Henson's office by 9:30 tomorrow morning. We have an appointment to buy our new home at ten."

The next morning Emmy and Callie sat in Mr. Henson's office. He carefully explained the details of each page to them. They had signed or initialed three copies of each page. He had explained they were signing two copies in order that they would have a copy of the deed; one would be kept at the courthouse; one in his office.

"Is there anything else I may assist you with, Miss Emmy?" he asked.

"Well, yes there is. My niece and I have been raised in the Presbyterian faith. I understand there is a lovely Presbyterian church in Lewisburg. Would you be so kind as to give me directions to the church? Perhaps you know what time services start on Sunday." Emmy replied.

"Why did she ask him that," Callie thought. "We rode by that church yesterday. She knows where it is."

"I'd be delighted to assist you with that. In fact, that is my church," he responded. He proceeded to give her the directions to Old Stone Church. Services he informed her began at 11:00 AM.

"That's exactly where we saw it yesterday." Callie thought to herself.

"If you and Miss Callie could spare the time, I could ask my clerk to take the deeds to the court house and record them. You could have your copy to take back to the Inn with you. I could tell you some of the traditions of the Old Stone Church." Mr. Henson added.

"That would be delightful," Emmy replied. "We really have nothing pressing to do today. Once my furniture arrives from Richmond next week, I won't be able to say that."

Returning to the room after delivering the signed deeds to the clerk, he said, "When you enter the church, the families and their children sit in the pews closest to the pulpit. You and Miss Callie will be escorted to a pew on the left of the main aisle behind the families. That's where the unmarried women sit. Unmarried men sit on the right behind the families on the right side."

"Well," she chuckled, "I certainly am glad you told me that! I would have been embarrassed to tears if I'd sat on the wrong side."

"Do you intend for your driver and your maid to also attend services?" he inquired.

"Yes I do." Emmy replied.

"Well then, as you enter the door of the foyer you will notice that there are stairs leading to a second floor on either side of it. Your driver will go up the stairs to the right; your maid servant the steps to the left. The stairs lead to a balcony where they are to sit during the services."

"I see."

"If it would not be too bold of me, I would be pleased to introduce you to some of the town people who attend the church after the service," he continued.

"That would be delightful, Mr. Henson."

There was a light knocking on the door.

"That must be my clerk bringing the deed back from the court house."

As they rode back to the Inn, Callie asked Aunt Emma why on earth she had asked Mr. Henson where the church was when they had driven by it yesterday.

"My dear," she replied patting Callie's hand. "In a town like Lewisburg, one does not act pushy. One has to appear helpless and seek advice from the men. One has to be courteous with the women, hold on to every word uttered from their mouths, but wait for the women to make the move to socialize with them. I can not emphasis enough that no matter what you see or hear, you show absolutely no reaction.

"Tomorrow afternoon after we return from our ride with Jefferson, we will decide which of our dresses we will wear to services on Sunday. First impressions are very important. And Angel, you decide which of your uniforms you want to wear."

Sunday morning, the congregation of the Old Stone Presbyterian Church lingered on the sidewalk in front of the church longer than usual. All had heard that the new women in town would be attending church that morning. They chatted about wooly worms, spread more gossip about the trouble that was coming and waited to see if they could get a close up glimpse of the new women.

Rounding the corner of Washington and Church Street, Emmy turned to Callie and Angel. With a chuckle and grin on her face, she said, "OK girls, show time!"

Jefferson chuckled too but held in a full fledge fit of laughter.

The church filled quickly after Emmy and Callie had been escorted to a pew on the left. Angel found a space on the front pew on left side of the balcony. Jefferson knew he was to sit on the right after he had taken care of parking the carriage.

Callie looked around the interior of the church. The windows she estimated to be at least a foot and a half deep. In each window sill there was a single silver candlestick with a white candle in it. A young man was lighting the candles in preparation for the service. The simple, yet elegant pulpit was in the center of the front of the church on a platform. She saw Mr. Henson sitting on the right side where the unmarried men sat. Callie turned to look up in the balcony to find Angel.

The congregation had been conversing in soft tones among themselves awaiting the beginning of the services. Suddenly a quietness started in the back of the church and drifted slowly towards the front as a ripple would drift towards a shoreline. Callie started to turn to see what was causing the silence but Aunt Emmy tapped her on her hand and barely visible even to Callie, shook her head no.

The pew behind her stopped their whispering. Out of the corner of her eye approaching her pew, Callie saw a very old woman, bend over and supporting herself with a cane in her left hand. She saw that the woman had her right arm wrapped tightly around the biggest ebony arm Callie had ever seen.

As this odd couple became parallel with her pew, Callie glanced up beyond the arm and saw him. There was the huge man with the gold hoop earrings in his ears, the man who had been so kind to her at the Garman Inn, the man to whom Uncle Jim had given Rim.

The couple proceeded to one of the front pews on the right where a man waited for them. It was Mr. Garman, the owner of the inn. "The lady must be his mother or his wife's mother," Callie thought.

Mrs. Garman was seated by Mr. Garman. The gentle giant turned and walked back down the aisle.

After the service, the gentle giant again came down the aisle before anyone left his or her pew. Mr. Garman handed over his elderly Mother to his care. They started slowly walking down the aisle when Callie noticed that the giant glanced up at the balcony and touched his gold hoop with his free hand. "I wonder if Angel sees him, sees what he just did," she thought.

Mr. Henson waited for them outside the church. The church was emptied first from the area in front of the pulpit and then to the back. He had left before their pew was empty. There was a large gathering of people near him.

He motioned to Emmy and Callie. "Oh there you are, Miss Morris. You and Miss Callie please come and join me. There are people here who are anxious to meet you."

One by one, he introduced the people from the gathering by families or individuals. Emmy was most anxious to see which of the women who were assessing her and Callie's attires was Sarah McKinney.

Callie was more interested in having the opportunity to ask Mr. Henson about the inscription she was trying to read on one of the stones in the church. However, she smiled sweetly, followed Aunt Emmy's lead and behaved in an appropriate manner. Amber stood off to the side next to Jefferson.

On the way back to the Inn, Callie asked Angel, "Did you see the man who led the little old lady down the aisle? Did you see he was wearing the gold hoop earrings in his ears I was telling you about? Did you see him touch his gold hoop when he looked up into the balcony on his way back down the aisle?"

"Yes'em I'se did!"

"What's this all about?" asked Aunt Emmy.

Standing on the left of the chair, my mother, Reba
Standing on the right of the chair, my grandmother, Velma
Seated in the chair, my great-grandmother, Nancy
Baby being held is me, Velma Ellyson

Easter Sunday, 1985
My mother, Reba, and myself.

10

As early as 1783, the settlers of West Augusta had tried to break away from Virginia. There were differences over who should be educated, who should provide the labor for commerce and what it should be. The origins, culture and habits of the citizens of West Augusta were different from those of "flat land" Virginians.

In 1810, delegates from West Augusta had protested that there was unequal representation of West Augusta in the Virginia legislature. A controversy flared up again in 1829 at the constitutional convention. The western delegates maintained the new constitution favored slave-holding counties. There was only an average of two slaves per square mile in West Augusta.

The Wheeling Gazette proposed in 1830 that western Virginia separate from eastern Virginia. All this controversy died down in 1851 when Joseph Johnson of Bridgeport, West Augusta was elected Governor of Virginia by popular vote. A new Virginia constitution granted concessions to the west. The honeymoon did not last long.

The straw that broke the camels back happened ten years later when Virginia voted to succeed from the Union. At the West Augusta first Wheeling Convention, a legislative branch was formed and a name, the "Restored Government of Virginia," decided. It began making plans for statehood. To the Virginia legislature, this was an outrage; selective succession was tolerated if it was Virginia succeeding from the Union. It did not believe West Augusta had the right to succeed from Virginia. In August, the "Restored Government of Virginia" adopted the name Kanawha for a new state to be formed and called for a vote of the people on the issue.

Jefferson drove the carriage west on the Kanawha Turnpike Monday morning out of Lewisburg. Callie had explained to Aunt Emmy what she and Angel thought the connection was with the man with the gold hoop earrings.

"I remember now where I first saw him, Aunt Emmy. It was at the Garman Inn before we came through Lewisburg. Could we please take our morning ride west of town? Please?" Callie asked.

"I'se sures wood lak' ta talks wuth da man, Miss Emmy sum time. Please fo' me too, Miss Emmy?" Angel pleaded.

"Where's we's headin' today, Miss Emmy?" Jefferson had asked as the women climbed into the carriage.

"We're going west to see if Miss Callie can find a place she calls Garman Inn."

"Oh I'se know where dat place is Miss Emmy," he had replied.

Callie recognized Garman Inn immediately as the carriage wound it's way down from a knoll to another sink hole area on the west side of town. This time she knew for sure what a porch was and won't be ridiculed as she had been the first time she had seen the Garman Inn porch.

"There it is Aunt Emmy!" She screamed excitedly pointing at the house. "There it is Angel!"

"Why's you'se lookin' fo' Garman Inn, Miss Callie?" Jefferson asked.

"I met a man there that wore gold hoop earrings. My Uncle Jim left my dog Rim with him when we took my Mama's body back to Jackson River country. I think he was called Sammy." Callie explained.

"I'se knows him, Miss Callie. We's jest calls him Big Man."

They drove by the Garman Inn. Callie did not see Big Man. She did see Rim romping in the side yard with other dogs.

"You'se wants ta go in dare, Miss Emmy?"

"No, not today, Jefferson, just keep driving. We'll go a little further to see the lay of the land." Emmy replied.

Arriving back at the Inn, she was handed a note by Mr. Gumm. It read, "Your wagon trains have arrived with your furniture."

Emmy was very pleased with the way everything was working out; better than she had hoped. The house would be perfect for her activity with the Yankees. With everyone in town believing the house was haunted, a light seen moving back and forth in the second story bedroom window would be accepted as further proof that the house was haunted even with people living in it.

The furniture was placed in the rooms exactly where Emmy wanted. It fit like a glove and as if it had been specially made for the rooms. Callie and Emmy hung the sheers at the windows in the living room and dining room. Jefferson drove the nails into walls and hung pictures where Emmy said to hang them.

It was remarkable. After only one afternoon and one morning, it looked as though Miss Emmy Morris and her niece, Callie, had lived in the house for months!

There was a light tapping on the front door.

"Miss Emmy, we apologize for not sending word ahead that we were coming but we don't plan to stay. We met you and your niece at services Sunday." Mrs. Harold LaRue presented her card. Her first name was Josephine the card said. Josephine was printed under her husband's name.

"I had my girl make you a pumpkin loaf. I know you haven't probably had time to have your girl fix anything decent to eat with unpackin' and all." She handed Emmy the pumpkin loaf.

The other woman spoke. "I'm Mrs. John Lewellyn," and handed Emmy her card. "Please call me Betty. You must let me know if you would like my recipe for these cookies."

Both women were straining their necks trying to see past Emmy and into the house.

"Oh by all means, do come in. I could use a break from all this work. Angel, put some water on to boil in the kitchen. And see if you can find where you placed the tea in the pantry." Emmy motioned to the two women. "Please follow me to the drawing room."

Josephine and Betty were flabbergasted. Tea was served in fine white china cups with roses rimming the top and outlining the edge of the saucer. Angel had sliced the pumpkin loaf and placed a slice of it on matching dessert plates. Ornate silver spoons and forks and linen napkins finished the presentation.

"Pardon me, Josephine, for serving you the pumpkin loaf you brought. I promise you if you will return someday, I will offer you a sample of one of my favorite recipes."

"My dear, I brought you the pumpkin loaf to be eaten. Frankly, I just don't know how you have put this place together so fast." Josephine spoke. "It took me months to get my house together and I'm not certain it's how I want it even now."

As their carriage neared the bottom of the knoll, Josephine said with delight, "We did it, Betty! We got inside the house before Sarah. She's going to be so jealous! She'll throw a 'hissy' fit."

"Jefferson, please decide which of the men from the wagons would make a good butler. This is just the beginning of a long line of carriages that will climb the knoll to check out what our furnishings are; check us out!" Emmy said after the women left.

"I'se don't have to Miss Emmy. Capt'n Simmons done take care of dat'; picked da' man, fitted him in a suit frum place in Virginia. I'se go tell him get it on an' comes ta stay in da house now."

"Wasn't that a lovely service at the church Sunday?" Sarah asked the assembled Wednesday afternoon tea group.

"I found the new women in town to be quite refined. Mr. Henson introduced them to Mr. McKinney, George and me." Sarah announced.

"Humm," Sarah thought to herself. "This may be a difficult day to get any real conversation going." She ate some cookies, sipped some tea listening to talk about the weather, getting flowerbeds ready for winter, small talk; not the gossip that could give her a subject on which she could elaborate.

Finally, she spoke again. "I hear the wagons arrived with the furniture for the ole Smithson place."

Betty looked at Josephine and gave her a sly wink.

"It's quite lovely." Betty announced.

A silence filled the room.

"Lovely?" Sarah asked. "You've seen it?"

This time Betty took a long sip from her teacup and slowly ate a cookie.

After a silence that seemed like an hour to Sarah, Josephine said, "Oh yes. Betty and I called on Miss Morris yesterday afternoon."

A servant from the McKinney house knocked on the door of the ole Smithson house, within an hour of end of the tea.

"Miss McKinney axed me ta bring dis ta da lady of da house." The man handed a card to the properly attired butler who answered the door.

"Wait's heah. I's give it ta Miss Emmy."

Shortly, the butler returned with Miss Emmy's card and handed it to the man. On the back Emmy had written, "Miss Callie and I would be delighted to receive you and George tomorrow afternoon around two."

The McKinney carriage arrived at exactly 2:00 pm the next day. George trailed dutifully behind his mother as she entered. Emmy greeted Sarah attired in one of her most flattering dresses from Richmond. Callie stood beside her similarly attired.

The conversation that afternoon was pretty one sided. Sarah expounded on the McKinney family history that made her the "toast of the town" and gave her the ranking in its social structure. She indicated that George was probably the best catch a young woman of Lewisburg could capture and what wonderful plans she and Mr. McKinney had for George.

All the while, George sat beside his mother and did not utter a word. He had trouble swallowing the cookies because it seemed his heart had entered his throat. He could not keep his eyes off Callie.

As she was getting ready to leave, Sarah said, "Emmy, I'm having tea at my house next Wednesday at 2:00 p.m. I would be honored if you could attend. It's just a little gathering of the women of Lewisburg to keep in touch."

"It would be my pleasure, Sarah." They were on first name basis now.

"He looks like a toad, Aunt Emmy!" That was Callie's response to Aunt Emmy's comment that George had appeared to be quite smitten with her.

"Did you see his cheeks? They puff out just like a toad! And his eyes are too big for his head, just like a toad!" Callie stamped her foot for emphasis.

Emmy broke into a fit of laughter. "No one is saying you have to marry him, Callie. You just have to be nice to him to pick his brain and get information for the Union."

That night the ghost of Smithson house appeared in the second story windows that faced west.

Early in the morning two days later Callie woke and was unable to go back to sleep. She slipped down the stairs to get some milk. As she entered the back hall, a thin ribbon of light was shining beneath the library door. Thinking that Angel had forgotten to blow out the lamp, Callie opened the door and stood shocked at what she saw.

Two men in blue uniforms sat across the desk from Aunt Emmy. Maps and papers were scatter on top of the desk.

One was speaking. "This is where we expect the Rebs to make their supply depot. Their ammunition base will probably be here. We would like you to find out if these will be the locations." His finger pointed out the places on the map. He had not heard the door opening behind him.

"Callie Dear!" Emmy was startled to see her in the doorway.

Callie stood transfixed and rooted to the spot as she met the gaze of the man who stood up from his chair on Emmy's right. Her deep, red lips parted. Her eyes opened in amazement. She couldn't see two men standing, only one. She could only feel the tremendous vibration near her heart as his ice blue eyes locked with hers and a crescendo of heartbeats mounted in her. She stood absolutely motionless held by the warmth of those eyes.

Emmy was around the desk in a streak. She took Emmy's arm and started to turn her around to lead her back into the hall.

"This is no place for you now, dear. Go back upstairs to bed." She said gently to Callie.

"Just a minute, Miss Morris, I should like to be presented to the young lady." The mouth below those eyes had spoken.

The room seemed to revolve with the beats of her heart. Callie gasped as the furniture, light, men, Emmy all seemed to quiver and shimmer, then fade away leaving only the tone of his voice.

Then he was in front of her and the ice blue eyes held her helpless. She noticed, as she looked up that he had laugh lines in the corner of his eyes.

Time stood still and suspended until Emmy began the introductions.

"Callie, may I present Captain Alex Garrison, and Captain..." Callie only heard one name.

Captain Alex Garrison stood before her. His skin was tanned from days in the sun. His wavy hair was strawberry blonde with gold streaks bleached by the sun. The blue uniform covered a lean, muscular body. "He stands like Uncle Jim," she thought.

"Again, may I present Captain Howard Archer and Captain Alex Garrison. My niece, Miss Callie Morris."

Alex Garrison stepping forward, catching her hands in his said, "It is a pleasure to meet you, Miss Morris. I hope that I may see more of you when we come for our visits with your Aunt."

"Thank you Captain Garrison." She responded with the proper words to his comment like a robot. Inside, she was screaming, "Please, please, come back to see Aunt Emmy. I want to see you again."

Angel and Callie were sitting at the kitchen table the next day stringing beans for supper.

"Angel, how do girls know when they are in love?" Callie asked.

"In luv, Miss Callie? Whut's put sech a fool question in yo' head?"

"Oh, I don't know Angel, except Janie Pack asked me last Sunday after services if I'd ever been in love."

"Of 'cose yo' hasn't."

"Well, how will I know when I am?"

"You'll knos', Miss Callie. Yo' sho' knos' all rite, baby. They's a feelin' hasn't got no match. Sum times yo' feel so lonesome an hevy de misery so bad yo' jes' knos' nothin' will evah be da' same 'gin. Den' de' nex' minute yo's happy. Yo' mite say luv is bein' yes an' bein' no. But de's one thin' sho nuff, yo's knos' when yo' is in luv."

"Mercy, Angel. You talk in riddles. You make love sound very interesting. But I still don't see how I'll know exactly if I'm in love or not."

"Luv Miss Callie? How'll yo' no yo's 'n luv? Baby, days no need fo' me to be tellin' yo'. Yo's know'."

She wondered. "All that fluttering of my heart last night, the way his eyes could hold mine and not let them go, could this be the love Janie asked about?" At almost sixteen years of age, Miss Callie Morris was beginning to think about love.

"Jefferson, I would like you to take this note to Mr. Henson's office and wait for his reply." Aunt Emmy said.

The note said, "Mr. Henson, Miss Callie and I would like to hire you for another legal matter. When will it be convenient to meet with you? Sincerely, Emmy Morris"

Jefferson handed her Mr. Henson's note of reply. It read, "Miss Morris, I am available tomorrow at 10:00 AM. Unless I hear otherwise, I will look forward to meeting with Miss Callie and you then. Sincerely, Jonathan Henson."

The law clerk ushered Emmy and Callie into Mr. Henson's office. He stood by his desk awaiting their arrival. When Emmy reached out her hand to greet him, he took her hand and placed it between both of his.

"It is so very nice to see you again, Miss Emmy. How are you getting along with moving into the new house? Have you and Callie settled in? bla bla bla bla..." Mr. Henson was looking into Emmy's eyes as he spoke to her.

"Listen to him," Callie thought. "He isn't giving Aunt Emmy a chance to get a word in edgewise."

Finally seated behind his desk, Mr. Henson asked, "Now what may I do to help you ladies?"

Aunt Emmy explained that her brother, Callie's father, Calvin Morris had purchased land near the Gauley Bridge on Calico Creek. Because both Callie's mother and father were now deceased and she no siblings, Aunt Emmy was asking him to pay any taxes due on the property and transfer the title of the property to Callie's name. She was wondering if on one of his trips to Charleston if he could take care of the matter for them.

"Here is some gold to pay any taxes due." Aunt Emmy reached into her drawstring purse and then offered a small brown leather bag to Mr. Henson.

"Put that away, Miss Emmy. I will let you know the cost once I know. It just so happens I am going to Charleston on business next week. I will report to you after the trip."

Sarah stood behind the sheers in the entry watching as Emmy's carriage entered the semi-circular driveway leading to her home.

"This will show that Betty and Josephine! They may have seen her home first, but I'll be first to have her for tea!" Sarah was thinking. "I can hardly wait for them to walk into the drawing room and see Emmy."

Emmy was surprised to discover that she was the only one in the drawing room with Sarah. "Surely I'm remembering correctly that she said tea at two," Sarah thought.

"My dear, I asked you to come early today so we could have the opportunity to converse more and I could take you on a tour of my home. I thought it would be a good chance for me to fill you in on the upcoming social events that will take place in Lewisburg. The other girls will begin arriving at three." Sarah was speaking.

"Whew," thought Emmy. "I have not made the social blunder of arriving at a home too early after all."

"Perhaps we should take the tour first." Sarah rose from her chair and began leading Emmy through the various rooms. Of course Emmy "oo'ed and aw'ed" at each item Sarah pointed out and used words like exquisite, charming, unusual and the standard, beautiful.

"You have exceptional taste," Emmy heard herself saying as they were seated again in the drawing room.

"Well thank you, Emmy," Sarah replied pleased with herself. "George and I were wondering just how much of the area you have been able to see since your arrival. The leaves this time of year are quite beautiful."

"Mr. McKinney, George and I have a fall tradition of taking lunch at Sweet Springs this time of year. It affords us the opportunity to observe the fall foliage and lunch at one of the fine resorts of the area. Have you and Miss Callie visited Sweet Springs?"

"I've never heard of Sweet Springs." Emmy replied.

"Oh then, you and Miss Callie must join us next Thursday when George and I go for our traditional ride through the fall foliage. I'm afraid Mr. McKinney will be unable to go this year due to pressing business matters.

"Sweet Springs is in Monroe County south of Lewisburg. It's a charming resort built in the Jeffersonian style of architecture. If it were earlier, we would take appropriate wear to bathe in the mineral water pool there. I'm afraid it's a little chilly for than now." Sarah commented.

"That would be wonderful, Sarah. We will be happy to join you and George next Thursday."

"Oh, the butler has motioned that some of the other ladies have started arriving. Please excuse me momentarily while I greet them." Sarah stood up and walked towards the entry.

She was pleased as punch with herself. George would be so delighted that she had gotten Emmy to accept the outing to Sweet Springs. Then too, she still had the waiting thrill of watching the shocked expressions on Betty and Josephine's faces when they saw Emmy sitting in the drawing room.

The only interesting item of conversation at the tea for Emmy that day was that there was going to be a vote by the people next week to decide if West Augusta should become a separate state from Virginia.

"AUNT EMMY!" Callie stomped her foot! "You know I can't stand that toad! I'll have to ride in the carriage seat beside him all the way to and from this Sweet Springs place!"

Emmy chuckled. "Now don't be so dramatic, Callie. You know our objective is to learn as much as we can to help the Union."

Callie took a deep breath. Aunt Emmy had just said magic words, the Union. That meant Captain Garrison would come again.

"Oh alright, Aunt Emmy. I'll go and be a good girl. I'll even be nice to the toad!"

11

"Angel," Emmy was saying, "Jefferson and I have a wonderful surprise for you today. The two of you will go to the local orchard to purchase apples for the house. But the big surprise is that Big Man will be going to the same orchard to purchase apples for the Garman family."

Angel's body went numb.

"Don't speak or make any sign of recognition at the apple stand. Jefferson will drive you to a place where you and Big Man can talk after you buy the apples, Angel."

Angel hugged Emmy.

"Is dis' somethin' I'se dreamin', Miss Emmy?"

"Bless your heart Angel. No, this is not something you're dreaming. Now get yourself together. You and Jefferson need to leave soon." Emmy said.

She watched as the carriage left the lane. "Oh I hope everything will be alright for Angel."

"Aunt Emmy, I thought you said the men would be coming to talk with us about what we need to learn on our outing with the McKinney's." Callie had come up beside her.

"They will be dear. They sent word back that they are involved right now in another matter. They will be here one night this week."

"I don't think I can stand it!" Callie was thinking. "I have to wait maybe two more nights until they come." To Aunt Emmy she said, "Alright Aunt Emmy, I just don't want to have to sit by the toad and not have a reason to be sitting there."

Aunt Emmy just chuckled and shook her head.

When Jefferson and Angel arrived at the apple stand, Big Man was loading apples into the Garman carriage. Angel's heart started racing. She was standing frozen in the spot where she had stepped out of the carriage.

"De's looks good, Angel. Cum ovah heres an' look at de's." Jefferson yelled to her.

Mechanically she walked to where Jefferson was standing in front of bushel baskets full of bright red and yellow apples. Behind her, she heard the Garman carriage pull out onto the lane that led back to the road.

"Which ones does yo' cook wuth Angel? De's red ones or de's?" Jefferson was asking.

The woman behind the stand spoke. "Perhaps I can help you decide. These are a local apple. Women like to use in pies. They're very firm and tart."

"I'se take de's, Jefferson." Angel pointed to the ones the woman was showing her. She didn't really care what kind of apples they were or what she would use them for in cooking. All she cared about was getting in the carriage and meeting Big Man.

As they pull out of the lane onto the road, Jefferson turned and said to her, "Angel, yo' wills hav' ta listen very careful ta Big Man. Da' master he had done 'for cut his face so bad, messed wuth his talk box too."

Angel almost started to cry. "Oh my po' big brother. What's yo' bin through since Mama an' me's sees yo' leave dat horrible place in Richmond," she was thinking.

Jefferson turned onto a smaller road that turned, twisted and climbed a small hill. There were large boulders scattered about which had fallen from cliffs. He stopped the carriage and made the sound of a hoot owl. Almost immediately, the same sound came from behind a boulder not far up the hill.

"Angel, when we's gets dare, I'se gonna drive 'way fo' a little bit. You'se hav' Big Man hoot fo' me when he's wants me ta cum get yo'. He's kent stays long. Yo's git ou' da' carriage quick when's we's turns da' corner 'round dat boulder up dare."

Angel's breathing came in short spurs. She felt her heart pounding. She said, "Feets yo' ta gets me out dis' carriage when's I'se git dare."

There he was, Big Man; standing by the boulder, his gold hoop earrings gleaming in the sun. Angel approached him on legs that felt like they would fall out from under her at any minute.

"I'se Angel."

He nodded.

"My Mama's an' me's wuz sold 'n Richmond. I'se hab a brother older den me. He wuz sold dare too."

He nodded.

"My Mama, she's putt de's gold hoops in mys ears," her hand rose to touch one, "an' she's putt 'em in mys brother's ears."

He nodded but this time he reached up and touched a gold hoop in his ear. Then he opened his big arms and motioned for her to come into them.

Angel let out a deep breath, started sobbing and ran into those big arms. He held her so tight she thought the breath would be squeezed out of her. She could not control her sobbing. He stroked her hair and murmured softly, "AHH, AHH."

He picked her up in his arms and carried her to a rock where he could sit down. He cradled her in his arms as she sat in his lap. His hand gently stroked away the tears that were running down her face.

Finally, her tears stopped; she looked into his eyes, touched one of his earrings and her other hand touched one of her.

"Oh Big Boy, Mama's up dare in heb'en' lookin' down on us an' smilin'. She's hopes so much fo' she's dies I'se fin' you'se. She's says wuth her last breath, tells Big Boy I'se luvs him." Angel told him.

Angel saw tears form in his eyes. He hugged her closer to him.

He stood her on her feet. Then he patted himself on the chest. He made a guttural sound that sounded like "I'se"; waved one of his big hands as if saying goodbye. Next, he took two fingers, tapped them near his one of his eyes and then pointed at her.

"See's me?" Angel asked.

He nodded. Then he held up a hand showing five fingers, made a gesture that with a shrug of his shoulders that suggested he was questioning. He held up both hands showing ten fingers and the made the same gesture.

"You'se sees me in five ta ten days?" Angel asked.

He nodded, patted him self on his chest, pointed to his eye and then to her. Then he wrapped her in his big arms once more.

Gently taking her by her arms, he stood her in front of him. He cupped his hands and made the sound of the owl. Then he touched the gold hoop in his ear and disappeared around the other side of the boulder.

SOMETHING TO LIVE FOR

"Why's yo' cryin' Angel?" Jefferson asked as the carriage turned back onto the road again.

"'Cause I'se so heppy! 'an Mama's heppy ups dare in heb'en too."

Jefferson just shook his head. "I'se nevah gonna unda'stand women," he said to himself. "Cryin' 'cause they's heppy."

Thursday afternoon Aunt Emmy told Callie that the Captains would be coming that night to talk to them about the outing. Callie could not concentrate on a single thing she was doing all day long. Emmy had said that Callie was to go to bed at the regular time as every night but to stay dressed. She would hear a soft knock on the door. Emmy would enter the room and motion for her to follow her to the library.

"I'll fall down the steps." Callie thought. "Or I'll trip on my dress and fall flat on my face right in front of those ice blue eyes."

"Angel," she said. "Let's try fussin' with my hair this afternoon. I want to try different styles. You have to help me pick the one that looks best on me."

"You'se must hab tries on evah dress yo' own Miss Callie. Look at's yo' bed! An' yo' hair bin fixed hundred ways!"

Angel assumed this was dress rehearsal for the big outing with the Mc Kinneys.

"You'se gonna makes yo' self sick fo' da outin'gets here."

Callie heard every possible sound she could hear that night. She was listening intensely for Aunt Emmy's knock at the door. She must have looked at her reflection in the mirror a thousand times, pulled on the dress here, pushed on a strand of hair there. She was certain it must be approaching sunrise because it had seemed like yesterday when she had come into her room.

Then she heard it, a soft knock on the door. It opened. There stood Aunt Emmy holding a candle and motioning for her to follow. "Be still my heart," she said to her body. "Legs don't go all crazy on me now. Get me down those steps and into the library."

There HE stood by Aunt Emmy's desk. His eyes immediately grabbed hers and held them. A smile formed on his face. She supposed the other Captain was in the room but she could not tear her eyes away from his to look.

The eyes moved towards her. She felt a warm hand take hers into it.

"It's so good to see you again, Miss Callie," the voice was coming from the mouth below the eyes again.

"Please Lord," she was saying, "Don't let that black smothering velvety curtain come and get me now."

"Let's all sit down," Aunt Emmy was saying.

Captain Alex Garrison pulled a chair slightly away from the desk, motioned for Callie to sit and then pulled another chair over to sit beside her. "I'm going to die right now," she thought, "My heart can't pound this fast and not explode."

"Callie," Aunt Emmy was speaking to her. "Can you see the map on the desk alright?"

"Yes Mam."

"Then let's get started Captain Archer." Emmy said.

Captain Archer proceeded to place his finger on the map and start tracing the road that would lead from Lewisburg to Sweet Springs. "You will proceed east out of Lewisburg," he said. His finger stopped at the Greenbrier River. "It is important that you take careful notice here to see any evidence that the Rebs are setting up camp, plan to or have set up a camp."

"I know that spot Aunt Emmy. Uncle Jim and I stopped there on our way to Jackson River country." Callie interjected.

"That's great!" said the voice that went with the ice blues eyes, "Seeing it a second time will definitely help you remember details that may have not been there before. That will be helpful to us." The voice almost seemed to be smiling.

"I don't dare look at him," thought Callie. "I'll just die; I know I will."

Captain Archer continued. "After you cross the river, there will be a road that turns to the right almost within sight of the river beyond a brick two story house; for certain not more than a quarter mile. This is the road that will go by Organ Cave."

"Organ Cave? Uncle Jim told me about that cave, too." Callie blurted out.

"What did he tell you, Miss Callie?" the eyes voice asked.

Now she had to turn and face those ice blue eyes. HE had asked the question.

"Uncle Jim told me there were Confederate soldiers there for the salt peter. And he told me that the salt peter is made of ..." she stopped in mid sentence. "is used to make gun powder." She felt her face turning red from what she almost said.

A huge smile came on his face and she heard a slight chuckle. "That's alright Miss Callie. Captain Archer and I know what salt peter is made of."

Captain Archer asked, "How long ago did he tell you this Miss Callie?"

"It was in April, Captain Archer."

He continued. "That is one of the questions we would like answered. Are there Rebs there now; if so how many if possible; if not, do they plan to return? Here, let me show you on the map where the road is leading to Organ Cave."

Callie felt the warm hand take hold of her arm her to assist her from her chair. "I'm going to faint, I swear I'm going to faint," she thought knowing it was HIS hand.

"Let's count the roads on the left once you turn onto the road just beyond the Greenbrier River. Then on the day of your trip one of you can start asking where roads lead before you get to the Organ Cave road and no one will be the wiser for your question," Captain Archer continued.

"Captain Garrison," he said, "you explain the next major questions we have about the area in which they will be traveling."

HE stood up and went to the front of the desk beside Emmy.

"We have reliable sources who have told us that the Confederate troops are planning a major offensive next spring that will come from this direction into the Greenbrier Valley." His finger pointed to a spot below Organ Cave and moved along the road where they had been shown the location of the cave.

"We are interested in any information on how many troops will be sent, of course, but just as important is information on possible places where we could hide to either intercept these troops or send scouts to spy on the troop's movement. Please note possible locations in your minds by objects that are easily recognized; a house, a barn; anything that the scouts will need to avoid to in order not to be seen." The voice continued.

"Do you have any questions, Miss Callie?" HE may have also have said, "Or Miss Emmy" but Callie only heard him say her name. It sounded like music when he said it.

She might as well never have gotten undress and changed into her nightgown when the meeting was over. Callie was having a difficult time falling to sleep. When she closed her eyes, every detail of his face appeared. She heard his voice saying, "Miss Callie" over and over again.

There was a grey cloud hanging over the Wednesday afternoon tea group. The unthinkable had happened. Voters in West Augusta had overwhelming approved statehood. The ladies were certain the men of Lewisburg had not voted for statehood.

"Emmy, may I speak with you for a moment before you leave." Sarah had said to her as she was leaving the tea.

"We will arrive at your house at ten tomorrow morning. George and I are so looking forward to our little trip to Sweet Springs."

"So are we really looking forward to the trip as well, Sarah." Emmy said to herself, "but for an entirely different reason."

When Emmy arrived home, she was handed a note. Mr. Henson had written, "I have information for you concerning the matter of the land on Calico Creek. May I call on you Thursday afternoon to explain the details? Sincerely, Jonathan Henson."

Emmy handed Jefferson a note and asked him to take it to Mr. Henson's office. It read, "Callie and I have a previous engagement for Thursday afternoon. Would it be convenient for you to have tea with us at three on Friday? Sincerely, Emmy Morris."

His reply, "Friday at three will be perfect. I look forward to having tea with you. Sincerely, Jonathan Henson."

"Wipe that frown off your face, Callie." Emmy said as they watched the McKinney carriage climbed the knoll. "Remember why we are taking this trip. The Captains will be anxious to receive the information we get."

"That's right. HE will have to come back to get the information." Callie thought. That thought put a smile on her face and she said, "Here comes the toad!" They both broke into a fit of laughter.

A clammy hand assisted Callie into the carriage. "Thank you, George," she said sweetly smiling at him.

Aunt Emmy and Sarah sat in the back seat; George and Callie were in the seat behind the servant driving the carriage. Sarah informed Emmy who lived in which house, and if there was any, told her the gossip about the people, as they rode out of town. Callie looked up in the sky to see if she could find any pictures.

SOMETHING TO LIVE FOR

"That's the Greenbrier River," George was saying as they descended the hill. "I've caught many a fish in that river. There's also a good swimming hole where we boys go too."

"Really, where?" Callie looked in both directions. She wasn't looking for a fishing spot or a swimming hole.

The carriage turned onto another road after they crossed the bridge. "Do people live down that lane, George?" Callie asked pointing to the second lane they saw. Finally, they came to the one that really interested her. "And where does that road go?"

Now was his time to impress her. He knew lots about the cave that was at the bottom of the hill where the road led. She only made a mental note to remember certain details. "Where the Confederate commander and his men stayed when they were collecting the salt peter for gun powder…" George was saying.

Callie turned to Aunt Emmy, "Listen to this Aunt Emmy. George is telling me some interesting things about a cave at the bottom of that road. Do you think Jefferson could bring me here sometime?"

"Oh I don't think you would want to go into the cave by yourself, Miss Callie. Perhaps I could show you the cave. My father and I came here when the Commander was here. In fact, they are coming back next spring and I'm thinking about joining them." He had turned so Miss Emmy and his mother could hear him.

"You know your father and I are still discussing whether we will allow you to join them for the battles next spring. It is one thing to fight near home, but an entirely different matter to go where you'd have to camp overnight to fight. They will leave Lewisburg after they defeat the damm Yankees." His mother had spoken from the back seat.

The carriage continued through a valley of rolling hills and sinkholes. Here and there a home dotted the landscape. Both Emmy and Callie were taking mental notes on their locations. In Union, the carriage turned to the left and continued through the valley. It went through a gap between two mountains and into another valley.

"There it is, Emmy, Sweet Springs. Isn't it beautiful?"

Sarah was pointing at a brick three story building. On the ground level, arched openings supported a porch that ran the entire length of the building. Three grand stairways led from the ground to the second level. At the landing, huge white columns supported a roof at the third floor that covered the entries.

"I've never been to Charlottesville," Sarah was saying, "but I'm told that Jefferson used this same arched breezeway design at the University of Virginia. It's amazing the people who have been vacationing through the years here. I actually believe Sweet Springs is prettier than the Old White, don't you George?"

Sarah was talking to Emmy as they strolled across the lawn lined with huge trees. Callie and George were walking behind them. "Tell Callie about the Old White, George. Come, Emmy, I want to show you the bath house."

George slowed his pace and began telling Callie about the Old White near Lewisburg. "Those were the cottages and big Inn I saw from the road that Uncle Jim told me about," she thought. However, she looked at the toad as though she had never heard a word about the Old White and held on to his every word.

"There it is Emmy." Sarah was pointing to a rectangular brick building. The entry had the same arched design as the main building except only the front entry arches were open. Arches to the sides and back had glass windows in them.

"The arches with the windows are dressing rooms, Emmy. One changes there to partake of the healing waters in the pool; see there." Sarah was pointing at a pool in the center of the rectangle. It had no roof over it. "Even the Indians knew of the healing qualities of this spring. This was one of their favorite camping spots. I've heard people tell of miraculous cures from soaking in this water or drinking it from the spring itself. We must come back next summer when it is warmer and bathe in the pool."

Back home, Emmy was saying to Callie, "I think the Captains will be very pleased with the information we gathered today, Callie. Come to the library and we will write down what each of us recall."

"We won't write down what the toad asked me, will we Aunt Emmy?" Callie asked.

"What was that?" Emmy turned to look at Callie.

"WELL," she said with disgust in her voice, "the toad asked me if I would go with him to the Christmas Ball at the Old White."

"Callie, you have just received the invitation that every girl in Lewisburg hopes will come her way. What did you tell him?"

"I told him that I needed to discuss this with you before I answered; that I would tell him after church services Sunday." Callie's eyes rolled up in her head and she threw her hands up in disgust. "Can't you just see it now, Aunt Emmy? The toad probably can't even dance. He'll just hop around the dance floor!"

Callie started laughing and hopped past Emmy into the library. Emmy started laughing and hopping behind her.

"She laughs just like her mother," Emmy was thinking. "Oh how Calvin loved to hear Caroline laugh."

12

Punctually at exactly three, Mr. Henson dismounted from his horse in front of Emmy's house and handed the reins to the butler. Emmy greeted him at the door.

"My, that's a fine looking horse you have, Mr. Henson," she said as she led him to the drawing room.

"Thank you Miss Emmy. He's the brother of Robert E. Lee's horse, Traveler."

"Really, I thought there was something that looked familiar about him. He has the same coloring and that black mane and tail as Traveler." Emmy commented.

"Yes," Mr. Henson replied, "He was born and raised by Captain Johnson here in the valley along with Traveler. Did you ever hear the story about how General Lee acquired Traveler?"

"No," both Callie and Emmy responded. Callie didn't think Mr. Henson had even noticed she was in the room until then.

"General Lee first saw Traveler when he came here. The horse was called Jeff Davis then. Major Broun owned him at that time. Lee admired Traveler's muscular strength and high spirit.

"He saw Traveler again when he was stationed with Major Broun in South Carolina and continuously commented on what a fine looking horse Traveler was."

"Well that is certainly true, Mr. Henson." Emmy said.

"Major Broun offered to give the horse to General Lee but he insisted he would buy him. Then he changed his name to Traveler after the sale. General Lee said once that an hour on a horse like Traveler was never wasted. I agree with General Lee."

"That's a fascinating story, Mr. Henson," Callie said.

"I believe you said you had information concerning the property on Calico Creek, Mr. Henson." Emmy was speaking.

"Indeed I do Miss Emmy. In checking the deed, I discovered that your brother, Calvin, was very wise. He had listed the deed in his name, his wife's name and Callie's. It will be a simple matter to update the deed and put it solely in Callie's name. I will be happy to take care of the matter for you."

"That's wonderful, Mr. Henson," Emmy said. She wasn't surprised though that her brother had listed all three names. Her father had carefully explained business dealings to both Calvin and her.

"I want you both to know how business and legal matters work," he had said to them. "A person can never know too much about the workings of these matters to protect what you own."

"And the taxes?" Aunt Emmy asked.

"They were not due until the first of the year. However, I paid them and will include them in my bill when I update the deed." He replied.

The conversation turned to matters such as the apple harvest; wooly worm predictions that it would be a severe winter this year.

As he was leaving and thanking Emmy for her gracious hospitality, Mr. Henson said, "I have been meaning to thank you and Miss Callie for selecting me as your lawyer. To show my appreciation, I have been wondering if I might invite you two for dinner at the Old White."

"That would be very kind of you, Mr. Henson. Callie and I have heard so much about the Old White but neither of us has been there. We accept your invitation," Emmy replied.

"Good. Next Saturday? I would pick you up in my carriage."

It was arranged. Emmy and Callie would dine at the Old White next Saturday night with Mr. Henson.

Captain's Archer and Garrison were in the library when Callie entered with Aunt Emmy. She had promised herself all day that she would not embarrass herself again as she had at the last meeting, would look at Captain Archer as well as HIM and have total control of her heart.

"Miss Emmy says you have some information to report to us, Miss Callie." The eyes voice was speaking again.

"Yes sir, we do." Callie replied trying to be very calm. "I wish he'd just talk to Aunt Emmy," she was thinking. "I get too flustered when he talks to me."

"This is very valuable information you have provided us, Miss Emmy and Miss Callie," Captain Archer was saying. "You are to be commended on your report. I hope the day was an enjoyable one for you both as well."

"All except I had to sit by the toad and I have to go to the dance with the toad," Callie blurted out. "OH NO CALLIE, look what you have done now," she said to herself as she felt her face getting red.

Both of the Captain's chuckled and spoke simultaneously, "You what?"

"Let me explain," Aunt Emmy was saying.

"THANK YOU Aunt Emmy. I am too embarrassed to speak." Callie was saying silently to her.

Aunt Emmy was walking beside Captain Archer in the back yard, escorting him to his horse. Captain Garrison fell behind to walk with Callie.

"So you like to dance, Miss Callie?" he asked.

"I love to dance, Captain Garrison." She replied.

"So do I. It would be my pleasure to take you dancing sometime, Miss Callie, if and when, this war is over. I promise you I do not dance like a toad." He smiled.

"Aunt Emmy, Angel. The most wonderful thing happened to me last night. I didn't sleep a wink all night thinking about it." Callie said as she rushed through the kitchen door.

"What?"

"Captain Garrison said it would be his pleasure to take me dancing sometime when this war is over!" She spun around the kitchen as if she was dancing with him now.

"Oh mys" Angel thought. "Dis girls in luv."

"Can you believe what that second Wheeling Convention did?!" Sarah said.

"No, what?"

"Well, after the people in the west were foolish enough to vote to succeed from Virginia, they started working on a draft of a constitution. AND…" She, of course, stopped to sip her tea.

"AND?"

"They changed the name of what the state would be called from Kanawha to West Virginia. But that's not the worse part." She started to reach for another cookie from the tray.

"SARAH!"

"Well they had the audacity to change the boundaries of land to be included in the new state AND." Sip Sip Sip

"AND?!"

"Greenbrier County will be included in the new state!"

"OH NO!" a chorus of voices rang out.

"Do you know the story of the Old White, Miss Emmy?" Mr. Henson was asking.

"It's just like it was at the house," Callie was thinking. "He doesn't even know I'm here."

Callie was riding on Aunt Emmy's right, Aunt Emmy was in the middle and Mr. Henson was seated on Aunt Emmy's left.

"No, Mr. Henson, please tell me."

"Well, Indian legend says two lovers who would meet in the woods there. One day they were followed by the chief of the tribe. He did not approve of their romantic interludes. With the first arrow he shot, he killed the Indian brave. His second arrow missed the squaw and lodged into the ground. The squaw pulled that arrow from the ground and a spring sprouted from the ground.

"Legend says that when the spring is completely dry and no more water comes from it, the brave will live again and return to his Indian squaw. People have been trying to drink it dry for a long time so he can return."

"Can that happen?" Callie asked, "I mean can people drink a spring dry?"

"I guess there are enough people who think they can. They still come from all over to stay at the Old White to try, Callie." He answered

"The Indians discovered this spring as well as the one at Sweet Springs. I believe you were there last week, Miss Emmy?" She nodded in the affirmative.

"Huh, he's keeping his eye on Aunt Emmy." Callie thought.

Mr. Henson continued. "About 50 years ago, cottages were built around the spring; then a two story Inn. But just like Lewisburg, wealthy plantation owners from the south started building what they called private cottages. A man from Georgia built a two story colonnaded house. It was so popular with Presidents who vacation here in the summer it's called The President's Cottage now.

"In 1830 the spring was covered because so many people were coming. It is believed that if one drink's from the spring three times a day, good health will be theirs. I'll show it to you. It's quite attractive. The sculpture of the Greek Goddess of health, Huggeta, is on the peak of the roof."

"Will we take a drink Mr. Henson?" Callie asked.

"You can if you want, Miss Callie."

"Where we're going to dinner tonight was originally called the Grand Central Hotel and built in 1838. It's called simply the Old White now because of its exterior. The dining room can seat 1,200 people." Mr. Henson explained.

The carriage turned left into a beautifully manicured lawn that covered acres and acres. There were neatly placed flowerbeds everywhere. Huge purplish black pine trees with drooping branches stood gracefully in front of the cottages. In the distance, Callie could see the Old White.

As the carriage turned a corner Callie exclaimed, "Look at that." Callie was pointing to a concave roof supported by a circle of white columns. On top was the Goddess Huggeta. "That's the spring, isn't it Mr. Henson. May we go there first? I want to have a drink of the water to help dry it up."

Mr. Henson chuckled to himself. "Certainly."

"It stinks!" Callie said with a frown on her face.

"Yes, Miss Callie. That's the sulfur in it. You can have that drink now." he said and started to turn towards it

Callie had covered her nose and said, "NO THANK YOU!"

At the Smithson house, Big Man had come to help repair the axel on one of the carriages. That was the story that Mr. Garman was told when Jefferson had asked for Big Man's help. Miss Emmy and Miss Callie had no use for the carriage this afternoon. Mr. Henson was taking them to the Old White. This would be the perfect day to repair it. Mr. Garman often allowed Big Man to help in the community where strength was needed. Of course, there was nothing wrong with the axel on the Morris carriage.

Angel and Big Man sat at the kitchen table. She insisted he sample her baking specialties and served him tea. He finally patted his stomach and shook his head no when she brought another tray of cookies for him to sample.

Angel was babbling on and on about her life with Mama at the Hill plantation. She'd told him Mr. Hill was a good man but his wife was a crazy, spiteful woman. Mama, she told him, had been a house servant mainly in charge of the kitchen. Miss Hill had not been that kind to Mama and her eyes started filling with tears. He had patted her hand then and made the sound, "AAH AAH."

She had been luckier and was Miss Caroline's personal maid. "Dat's wuz Miss Callie's Mama," she told him, "an' Miss Callie jest lik' her Mama; jest as pretty an' jest as heppy now she away's frum ole Miss Hill." Angel went on to tell him about Caroline marrying Miss Emmy's brother and them running away to West Augusta.

"Dat's whys I'se so heppy ta bee's here. Miss Emmy jest like lik' her brother, kind an' good ta me. An' she's hep me finds mys brother a' gin." She gave him a big hug around the shoulders as he sat beside her.

He stood up then, patted his chest, touched the corner of his eye and pointed at her.

"Oh no, you'se got ta leaves so soon?" Angel hugged him. "I'se prays it be soon I'se see you'se a 'gin."

He wrapped her in his huge arms and almost squeezed the breath out of her. She watched from the porch as he rode down the knoll. It didn't look like the horse could possibly carry him. He was such a large and imposing figure.

Callie entered one of the most gorgeous rooms she had ever seen. In the center hung a chandelier with many more sparkling crystals, probably a thousand more, on it than the one at Calico Place. It was much larger than that one. The hardwood floors were so polished one could see their reflection in them. It was a huge room. Around the room were delicate chairs of gold gilt. An alcove was set up for a musical ensemble.

"This is the ball room." Callie had walked ahead of them. "This is where the Christmas ball is held each year. The decorations are unbelievable for the ball," Mr. Henson was telling Emmy.

"It may just be worth it to dance with a toad to be able to come here," Callie was thinking.

Mr. Henson was a gracious host at dinner. He entertained them with other stories of the history of the Old White, a list of famous guests who had stayed there and insisted on ordering for them the most delicious meals Calico thought she had ever eaten in her life.

Callie was in awe at how the white gloved waiters served the meals. At first, the plates had been a dark green, on the outside rim with rhododendron in the center. As each course came, the place setting gradually changed from dark green to a paler green, then through shades of pink to the dark rose of the dessert plate.

Soft string music filled the room. Callie heard Mr. Henson say to Aunt Emmy over the music, "I admire you, Miss Emmy. You have a good head on your shoulders and a pretty one too I might add. Most women I deal with have no idea that taxes need to be paid on properties; let alone about deeds or any other legal or business matters. It's refreshing to have a client as knowledgeable as you in these matters."

"Well thank you, Mr. Henson." She smiled at him and said, "Most men find my knowledge in these matters a threat."

"Sarah," Emmy said at tea on Wednesday. "Have I told you how much I have enjoyed having Mr. Henson handle my legal affairs for me?" She got the response she was hoping to get.

"Mr. Henson is recognized as one of the best lawyers in town. But it's such a shame about his wife." Sarah stopped to sip her tea and ate a cookie.

Emmy didn't respond as Sarah expected her to respond. She didn't beg Sarah to continue as the other women would have done. Sarah had to continue without the usual encouragement.

"I understand she was in her early twenties when she died in childbirth. The baby boy died as well."

Emmy sipped her tea and ate a cookie without commenting.

"Poor Mr. Henson. He owns a lovely farm just beyond the Garman Inn where they were living at the time but since then he has lived in a small house on Jefferson St. I understand the house on the farm has since burnt down." She stopped to sip, and sip and sip on her tea.

There was no comment from Emmy.

"Emmy certainly is different from the other women here," Sarah thought, "She doesn't appear to be interested in gossip at all." Sarah continued whether Emmy was interested or not. She loved letting everyone know she knew more about more people, what was going on in Lewisburg than anyone else.

"Mr. McKinney said when he asked Mr. Henson why he never married again, Mr. Henson told him he had not met the right woman."

In all the kitchens of Lewisburg, wonderful aromas were filling the air. Every house was preparing for the upcoming round of pre-Thanksgiving, Thanksgiving Day and post-Thanksgiving dinners. Wild turkeys were being located to be shot for these dinners. Hogs were being butchered, deer were being skinned, vegetables and fruits were being stored in root cellars. Outside the homes, one could smell apple butter being stirred in big pots over fires or apple cider being made.

SOMETHING TO LIVE FOR

There was so much excitement in the air. Servants were placing corn shocks in arrangements on the lawns where the lady of the house showed them to be placed. They gathered pumpkins and squash from the gardens to add to these arrangements. Scarecrow figures, stuffed with straw, completed the three dimensional pictures on the lawns.

Fall wreaths were made to hang on the outside doors; placed at specific locations in the house. Flowers from the gardens had been dried for this purpose. Other dried flowers were used for floral arrangements where fresh flowers had previously been displayed. Mother Nature may have ended her display of the multi-colored wonderland of leaves, but the ladies of Lewisburg had learned how to extend the beauty of fall beyond the last leaf to fall to the ground.

Emmy was busy accepting invitations for herself and Miss Callie to come to this dinner or that dinner. Sarah had advised her to not to have a dinner at her house this year but rather, she and Callie should attend as many of the dinners by others as possible. Without telling Emmy, Sarah also spread the word about what she had advised Emmy to do. No one could criticize Emmy when she was following Sarah's instructions.

Sarah had an ulterior motive. She wanted as many of "the" families of Lewisburg to meet Miss Callie; realize her charm and beauty as possible. George was becoming more and more smitten with her.

Callie had to be very careful when she was reviewing her week with her girl friends after Sunday services. They were all being trained to follow the example of their Mothers and let the kitchen maid prepare the meals, give directions to the house servants on what needed to be done in every room. "What a boring life they must have," Callie thought as she would hear them discussing this life they were leading. She, Mammy and Mama had worked side by side in the kitchen and she had enjoyed learning how to bake pies, prepare meals, made her own bed. To her, that was what young women were supposed to do.

"I bet there's not a one of them who could take care of themselves without someone doing something for them. Aunt Emmy won't have me be like that. I bet this is why everyone said that after Papa's folks freed their slaves, the slaves remained loyal to them and stayed with them." She thought then, "Oh my, I bet Angel has never been freed."

"Aunt Emmy, if I inherited the place on Calico Creek from my Papa, and because Mama is also dead, does that mean I inherit everything that Grandmother Hill owned? I am her only survivor." she asked.

"Yes, Callie, that is true." Aunt Emmy replied.

"Well then, I want Mr. Henson to draw up papers making Angel a free woman!"

"That's an excellent idea, Callie. I shall contact Mr. Henson."

The note read, "Mr. Henson, Miss Callie would like you to handle a legal matter for her. When will it be convenient for her to meet with you? Sincerely, Emmy Morris."

His reply read, "Miss Morris, I could see Miss Callie on the Monday after Thanksgiving at 10:00 AM. Perhaps it would be a good idea if you would accompany her. You could explain any questions she may have in the matter later. I look forward to seeing you both then if I do not hear from you otherwise. Sincerely, Jonathan Henson."

Aunt Emmy smiled when she read the part that he would like her to accompany Callie. She did not want him to think she might be interested in him in any way except as her lawyer.

Mr. Henson had written his note of reply three times until he was satisfied with it. He was concerned that it be written in such a way that Miss Emmy would not think he was interested in her in any way except as his client.

13

The women of Lewisburg were exhausted but energized. They had made it through the Thanksgiving dinners. It was now time to plunge into decorating their homes for Christmas, prepare for Christmas gift exchanges, and "little get togethers" during the season. Most importantly, they needed to make negotiations to be certain that their daughters had an escort for the Christmas Ball and their sons chose an appropriate girl to escort. Of course, the prettiest dress at the ball for their daughters was a top priority.

They were also praying that the deep snow would hold off until at least the end of December. The wooly worm's prediction appeared to be correct this year. Snow had been a part of the scenery since the end of October; not deep but present.

"Miss Callie will explain the legal matter she wishes you to handle, Mr. Henson." Aunt Emmy was beginning her training of Callie in legal and business matters, how to deal with lawyers as her father had trained her.

"That will be fine. Miss Emmy. May I say I was very pleased to see the two of you attending so many of the Thanksgiving festivities. You have certainly been accepted by the people of Lewisburg quickly and that is not always an easy task to accomplish." Mr. Henson was saying as he escorted Emmy to her chair holding her hand.

Emmy was pleased with Callie's presentation to Mr. Henson. Callie explained that she was the only survivor of Mrs. Letchia Hill who owned Angel. As her heir, she wished papers drawn up that would allow Angel to be a free woman.

"You have made a very generous decision, Miss Callie; if only more people would make the same one. It is always my pleasure to assist people in this decision." Mr. Henson replied.

"Mr. Henson, I was wondering if you might be able to help me with a personal matter." Emmy asked.

To Mr. Henson's surprise, his heart skipped a beat. "I'd be delighted if I can."

"Callie's sixteenth birthday occurs in January. I've been informed that is a horrible time to try to hold a birthday party because of the deep snow possibility. I have been considering a delayed party until perhaps the 1st of April. Does the Old White rent space for such parties?"

"Indeed it does, Miss Emmy. I personally know the man in charge of renting space. I would be delighted to assist you in making the arrangements. Perhaps you and I could meet with him sometime." Mr. Henson replied. "And congratulations to you Miss Callie. This is an important birthday in a young woman's life."

Callie made note of the fact that she was not included in the meeting with the person at the Old White.

The women were busy at tea exchanging all the recipes that had been requested after the Thanksgiving dinners.

There was other small talk about the weather; plans for distributing the food baskets to the "po folks" purchased with the money raised from the ball each year. Aunt Emmy remained quite listening for any important information.

It came when Sarah said, "I am so thankful General Lee has decided to station two regiments here in Lewisburg to protect us. We must invite the officers to the ball. It will also be helpful having those five regiments stationed at Camp Allegheny. If the 'damm Yankees' decide to attack, they can protect us."

"This is very valuable information, Miss Emmy." Captain Archer was saying. "Please find out the exact location where the regiments are to be encamped here in Lewisburg and when they will arrive. If you can, it would be helpful to know if they have brought artillery with them. We have information about the regiments at Camp Allegheny.

"Miss Callie, perhaps your young man will be a good source of information at the Christmas Ball." Captain Archer concluded.

"Yes Miss Emmy and I hope you enjoy your dancing at the Old White." the eyes voice said in a teasing manner.

"I may not enjoy the dancing at the Christmas Ball but I can assure you I will at my birthday party there the first of April!" Callie blurted out in response to his teasing.

The eyes voice man put on his thinking face.

"Captain Archer," the voice asked Captain Archie, "Wouldn't the first of April be the perfect time to gather information about the plans the Rebs are making for the summer offensive?"

"It would indeed." Captain Archer replied. "Miss Emmy, please add Captain Garrison and my name on the guest list. We could pose as friends from Jackson River country, mingle among the guests and hopefully gain very value information."

"BE STILL MY HEART!" Callie said to herself. "He had promised to dance with me after the war but now I'll get the best birthday present I could ever hope to get. I'll get to dance with HIM at my birthday party!"

"After the Christmas Ball," Captain Archer was saying, "Please signal us if you also gather information there."

Callie was trying to slow down the rapid beating of her heart.

"I certainly will, Captain. I'll also signal when I know the exact date of Callie's party. A friend of mine and I will have a meeting with the man at the Old White soon to make arrangements."

"A friend?" Callie though. "I thought Mr. Henson was just her lawyer."

The note read, "Dear Miss Morris, I have arranged for us to meet with the gentleman at the Old White to discuss the matter of Miss Callie's birthday party at four this Friday. Perhaps we could stay for dinner after the meeting. I will pick you up in my carriage at three if these plans meet with your approval. Sincerely, Jonathan Henson."

Her reply read, "Dear Mr. Henson, Your arrangements are satisfactory. Thank you for assisting me in this matter, Sincerely, Emmy Morris."

Now Emmy was the one saying, "Be still my heart."

"Miss Callie," George was saying after church services Sunday, "My Mother, Father and I will arrive at your house at six to take you to the ball."

"I wish he wouldn't keep reminding me constantly that he will be my escort to the ball." Callie was saying to herself. To him she said smiling sweetly, "I will be ready."

"I declare, I don't know how you managed to get him to ask you to the ball, Callie." her friend Janie was saying. "We were all dying for him to ask us."

"I didn't know who he was." Callie replied. "And he was the first one to ask me."

She was saying to herself, "Do you think I would want to go with a toad like that? It's a good thing Aunt Emmy reminded me it was good for the Union cause. Who would want to hop around a dance floor with a toad?"

"Well I wish he had asked me," another girl said.

The arrangements were made that Callie's birthday party would be held on April 2nd at the Old White. Emmy and Callie would greet the guests in the parlor, twice as large as the East Room in the White House. There would be finger foods located in the rooms leading to the grand ballroom. The guests could enjoy the finger foods and small talk here until all the guests had been greeted, their "Happy Birthday Callie" wishes had been acknowledged. The string ensemble would be playing soft background music from the grand ballroom during these proceedings. When all the guest had arrive, they would move to the ballroom for dancing.

"If you could return in early March, Miss Morris, our staff will assist you in selecting the finger foods and discuss the decorations you would like." the man said.

"We will make an appointment for early March before we leave tonight," Mr. Henson replied.

At dinner, Mr. Henson said, "I apologize, Miss Emmy, if I have over stepped my boundary in this matter by suggesting that I would escort you to the meeting here in March. I do not have children," she saw his eyes mist, "of my own. I have regretted that I have not had the opportunity to be involved in important times like this in a child's life."

"It will be to my advantage, Mr. Henson." She paused. "May I call you Jonathan when we are not discussing legal matters? Please feel free to address me as Emmy at such times. And you may refer to my niece as Callie."

He nodded but his heart skipped a beat.

"I will need assistance in preparing a guest list and the appropriate dress for Callie to wear. Keeping her feet on the ground will be no small feat in itself." She laughed as did he.

"I certainly don't envy you in trying to keep her feet on the ground, Emmy." His heart skipped a beat again. There he said it! Emmy! "Callie certainly is a high spirited but charming and intelligent girl. You and her parents have done a great job raising her."

"Thank you, Jonathan." There! "I have said his name." she said to herself.

"Emmy, do you have someone to escort you to the Christmas Ball? Callie will be riding with the McKinney's I would imagine."

Her dress had been selected; the best hairstyle to wear with it; the appropriate jewelry. Callie was ready for the season's big social event. Aunt Emmy was paying particular attention to her dress, hair and jewelry as well. Callie wasn't surprised now or when Aunt Emmy told her Mr. Henson would be escorting her to the Christmas Ball. She had seen how Mr. Henson didn't even know she was present at times. She was happy for Aunt Emmy. She seemed to become prettier with every passing day.

"Ain't yo's a pitcher Miss Emmy an' Miss Callie! I'se bet dares ain't gonna be no two purttier ladies at da ball ta'nite." Angel exclaimed as she surveyed them both in the foyer waiting for their respective carriages to arrive.

"At least Aunty Emmy doesn't have to dance with a toad." Callie said with a scowl on her face.

"Now Callie, calm yourself. You know I've explained that George, PLEASE call him George and not 'toad', will not be your only dance partner tonight. He is escorting you BUT other young men will ask for a place on your dance card. You only have to fill his name in on the first and last dance lines." Aunt Emmy reminded her.

"THANK HEAVENS!" Callie responded. "Is it alright if I get sick on the refreshments before the last dance and am unable to dance?"

They all broke out laughing.

"Angel, I am going to give you your Christmas present from me to you tonight." Emmy gave her a big hug. "Tonight you will have dinner here with Big Man, just the two of you. Jefferson has asked Mr. Garman if he could borrow Big Man to help him with another problem with our carriage not be needed tonight.

"All the men know that Big Man is coming just to have dinner with you; that wonderful meal you have prepared for all of them. They will come before he arrives, pick up their supper. You and Big Man will have the run of the house all to yourselves and can eat anywhere you like."

Angel stood as still as a statue. She could not believe what she was hearing. Tears started to form in her eyes.

"Oh Miss Emmy. Ain't nothin' betters I likes in dis whole wide world than to eats wuth mys brother'; jest da two's of us."

"And I have a special gift for you too, Angel." Callie handed her a folded paper. "This paper that Mr. Henson drew up states to the whole world that you are a free woman owned only by yourself."

Angel's tears began to flow. She hugged both Emmy and Callie. "Ain't no ones on dis earth happier den me's rite now." She look up at the ceiling and shouted, "You'se hear dat Mama? Miss Callie done made me's a free woman. An' Miss Emmy done fixed it so's I'se have supper wuth my brother." She paused. "Only thing dat makes it betta is if'n yo's cud bee's here's wuth us, Mama."

The Old White decorations were almost indescribable in their beauty. Pots of red poinsettias lined the steps of the entry. Garlands of fresh green pine were draped around the banisters of the steps with big red bows placed at intervals. A decorated tree stood on either side of the porch and the entry doors. These trees held little candles in foil plates, clipped on every limb and lit. They gave off enough light that the chandelier hanging in the center of the porch didn't need to be lit but was. It too was draped in garlands of fresh pine with huge red bows. Butlers waited in the formal uniforms at the doors.

"My goodness" Callie thought with excitement, "If this is what it looks like just to get to the door to go in, I can hardly wait to see what the ball room looks like."

The butler opened the door; she took George's arm.

"Evenin' Suh. Evenin' Mam. Enjoys da dance." The butler said as he bowed.

The hall leading to the ballroom had pine shaped trees made of potted poinsettias. Gold ribbon was draped on the poinsettia trees with white bows randomly placed. A gold angel topped each tree. Between the trees were large gold compotes of fresh dark waxy leafed holly with bright red berries.

"What could be more beautiful than what I've seen already." Callie said to George. "Oh please stop."

They were about to enter a room of silver and gold. Surrounding the room were tall Christmas trees with gold ribbon garlands, little gold plates holding lit white candles and every imaginable size of gold ornaments with silver and gold glitter on them. The angel on the top of each tree was dressed in a white and gold gown. There were white wicker birdcages on stands between the trees. The two white doves in the cages were alive. Large widths of sheer white fabric were draped from the corner of the room and the sidewalls to the huge chandelier to the middle of the room. The widths of fabric were gathered at the corner of the wall where it originated and the largest bow of gold lame' Callie had ever seen held it in place.

Gold lame' bows ringed the top of the chandelier and held the gathered fabric in place. This gold and white theme was continued in the alcove off the ballroom where refreshments were served.

It was the perfect setting to show off the colorful ball gowns the ladies were wearing. Their escorts black evening suits highlighted the ladies gowns even more. When they were whirled around the dance floor, the ladies colorful gowns looked as if a wind devil was blowing around all the colors and hues of the rainbow.

Callie's dance card began filling as soon as she entered the room. She was so thankful. Her greatest fear was that there would be too many spaces left for George to enter his name.

She noticed Aunt Emmy and Mr. Henson dancing. "Well look at that. You'd think they had been dancing together for years." she thought.

Snow began falling in big puffy white flakes on the ride back to Lewisburg. "Let it snow, let it snow, let it snow! Mother Nature didn't spoil the Christmas Ball this year" she said to George.

Angel and Big Man sat at the kitchen table. She had so many plates of cookies, cakes and pies after dinner before him that they almost covered the whole top of the table.

Big Man shook his head back and forth to say "No" to an offer of one more dessert. He motioned for her to come and sit in his lap and hugged her tightly.

"Brother, tells me whut happen ta yo' afters dat man gets yo' in Richmond." She had told him of her journey through life that had resulted in her being here in Lewisburg.

He held her so he could look into her eyes, shook his head back and forth to say "NO," motioned that she was not to cry when he told her the story. She had learned to interpret his guttural sounds and motions. He said next that he was just so happy that his journey had led him to find her.

The man who had bought him in Richmond was very cruel; not only to Big Man and his other slaves but to his own family as well. When it became apparent that his only child, a son, was mentally retarded, he gave the son to the slaves to raise. He forbid his wife to ever see the child again. In his world, there had never been the birth of a child.

Big Man and the son were the same age. They played together, fished together, lived in the same house. One day when the Master had gone on a trip to Richmond, as he often did, Big Man and the boy went to the big house to see the boy's mother. These visits were the highlight of her life. She was dwindling down to a skeleton of herself, paced the floors at night and would not communicate with anyone.

Unexpectedly, the Master returned from the trip early. He heard Big Man, his son and wife in the kitchen laughing. Barging through the door, he picked up his son and threw him against the wall breaking his arm. The wife was his next target. He struck her so hard across the face that she was knocked her out of her chair to the floor. She lay there motionless in a fetal position.

Then he turned his attention to Big Man. "You like to laugh boy? I'll fix your face so it looks like you're laughin' all the time." He picked up a knife from the kitchen table, made one swipe that cut Big Man's face from ear to ear.

Big man had reached up with both hands to try to stop the bleeding. In an instant, the man raised his fist and hit Big Man in the throat so hard it not only crushed his larynx but sent him crashing into the wall.

"Now let's see if you will ever tell anyone what is so funny to laugh about."

The man grabbed his screaming son from the floor by the broken arm; dragged him to the barn. There he instructed the stable slave to chain his son to the barn wall by his ankles. He instructed the slave to build a wire cage, when it was completed, to put his son into it.

Big Man said to this day he wondered what ever happened to the boy who was put in the cage in the barn. He also told her that the wife died soon afterwards from starvation. She never ate another bite of food after that day in the kitchen.

It was almost more than Angel could do to hold back the tears. She hugged him tightly; he stroked her hair. Finally, she asked him how he arrived in Lewisburg and with Mr. Garman. Big Man explained that after his face wounds had healed, he was taken to Richmond to be sold again by the man. That's when Mr. Garman bought him and brought him to Lewisburg.

Mr. Garman was a good man, Big Man told her. He had actually given him his freedom shortly after they arrived in West Augusta. Because of the kind way Mr. Garman had treated him, he decided not to leave.

"We's both free, Mama!" Angel raised her arms to the ceiling. "Yo's hears me? We's both free!"

Pulling him to his feet they swirled around the room to her chats of "We's free! We's free!"

That night Angel, Emmy and Callie sat at the kitchen table drinking hot cider discussing all the events of the dance.

"Aunt Emmy, you and Mr. Henson made a perfect couple dancing together. It looked as though you all had been dancing together for years." Callie said.

"I noticed Callie, you and George didn't exactly hop around the room like toads."

Callie chuckled. "Not exactly but his belly shook like a bowl full of Santa's jelly!"

They broke into uncontrollable laughter.

14

Christmas and the days leading up to it were again a whirlwind of activities. There were the "little get togethers" to attend, presents to wrap, preparations to be make for Christmas dinner.

Emmy had declined every invitation to dinner. Her reply simply mentioned that this was the first Christmas she and Callie would have ever had together and she wanted it to be special for them. People seemed to accept this reason.

Callie made the suggestion one night at supper. "Why don't we invite the people who have helped us or who are special to us for Christmas dinner Aunt Emmy? We could invite Mr. Henson. Angel could invite Big Man."

"That's an excellent idea. Mr. Henson has no family with whom to share Christmas dinner; Angel has found her family" Aunt Emmy was excited that Callie had suggested inviting Mr. Henson. It meant that Callie like him too.

Emmy, Angel and Callie were sitting at the kitchen table preparing the foods for the night's supper. Callie stopped peeling the potatoes, got up and gave Aunt Emmy a hug.

"My goodness, Callie, what was that all about?" Emmy asked.

"I had so dreaded even the thought of Christmas at Calico Place with Mama, Uncle Jim and Mammy gone. I was thinking about that just now and realized this Christmas has been as wonderful as the Christmas' I had with them on Calico Creek. Thank you Aunt Emmy." She hugged her again.

"Wells, I'se gots ta giv' mys hugs ta boths of yo'. Plez stand up Miss Emmy." Angel said rising from her chair. "Miss Emmy dis fo' makin' sech a niz home fo' Miss Callie an' me. An dis one fo' heppin' me's fine Big Man." Tears were forming in her eyes.

"An' Miss Callie, dis' hugs fo' makin' me's a free woman." The tears came as she hugged Callie.

Callie hugged her really tight. Then she held Angel's chin to look at her in her eyes and said, "You always were a free woman in my heart, Angel. I just took care of the paper work."

"Aunt Emmy, I know what I want my dress to look like for my birthday party. I remember Mama and Uncle Jim talking about her 16th birthday party dress. It was lavender taffeta and had pearl trim around the neck." Callie announced.

"I'se remember dat dress, too. Mama hepped her dress dat nite. I'se peak threw da kitchen doo' ta see yo' Mama an' da dress. My she wuz a pitcher." Angel chimed in.

"Mammy said she put fresh flowers in Mama's braids after she wound them around the crown of her head. Then she made ringlets to hang down her back."

"Dat's rite! An' ole Miss let's yo' Mama wears da' danglin' pearl earrings, pearl necklace, bracelet an' ring. I'se remember da' too." Angel added.

"Angel, can you fix my hair like that?" Callie asked.

"I'se sho' can. An' I'se ken makes yo' a dress jest lik' dat one."

"What color do you think the lavender was Callie?" Aunt Emmy inquired. "I could ask Jonathan to buy the taffeta on one of his trips to Charleston."

"I'm not sure, but I'd like it to be almost the color of a spring violet."

"Very well, I will invite Jonathan to dinner one night this week. You can tell him the color you want. Angel can tell him how much fabric to buy in Charleston and anything else she will need to make the dress."

The note read: "Jonathan, There are some items I would like you to purchase for Callie's birthday party on your next trip to Charleston. Could I discuss these items with you at dinner Thursday? Emmy"

His note read: "Emmy, Thursday night will be perfect. I'd been meaning to ask you how the plans are coming for her party. I will be happy to shop for you in Charleston. Jonathan."

"Angel, please have supper with us tonight. We will be discussing with Jonathan what he will need to find in Charleston for Callie's dress." Emmy requested.

House servants didn't eat at the table with the owner of the house and their guests in Lewisburg. Early in his visits to Emmys, Jonathan had made it understood that he did not object at all to Angel eating with them in the dining room or at the kitchen table.

"Taffeta?" Jonathan had a puzzled look on his face and in his voice. "I'm not well versed in the different fabrics of lady's dresses." Then he laughed.

Emmy patted his hand. "Most men aren't."

"I brought one of my dresses made of taffeta to show you." Callie retrieved a dress draped across a chair by the fireplace. "This dress is made of taffeta. Listen when I twirl it around. It rustles."

Jonathan laughed again. "So I'm to ask the sales clerk for the fabric that rustles?"

Emmy laughed too.

"No Suh yo's ta ax fo' taffeta." Angel answered. "An's yo's to tell dem yo's need twelve yards." She placed her left hand pointing finger on her nose, stretched her right arm as far as it would go and continued. "Dat's a yard; so's dey's gonna giv's yo lots ov taffeta. An' I'se gonna need sum pearls ta put 'round da neck."

"How on earth am I going to remember all this?" Jonathan asked.

"I'll write it all down for you." Emmy responded.

"I want the taffeta to be the color of a spring violet or a Johnny jump up." Callie explained.

"Whew, these are tall orders Callie. But I promise you, for you, I will do my very best to find exactly what you want."

"Jonathan, let's go to the library. I would like to discuss when you can help me start preparing the guest list and I'll make your shopping list." Emmy too his hand and they left for the library.

"An' yo's come hep me's wuth da' dishes, Miss Callie."

In the kitchen Angel told Callie, "Dey's wants ta be alone. Day's don'ts wants us'en hangin' 'round."

"I know, Angel. I think Aunt Emmy is in love. Remember when I asked you how I'd know if I was in love? You told me it was sometimes like yes and sometimes like no. Remember?

"Yes'em I'se does."

"Well, I think I know what you meant now. I think I'm in love." Callie had a big smile on her face.

"Wuth George?" Angel teased.

"NO!" Callie stamped her foot.

"Bet's I'se in guess den'. He be da' han'sum Capt'n Garrison da' comes heah, ain't he?"

Callie's face turned bright red. "How did you know?"

"I'se sees da' ways yo' looks at him; how's yo' gets alls heppy 'round him. I'se see how yo' not heppy when yo' don't knows when he be comin'. An' I'se see da' ways he looks at yo'. I'se thinks da luv bug done bit him ta'."

"I can hardly wait for Mr. Henson to get here tonight for dinner with my dress taffeta." Callie said to Aunty Emmy.

"He's very concerned that the color is what you wanted." Emmy replied.

"It's PERFECT! Mr. Henson." when Jonathan showed her the fabric.

"How are these pearls, Angel? Are they what you wanted?" he asked.

"Yes Suh! Dey's perfec'. Miss Callie, af'ta supper yo's an' I'se go ta' da' kitchen an' I'se draw up a pitcher what's I'se 'member da' dress looks lik'."

Emmy and Jonathan retired to the library to start the guest list.

Jonathan suggested that he take a copy of the list home to review. "It's very important for the first big social event that you have, Emmy, not to leave anyone off the list."

"I understand." Emmy replied. Actually, she was delighted he made the suggestion. It gave her a reason for inviting him to supper again.

After Jonathan's next visit, the ghost of Smithson house appeared in the window.

"This is the list I've prepared, Captains. Aunt Emmy handed the list to Captain Archer. Captain Garrison handed her the list they had made.

"Perhaps we could have some hot cider while you two begin reviewing the lists, Miss Emmy. Miss Callie and I could bring it while you start comparing names. Would you assist me Miss Callie?" He had thought about he could get to be alone with Callie for days.

The black smothering velvety curtain was about to take over her body. Callie took a deep breath to stop it and said, "Certainly, Captain Garrison."

She led him to the kitchen; got the cider out of the pantry and placed it in a pot to heat. He watched her every movement and she could feel his eyes following her around the room.

"Perhaps we should also have some cookies that Angel and I made today." Callie suggested.

"This beautiful, vivacious girl can cook too? WONDERFUL!" he said to himself. To her he said, "May I get the plates and cups for you, Miss Callie?"

"This handsome man with the ice blue eyes is willing to help with 'woman's work'. WONDERFUL!" she said to herself. To him she said, "That would be very nice of you, Captain Garrison. They are in the cabinet to the right of the sink."

Placing them on the table he said, "May I call you Callie? Miss Callie seems so formal. Please call me Alex, if you wish, when it's just the two of us."

"Yes, please Alex." Her heart was racing.

From his jacket, he pulled a small object wrapped in brown paper. With it was a note. Handing it to her he said, "Callie, it will be your real birthday soon. I hope you will accept this from me. But you have to promise you will wait and open it first thing on your birthday when you wake up."

"My that cider smells good." Captain Archer said as Callie and Alex entered the room. "It's been forever since I've had hot cider."

Emmy smelled the cider too but what she noticed was that Callie looked radiant.

"I hope you will enjoy the cookies too, Captain Archer." Callie responded.

That night in her bedroom she looked at the package from every possible angle, squeezed it trying to determine what it was by its shape. She bounced it in her hand hoping its weight would give her a clue.

Temptation got the best of her. She opened the note first.

> "My shopping possibilities are limited,
> wrapping paper and bows, too.
> However, when I saw how this sparkles; it's beauty,
> I thought of you.
> Happy Birthday Callie
> Alex"

She opened the brown wrapping paper. Inside was a rock glowing with minerals that made it sparkle like diamonds. She clasped it in her hands and held it to her heart.

"This is so beautiful! It's like the rocks I use to find along Calico Creek. And the words in the note make my heart race. How will I ever get to sleep tonight? I'll tell Mama, Mammy and Liza all about it in my prayers tonight." she thought. When she finally fell to sleep, the rock and note were under her pillow.

Jonathan was invited to Callie's "real" birthday supper.

"There's no reason why a person has to have only one day for their birthday. After all, they are the only one with their body, their heart who will ever be born on this earth. They should have a birthday season!" Emmy had explained when she had invited him.

"You are absolutely right, dear. Everyone should have as many days for their birthday as they want." He had hugged her when he said that.

After supper, Emmy appeared with brightly wrapped presents in her hands.

Jonathan, Angel and Emmy sang, "Happy Birthday to you ... Callie."

Tears formed in Callie's eyes. She gave each one of them a big hug.

"You must open this one first." Aunty Emmy handed her a package. "It's from Angel."

Callie removed the paper carefully. She gasped and said, "Oh it's so beautiful Angel." and rushed to hug her.

"Yo's needs it ta' goes wuth yo's dress, Miss Callie."

Callie held in her hands an intricately embroidered drawstring bag made of the same fabric as her dress. There were violets of different shades embroidered on it and pearls. "I can put Alex's rock in this and take it with me." Callie thought. She hugged Angel again and said, "Oh Angel, this is truly the most beautiful bag I have ever seen. THANK YOU."

"Here is your dance card to put into the bag, dear." Aunt Emmy handed her the card.

Callie looked at it thoughtfully and then asked, "Mr. Henson, would you put your name on the first and last line, please?"

He swallowed hard and replied, "It would be my pleasure, Callie."

"My Papa and Uncle Jim are gone." Callie had thought. "Mr. Henson is the closest replacement for them that I know to dance the first and last dance with me."

"This one is from me, Callie." Emmy said as she handed her a present.

Callie burst into tears when she saw the contents of the package. Inside were dangling pearl earrings, a pearl necklace and ring. She ran crying to Aunty Emmy with tears of happiness. "You remembered from the night I told you about Mama's dress, didn't you Aunt Emmy? THANK YOU! I love you so much."

"Yes dear, you wanted to dress just like your Mama had for her 16th birthday party." Emmy was looking at Jonathan with a question on her face. Had he forgotten one item she had asked him to bring from Charleston.

He pulled a wrapped package from his pocket and handed it to Callie. "This one is from me, Callie."

Inside was the matching pearl bracelet. She gave him a big hug and a kiss on his cheek.

"I can't tell you how happy you all have made me on my birthday. I will always cherish the memory of this day. I love you all."

"Well, I'd like to see you in your birthday dress, Callie." Jonathan said. "After all it is your birthday."

"Yes, let's show Mr. Henson, Angel. It's so beautiful."

"I'se not gonna fix da' hair lik' da' way it's gonna be fo' da' dance. You'se gonna hab ta' 'magine lots ov violets in da' hair." Angel said as the two rushed out of the room.

Emmy gave Jonathan a hug. "That was wonderful of you to give Callie the bracelet."

"He gently tiled her head up and gave her a kiss. "Emmy, I had no idea two women could steal my heart but you two have."

Upstairs Angel was helping Callie into the dress. Callie said to her, "Angel, I'm going to tell you a secret that only Mamma, Mammy and Liza know. You can't tell anyone."

From under her pillow, she pulled the rock and note. She read the note to Angel.

"See's dare! I'se told yo' da' luv bug done bit dat Capt'n Garrison too!" Angel said.

Callie carefully placed the rock and note in her drawstring bag.

Downstairs Mr. Henson said as he saw Callie enter the room, "You take my breath away, Callie.

Turning to Emmy he said, "Let's start your birthday season now too, Emmy."

He pulled a small box from his pocket, dropped to one knee, opened the box and said, "Miss Emmy Morris, will you marry me?"

"YES, YES, YES Jonathan!"

He placed a beautiful diamond ring on her finger, rose, embraced and kissed her.

Angel and Callie were screaming with joy, had joined hands and were dancing around in circles. Emmy and Jonathan joined them. There was much happiness in the ole Smithson house this night.

In a cold army tent, Captain Alex Garrison was trying to imagine what was happening in that house tonight. He saw Callie's face in his minds eye, heard her infectious laughter. "Oh Callie, how I wish with all my heart, I could be with you tonight."

"The ball was a complete success." Sarah announced at tea. "We've raised enough money to fill forty baskets for Christmas."

'That's wonderful."

"I've gotten the list from the ministers of the churches on the families they recommend to receive a basket. We can pack them at the Old Stone Church. Betty and I will deliver them in our carriages on the 23rd." Josephine said.

"That's very nice of you Betty and Josephine. May I add that your dresses were beautiful." Sarah comment.

Turning to Emmy, Betty said, "I thought George and Callie made a handsome couple as well as you and Mr. Henson."

This comment had been careful scripted between Betty and Sarah before the tea. The two of them had buried the hatchet. Sarah had decided it was better to have Betty as a friend than as an enemy.

"Thank you Betty." Emmy replied.

"That's all? That's all she's going to say about Betty's comment?" Sarah was fuming to herself. To Emmy she said, "It was nice of Mr. Henson to escort you, Emmy."

Emmy was chuckling inside. "It's always best to keep them guessing." She was saying this to herself. "At least that way they will spend their little secret gossip sessions on me and leave everyone else alone." She did not respond to Sarah's comment.

"The information we heard at the Christmas Ball was, 'just wait until spring,' and soon, two regiments will be stationed here in Lewisburg. Emmy informed the Captains.

"Both Callie and I observed no evidence of any troop encampments on the route to the Old White or appearance of any possible beginnings for future encampments."

Captain Archer replied, "This confirms reports we've had from other sources that there are plans being made for a spring campaign in this area.

Our scouts will be watching for troop movements from the south and north as soon as possible in the spring. The information you gained from your Sweet Springs trip will be of great assistance in the southern observations. Thank you."

Emmy continued. "I have also made arrangements for Callie's birthday party to be held on April 2nd at the Old White."

Captain Garrison smiled slight and said, "We would like to review your list of guests. There are certain members of the community it would be helpful to invite."

"That voice." Callie was saying to herself. "It's getting to be as bad as his eyes making my heart flutter."

"We could just send the list to Miss Emmy," Captain Archer interjected.

"We could but I think it will be important to review the list to see if there may be someone we've forgotten that we think of at that time." Captain Garrison answered.

"That's a good idea." Callie blurted out for purely selfish reasons.

"Very well then, when do you hope to have the list prepared, Miss Emmy?" Captain Archer asked.

"We will start making plans as soon as the Christmas rush is over. I hope to have the list made by the first of February."

"Speaking of Christmas, I'd like to wish you and Miss Callie a very Merry Christmas and a Happy New Year if I do not see you again before then. The Union wishes you Happy Holidays as well." Captain Archer responded.

"I, too, would like to wish you both the same. As a token of my appreciation for what you both have done, please accept this gesture as an appreciation present from me." Captain Garrison walked to where Emmy was sitting behind the desk, took her hand, placed it in his and kissed the top of her hand.

"Thank you Captain Garrison. That was very sweet of you." Aunt Emmy said.

"BE STILL MY HEART!" Callie was saying to herself as he came toward her from behind the desk.

He took Callie's hand in his. Emmy noticed that he seemed to take longer to get to the kiss and held Callie's eyes with his before he stooped to kiss her hand. He then said the same words he had said to Emmy.

"THINK CALLIE!" she told herself. "What did Aunt Emmy say in response to his kiss." With her heart racing so hard it seemed to be ready to run up her throat and jump out of her mouth, she said to him, "Thank you Captain Garrison. That was very sweet of you."

All over West Augusta, both the Union and Confederate troops were settling in preparing for winter. All indications were the wooly worm's predictions would come true. It would be a severe winter.

Confederate forces were in the county north of Greenbrier, Pocahontas, at Camp Allegheny. They were there to protect the Staunton-Parkersburg Pike, an important transportation route for supply and troop movement. At years end, the two regiments were in Lewisburg to protect the Lewisburg-Huttonsville Pike and Kanawha-Staunton Turnpike.

15

President Abraham Lincoln had issued an order that authorized Union forces to engage the Confederate forces in a unified effort in January 1862. In February the capitol of Tennessee, Nashville, fell into Union hands. The first naval battle of ironclad vessels took place in March in the waters off Norfolk, Virginia. The U.S.S. Monitor engaged the U.S.S Merrimack, renamed the C.C.C. Virginia, and fought to a draw.

In April the voters of West Augusta approved the constitution for the new state of West Virginia. Plans were being made to petition the US Congress in May asking for recognition of this new state through the Restored Government of Virginia.

"Jonathan," Emmy had said to him on the night he asked her to marry him, "There is something I must tell you. I hope you will keep it strictly confidential. If what I am about to tell you, you cannot accept, please know that I will understand. I will not be offended if you wish your ring returned. I will love you until my dying day however this turns out."

"What is it my dear?" he asked.

She took a deep breath and said, "Callie and I were sent to Lewisburg by the Union to gather information for the Union cause."

"Well of course you were my dear. Who do you think told them that we needed someone to gather information in this area about rumored impending actions? If you recall, Captain Simmons recommended me to you in Jackson River country on recommendation of Captain Archer. He wanted me to keep an eye on you and Callie once you got here. Frankly I never expected it to turn out this way and I suspect, neither did Captain Archer."

She burst out laughing and ran into his outstretched arms.

SOMETHING TO LIVE FOR

"You are never to take my ring off, do you understand me Miss Emmy Morris! The next ladies tea will at least have a topic of conversation and just wait until Sunday services."

That Sunday, Mr. Jonathan Henson entered first and stood by a pew on the right where single men sit. Callie and Miss Emmy Morris entered next. Callie turned to take a seat in a pew on the left where single women sit. Emmy kept walking towards Jonathan and took his arm. He deliberately walked slowing as he escorted her to one the front row pews where married and engaged couples sit. This was the traditional way of announcing engagements.

The entire church fell silent. This time it was not at the sight of Big Man escorting the elder Mrs. Garman to her seat. This time it was because Miss Emmy Morris and Mr. Jonathan Henson were telling the whole world they were in love and engaged to be married. Within an afternoon, the whole world of the Greenbrier Valley knew about the engagement.

Spring was in the air that March. The trees were manufacturing sap and forming those tiny green buds for summer leafs. Snow, trying desperately to hold onto winter, dripped water as it melted from the creek banks swelling the streams. The word spread in Lewisburg that someone saw a robin in the yard.

The men of the North and South in West Augusta started practicing their drills with more fervor. General Lee and General Grant were at their respective camps planning campaigns with their subordinates for this territory of Virginia. Transportation of troops and supplies was a major concern and major transportation routes ran through this mountain territory of West Augusta.

It was imperative that the Confederate forces maintain control of the Staunton-Parkersburg Turnpike and the B&O Railroad in the north. South of Lewisburg it was just as critical to gain control of the East Tennessee and Virginia Railroad. It was anyone's guess if either side could truly control the much-desired Kanawha-Staunton Turnpike between Charleston and Lewisburg or the Lewisburg-Huttonsville turnpike. Both met at Lewisburg and led into the heart of the Shenandoah Valley through Covington.

"What wonderful news that you and Mr. Henson are engaged, Emmy," Sarah said at tea.

"Thank you, Sarah." Emmy responded.

"Have you set a date, dear?" Sarah asked.

"No, we haven't."

Betty spoke then. "Oh Emmy, you have so many exciting events coming up in you future; Callie's 16th birthday party at the Old White, and now a wedding to plan. How can you do it all? You know any of us will gladly assist you in any way we can."

"Actually, Jonathan and Callie are helping me with all the planning." Sarah and Betty wanted an entirely different answer.

After tea, Sarah said to Betty, "That woman drives me crazy. She has the tightest zipper on her lips I've ever known of anyone."

Captain's Archer and Garrison visits to the old Smithson House were more frequent. They both congratulated Emmy on her engagement to Mr. Henson. "I really didn't see that one coming Miss Emmy. But I am delighted for you both." Captain Archer had said.

"They are the perfect couple!" Callie had blurted out. "You should see them dancing together. It looks like they have danced with each other forever."

Captain Garrison managed to tell Callie privately on that trip, "Just wait until we dance at your birthday party. We'll be a perfect couple too; dance as though we've danced together forever."

On the previous trip to finalize the list of guests, he had asked her when the opportunity arose, "Did you like your birthday present, Callie?"

"I think it's the most beautiful rock I've ever seen and I've seen a lot of rocks like that one. I love to pick them out of Calico Creek where I use to live. Thank you, Alex." Callie had replied.

"Someday I'd like to go there with you, Callie, and we can pick up rocks together." He took her hand in his, with the other gently lifted her chin to look directly into her eyes.

"And the note Callie, I meant every word of it. You are the most beautiful girl I have ever seen. You sparkle like a diamond." Then he kissed her.

"Oh Angel, I thought that black smothering velvet curtain was going to throw itself over me and pull me right down to the floor when that happened." Callie was telling her about the kiss.

"Miss Callie in luv'; Miss Callie in luv'" Miss Callie in luv'." Angel chanted.

"Stop that teasin' Angel! I know I'm in love with the most handsome, sentimental man who ever walked the face of this earth.

SOMETHING TO LIVE FOR

"Remember when he told me that after the war he wanted to dance with me? It's happening early, next month! Oh if only that time when we pick sparkly rocks out of Calico Creek could come fast."

With that said, she grabbed Angel's hands and the two of them swirled around the kitchen chanting, "Miss Callie's in love."

The invitation read:

> You are cordially invited to
> a party give by
> Mr. and Mrs. Jonathan Henson
> for their niece
> Miss Callie Morris
> Old White 7:00 PM April 2nd
> RSVP no gifts

"George, you must at once send a note to Miss Callie telling her you would be honored to escort her to her birthday party." Sarah said to her son. She had been shocked to read the "Mr. and Mrs." part of the invitation but assumed it only meant they were planning their wedding before Callie's birthday party.

"But you know, Mother, I have tried so many times to escort Callie to various functions since the Christmas dance. She seems always to have a reason why I cannot. It is breaking my heart."

"My dear, some girls just like to play hard to get and I have a feeling that is just exactly what Miss Callie is playing with you. She's always very attentive to the words you're saying I've noticed. She does seem to be gracious and smiles around you. I think you just need to play along with her little game if she's the girl you want."

"Mother, I have never seen anyone more beautiful; met anyone with such an infectious laugh. I love everything about her. She's the girl I want."

"Well then, play her game, George. The time will come when she will realize what a wonderful catch you are; what a fine husband you will be!" she told him as she gave him a big hug.

As the invitations were being delivered throughout the Greenbrier Valley, Jefferson was driving Emmy, Callie and Angel over the Kanawha-Staunton Turnpike to Charleston. At the last tea Emmy had told everyone that they were planning this trip to Charleston. In her usual zipped lip fashion, she had not given the reason.

A few weeks before Aunt Emmy and Jonathan had asked her, "Callie, what would you like as a present for your second birthday? It has to be something that we can give you."

Callie had thought for several days and finally decided. "I would love for us all to go back to Calico Creek. I want to show you the cabin; how beautiful it is there."

"This will be perfect." Jonathan had said to them. "We've made all the arrangements with the Old White for the party; invitations have been addressed. I have an appointment in Charleston the third week of March. I could meet you all there."

That night Emmy and Jonathan had discussed their marriage plans. They would be married by a friend of Jonathan's in his church in Charleston. The ladies would have two days to shop for dresses. Callie would be maid of honor; a lawyer friend best man for Jonathan.

"Emmy, I have a dream for us and I want you to be a part of the planning for our dream. Next spring let's begin building our home on my land west of Lewisburg." He told her.

"It's so beautiful there." Emmy replied, "The perfect place for our home."

He gave her a hug. "Good we'll spend the summer and fall planning the house; begin construction at the first sign of spring next year. Then later that summer we can all go to Europe on a delayed honeymoon. You can shop for all the furniture and knick-knacks you'll want for your dream house."

The cabin on Calico Creek was no worse for wear having been empty during the past year. There was evidence that a stranded hunter or perhaps military persons might have spent a night or two. Only a few pieces of jerky were missing.

Jonathan had suggested that Jefferson take Callie and Angel to Calico Creek one day while he introduced his new bride to his friends in Charleston for lunch and afternoon teas. They packed a picnic lunch.

"Jefferson, Angel. You have to come down to the creek with me. I have to show you where the water sparkles like diamonds." Callie said excitedly.

"Yo's go' head, Miss Callie. I'se got ta git stuff out fo' us'ens ta eat." Angel replied.

"An' I'se got ta takes care da horse." Jefferson answered.

SOMETHING TO LIVE FOR

Before they hardly answered, Callie was running out of the cabin to Calico Creek. The sun was starting to rise high in the sky. There were only patches of snow at the edge of the woods and in the shaded part of the field. The smell of spring was in the air. There were birds singing once again in the trees.

Running across the field Callie stopped, stretched out her arms and looked to the sky, "Lord, thank you for helping me get through this year. I'm so happy to be home again."

She started giggling and spinning around and around across the field with outstretched arms. Suddenly she stopped; stood like a statue. Her heart pounded.

At the creek's edge, she saw a figure squatted and skipping stones across the creek. Slowly he rose, turned and stretched out his arms. Callie ran straight into the arms of Captain Alex Garrison.

"I've come to pick those diamond rocks with you, Callie. It has seemed like an eternity waiting for you to get here," he told her lifting her chin and looking into her eyes.

She reached up her hands and cupped them behind his head, pulled his face to hers and kissed him. They walked hand in hand along Calico Creek with occasional stops for another kiss.

In the distance, Callie heard Angel calling. Holding hands, they ran toward Angel.

"Look who's here Angel." Callie shouted.

Angel held the picnic basket in her hands. "I'se no's Miss Callie. Master Jonathan say dat he's kin mak' it happen. Yo's get to fine dim rocks yo' wants wuth Capt'n Alex fo' yo' second birthday gif' frum me. Yo's all go back ta da creek wuth dis. Me's an' Jefferson is at da cabin eatin'."

Callie and Alex spent that afternoon walking hand and hand over the fields and along the stream. He told her of his childhood near the place where the Kanawha River joins the Ohio River, about his family and his love of the outdoors. When the Union forces had recruited him, it was as a scout. Gradually he had worked his way up the ranks to Captain. His knowledge of the Kanawha Valley, the mountain country and his skills as a scout had for the most part kept him out of any of battles.

Captain Archer had recruited him to continue his work as a scout along the Kanawha Turnpike and into the Greenbrier Valley area where major offensives were planned for the spring of 1862.

The Union forces plan was to drive the Confederate forces out of Tennessee, Ohio, Pennsylvania and West Augusta and back into Virginia. A major part of the plan was to block the Confederates from moving west, from receiving supplies or reinforcements using the B&O railroad to the north, East Tennessee & Virginia Railroad to the south. The plan also included capturing and controlling the Staunton-Parkersburg turnpike as well as the Kanawha and Lewisburg-Huttonsville ones.

"This war won't last forever, Callie. This country will get back to settling the west. People will also continue settling in this beautiful country too. When they come through here or move here, they are going to need supplies.

"I have a dream that someday, I'll have my own supply store, my own family and raise them in the new state of West Virginia." He stopped, took both her hands, pulled her near him and gazed into her eyes. "I can't promise you when it will happen but I promise you it will. You're a very big part of my dream Callie Morris. Will you share my dream with me?"

Stay away black smothering curtain! I have to answer him she commanded her body as her heart raised. "Yes, Yes, Yes. And we could build that store right here on Calico Creek!"

He picked her up in his arms and they swirled around and around.

Sarah heard George scream in the foyer in pain as he had when he was a small child. She ran to him.

"Darling, what's wrong?"

"She's done it again! This time she says she has asked her Uncle Jonathan to escort her to her birthday party; says he's the closest thing to a father she's had since her own father died." George replied as tears fell down his cheeks.

"Now, now, darling" Sarah said to George as she cradled him in her arms. "If you think about it, she's right. Her father should escort her to her birthday party. And remember dear, she's playing hard to get."

"Well, she did say she's looking forward to seeing me there."

"See dear, I told you she was playing hard to get."

"You and Jonathan certainly surprised us all with your wedding in Charleston, Emmy." Sarah was saying a tea. We had all thought you would be married here in the Old Stone Church."

"Were there many people at the wedding, Emmy?" Betty asked.

"Only Callie, Angel, Jefferson and a couple of Jonathan's Charleston friends" Emmy answered.

"Did anyone hold a reception for you there? We were all planning on holding one here for you if the wedding had been at the Old Stone Church." Sarah noted with disappointment in her voice.

"Actually it was more of a tea than a reception."

Sensing that this topic was going nowhere, Sarah asked, "Do you have all the plans made for Callie's party next week? It looks like the weather is going to cooperate."

"Yes, and we're thrilled that a couple of our friends from Jackson River country will be able to attend."

"How nice. From what I hear, everyone in the Greenbrier Valley plans to attend. Remember, if there is anything at all we can do to help you, please let us know. Any of us would be delighted to help you." Betty enthused.

"Thank you. I know you would." Emmy zipped her lips again.

The weather was perfect for the party. It was almost balmy, one of those teaser spring days that promises an end to winter and nothing but robin egg blue skies in the future. All the carriages in Lewisburg were cleaned, the frantic last minute adjustments to dresses were made. The men's shoes were polished bright enough that one could see the reflection of their faces.

Jonathan noted as he filled in his name in the first and last lines of Callie's dance card that every third line had been filled in with the name, Alex Garrison.

"My goodness, it looks like your dance card is almost completely filled, Callie, and you haven't even arrived at the party." He teased. "And just who might this Alex Garrison be?"

She stomped her foot. "You know exactly who Alex Garrison is! Do you think that's too many times for his name? I really don't want to dance with anyone but the two of you. Aunt Emmy says that I must dance with some of the local boys though."

"That's true dear. Alex has other reasons for being at the party you must remember. But I'll see if I can get the quartette to play their long, slow songs every third dance." He chuckled.

The excitement created for the first huge social event of the season was contagious. Anxious parents desiring to make the best match for their children paired couples. Their fathers were teaching young girls the waltzes and other dances; young men were learning the dance steps from their mothers.

The Old White was filled with fresh flowers; tulips, daffodils, jonquils and potted violets. Lavender and purple bows held sprigs of baby's breath. Potted azaleas in shades of pinks, mixed with pots of cream and white ones graced every room and in the front of the windows. Single and three-tiered silver candle sticks with softly lit lavender candles were scattered around the rooms. Aunt Emmy had picked the decorations with one thought in mind. All would compliment the dress Callie would be wearing, her Mama's dress.

Polished carriages arrived with beautifully attired ladies bedecked with family heirloom jewelry. The men stood more erect in their evening suits. Each man was given violets to wear in his lapel. Women were given a wrist corsage of a single gardenia surrounded by violets. Riders on beautifully groomed horses handed their reins to the attendant and entered to receive their violets.

Callie, Aunt Emmy and Uncle Jonathan greeted each arriving group at the entrance to the parlor. The smell of the gardenia wrist corsages filled the air along with the tempting aromas of finger foods. Huge punch bowls held a blend of tea with fresh fruit. Cups were arranged around the bowls. Dainty white plates for the food, pale lavender napkins and small pieces of silverware were placed near the foods. Discretely the trays were filled; cups were replaced; used serving plates removed.

Emmy was the first to notice the arrival of her "friends" from Jackson River country. She immediately went to them, accepted their kiss on her cheek and led them to meet her new husband and reacquaint them with her niece, Callie. Each wished Callie a happy birthday and asked to have their name added to her dance card. Alex pretended to be writing his name in the spaces where his name already appeared. He was polite but reserved and Callie followed suit.

All the young women in the room used any method possible to position themselves to be in the vicinity where Aunt Emmy was escorting the two Virginia gentlemen and introducing them. They had their dance cards ready for a signature. After all, southern traditions were alive and well here. It was one's duty to make a friend of a friend feel welcome when they were away from home. The fact that the two were very handsome and older than most of the other young men who would be their dance partners that night, didn't make following tradition difficult at all for the young ladies.

Callie's partner for the first dance was Uncle Jonathan. Captain Archer danced with Aunt Emmy. Janie Pack was dancing with Alex.

SOMETHING TO LIVE FOR

"That's ironic," thought Callie. "Janie was the one who asked me if I'd ever been in love and I had no idea what love was. Wouldn't she be surprised if she knew that the man she's dancing with right now is the one I love! "

Finally, the time came for Callie to dance with Alex. She already knew how well they fit in each others arms but how well they danced together was remarkable. Her body seemed to feel ever move and turn he was about to make as they waltzed around the floor. Yes, they looked as though they had danced with each other forever. They did not speak a word. They didn't have to speak. Their hearts and souls were one.

Callie could have almost cried when the last dance started. Her heart ached to dance just one more time with Alex. For this dance, he danced with Aunt Emmy.

"You know I'm in love with your niece." He said quietly to Emmy.

She smiled. "I believe the feeling is mutual Mr. Garrison."

The Union forces were making plans to send the Rebs "packin'" back to the Shenandoah Valley and out of West Augusta once and for all. Troops stationed at Cheat Mountain in the north would defeat the Confederate forces and send them retreating to the Shenandoah Valley. They and other forces would continue south, meeting up with troops coming from the west.

From the west, Colonel George Crook would march two brigades across the Kanawha-Staunton Turnpike into Lewisburg. There they would set up camp on a hill on the west side of town. Once all the Union troops were in Lewisburg, they would proceed south to capture the Tennessee-Virginia Railroad.

In the meantime, the Confederates were making plans to capture Lewisburg. They would march from Pearisburg, Virginia, with heavy artillery attacking from the east. Once they were in Monroe County south of Lewisburg, they would follow the same route that Callie, Emmy, Sarah and George had taken on their trip to Sweet Springs in the fall. They intended to capture Organ Cave, Lewisburg and retrieve the law books from the law library in Lewisburg.

16

"WHAT ON EARTH WAS THAT?" A man sat straight up in bed. "Didn't sound like thunder." His wife replied.

"There it is again!" He jumped out of bed this time and ran to the window.

The people of Lewisburg were jarred from a sound sleep at 8:00 AM on May 23, 1862 by the sound of artillery before they had even had breakfast. Confederate Brigadier General Heth had fired from the top of "Hardscramble Hill," East Washington Street, on the east side of town. He bombarded the Union camp just as the men there were preparing breakfast. Shots, shells and canisters began to rain down on the town below before the people had a chance to escape the battle. In one home, a shell came down the chimney. While the battle raged at its fiercest, two girls of the home worked frantically to remove the burning debris and to keep the house from burning to the ground. One soldier remarked that the cannon balls fell on the ground like hail.

Children still dressed in bedclothes ran across their bedrooms to windows; pressed their faces against the windowpane to catch a glimpse of the fighting. They heard bullets whistling through the trees and shrubs in their yards.

The Confederate forces were divided into three groups on the east side of town. One group was perched at the top of "Hardscramble Hill" which was part of the Kanawha-Staunton Turnpike. It ran the width of the town from east to west. A second group was placed a little further down the hill on the left. The third group were located on the right side of "Hardscramble Hill" near the fairgrounds and Smithson House.

"Aunt Emmy, Listen! The battle has started." Callie rushed into Emmy's room and looked out the window facing Lewisburg. Soon Emmy, Callie and Angel were huddle together looking out the window.

Union soldiers advanced toward the fairgrounds. Emmy, Angel and Callie were hearing this battle. The soldiers delivered heavy fire on the Rebel forces. A Confederate Captain with this group described his men as falling like ten pins in a bowling alley.

The left flank in the back yard also collapsed as Union forces advanced from the west up the "Hardscramble Hill." There the gunners of the south fought bravely to protect their artillery but were eventually over-run by Union forces. More Rebel men were moved to reinforce the gunners and they too came under heavy fir. They broke rank and fled.

Brigadier General Heth had no recourse but to sound retreat for the remaining troops in the center. His troops suffered 80 deaths, 100 wounded and 157 were taken prisoner. The Union forces had 13 killed, 52 wounded and 7 missing. Heth pulled his troops back across the Greenbrier River and burned the bridge behind him.

The battle between the North and South had lasted a little more than an hour. The fighting, however, continued in Lewisburg. Snipers concealed in homes took shots at Union soldiers returning to the camp on the west side of town. One soldier was killed. The house from which the shot came was burned to the ground. Colonel Crook was heard to threaten after that he would hang immediately any sniper found at once on the main street of Lewisburg. None was ever caught after that threat and the sniping stopped.

Colonel Crook would not permit the Southern sympathizers in Lewisburg to bury their dead or conduct any funeral ceremony. Instead, Union soldiers placed the dead Confederate soldiers in Old Stone Church. Later they were moved to a trench in the churchyard.

Hospitals were established in the John Wesley Methodist Church, Old Stone Church and The Virginia State Law Library. The wounded from both sides were often placed in the same room. Soldiers wrote very emotion messages on the walls of the library to their loves ones at home.

That night Jonathan and Emmy heard a light knocking on the kitchen door. Jonathan found Captain's Archer and Garrison there. They went to the library and he asked Emmy to wake up Callie.

"Ladies," Captain Archer was saying, "the Union is forever indebted to you for the fine work you have done here in Lewisburg. The soldiers may have won the victory today; but not without the information you gave us, the outcome could have been very different. The Rebs did not have the element of surprise on their side that they thought they would have. Being able to scout their strength before they arrived here proved to be extremely valuable. Thank you."

Emmy and Callie smiled.

"We'll be leaving this area now for an assignment further north." Captain Garrison said.

Callie felt her heart fill her chest. "You're leaving?"

"Yes," Captain Archer replied. "We are needed in other parts of the battle. The Confederates are really on the run now."

"Does that mean that we have to leave too?" Emmy asked with concern.

He chuckled. "I won't want to be the person to tell Jonathan Henson that we are taking his wife and niece away from him."

Jonathan laughed at that remark.

Captain Garrison spoke, "You have made a wonderful home here. I feel you will all be safe. The possibility still exists that the Rebs might make another attempt to gain this territory. It will be good for you all to stay to learn of any possible campaigns planned for the area."

"Callie, let's get some cider from the kitchen to celebrate the victory." He took her hand and they left the room.

In the kitchen, he took both of her hands into his and looked into her eyes. "Callie, I love you more than life itself. I know I am asking you to believe in me and my promise that I will come back after this war is over. What I'm trying to say in such a clumsy way is that I would like you to be my wife. I'd like to spend the rest of my life with you once this war is over."

He paused to read the expression on her face. Her eyes were filling with tears but her mouth was smiling the largest smile he had ever seen on her face.

"Oh Alex, I have dreamed so many times you would ask me to wait for you and be your wife. I just can't believe my dreams are coming true!" Callie wrapped her hands around his neck and snuggled close to him.

"I promise you, my love, I will come back to you. We'll be married anywhere you want. I'll try to send you a message at least once a week. Any chance I get to scout in this area or come to see you, you'll hear me knocking at the kitchen door."

He held her at arms length. "Did you say yes?"

"YES, YES, YES!" She pulled him to her and they kissed.

July 14, 1862 the West Virginia statehood bill passed the Senate allowing for the gradual emancipation of slavery.

It was a very somber group meeting for tea a month after the battle. Tea was canceled for a month. Most of the women were busy offering nursing care, cooking and writing letters for the wounded from the battle. The wounded Confederates captured were first sent to a camp near Columbus, Ohio. By September 1862, they had been exchanged for Union soldiers held captive by the South. Wounded Union soldiers returned to their homes to recuperate or to hospitals near their homes.

For once, Emmy was the person who broke the somber mood with the news that she and Jonathan were planning to build their home in the spring.

"That's wonderful Emmy. I must tell you, if it's as well planned as Callie's birthday party at the Old White, it will be beautiful. That was one of the nicest parties I've ever attended." Sarah said.

"Thank you Sarah."

"Those were certainly two nice young men who came from Jackson River country for the party." Sarah continued.

"And very handsome too. Both were such good dancers." Betty added.

"I always enjoyed it when they came to my parties." Emmy said trying to stop this line of conversation.

"It seemed that Callie and one of them, I believe his name was Alex, had danced together before; probably at your parties there." Sarah said hoping to learn more of their relationship. She had noted that there seemed to be a special bond between the two of them.

"Yes, they always have danced well together." Then Emmy zipped her lips.

The fall months were filled with endless meetings with the architect designing their new home. As the plans developed, then were drawn over and over again, Jonathan was amazed at the details Emmy included. She wanted to be certain there was a place for every piece of furniture to be displayed to its best advantage. He actually believed she could see each room finished and filled with furniture in her mind's eye. She had begun her shopping list for pieces she wanted to add on their trip to Europe in the summer; made lists of pieces from the Smithson house she wanted moved to the new house.

She blossomed with happiness. He was convinced she grew more beautiful with each passing day.

One night at dinner Jonathan stated, "I am the luckiest man in Lewisburg. I have supper every night with the two most beautiful ladies in all of Greenbrier County, probably the world. The day I met you two was the beginning of nothing but happy days for me."

It was Sarah's scream; the sound of glass shattering and then a loud thud that caused the servants to run up the stairs to George's bedroom. There they found Sarah on the floor and a note clutched in her hand. It read, "Dad and Mom. I have been so humiliated by the defeat of our courageous forces in Lewisburg I cannot stand it. I have left to join up with them. Your loving son, George."

Alex managed to send messages each week as he had promised Callie. She always had a message ready to be taken back to him in reply. He was able to visit the week of Christmas. Once again, winter in the mountains had stopped all activities on the battlefields.

December 31, 1862 President Abraham Lincoln signed the statehood bill declaring that after a sixty-day waiting period, West Virginia would become the 35th state of the Union. June 20, 1863 would be its official first birthday.

17

Spring finally came to the Greenbrier Valley. Robins busily built nests, tulips and jonquils awoke from their winter sleep and poked their heads through the warm soil. The streams and rivers filled with melted snow. The warming rays of the March sun filled the air.

In Wheeling, excitement filled the halls of the Linsly Institute. It would serve as the new West Virginia capitol building. Decisions were being made that would alienate the supporters of the Confederacy in Greenbrier County but the legislators could care less about their feelings. Many legislators had fought or had sons who were still fighting in the Union blue; some had sons who were killed in the struggle.

"How is Mr. McKinney these days, Sarah?" Betty asked.

"Well the news from George that those two fine Generals Jones and Inboden had successfully sent those 'damm Yankees' running up north seemed to raise his spirits. George said one of the purposes of this raid was to capture Frances Pierpont, the Governor of the 'Restored Government of Virginia'. Virginia does not recognize a new state. They didn't find him but they did burn all of his personal papers. AND" sip…sip…sip

"AND" shouted a chorus of voices.

"And General Jones sat fire to oil wells, barrels of oil, and sent a sheet of oil and smoke floating down the Little Kanawha River."

"WONDERFUL!" the chorus of voices shouted.

Sarah continued, "I really think George's visit was the best medicine that Mr. McKinney could have had. He seems to be recovering from the consumption he got this winter.

"And George told him of plans General Echols has to move into the Greenbrier Valley area later in the summer."

She said that George had said to his father, "Just because that President Lincoln says there is going be a new state this summer, doesn't make it so! We plan to put these 'damm Yankees' in their place here in the mountains and then run them across the Ohio River. We'll tar and feather ever last one of them and that President Lincoln too when we get to Washington. That'll be the end of it!"

Emmy made a mental note of the General Echols information before saying, "I certainly wish Mr. McKinney a complete and full recovery. As you know, Jonathan, Callie and I will be leaving in two weeks to go to England and France to select furniture for the new house."

"We can hardly wait until you have it totally completed," Betty said. "You must promise us you will have a big open house when it's totally finished and furnished."

That night the ghost of the Smithson house appeared with lit candle in the window. The usual Captains did not arrive to receive the information.

"Aunt Emmy would you and Uncle Jonathan be too disappointed if I didn't go to Europe with you looking for furniture? I don't want to be so far away from Alex. I hate big cities and that's where you'll be shopping. I'd much rather spend the summer on Calico Creek." Miss Callie was holding Emmy's hand and looking straight into her eyes as they sat at the kitchen table.

"An' I'se say I'se go wuth her, Miss Emmy." Angel spoke up.

Callie continued. "There are so many things I'd like to do at the cabin, Aunt Emmy. It's not too late to plant a garden. I'd be close to Alex's unit now in the Kanawha Valley. I never had a proper burial service for Mammy and I want to fix her gravesite. Oh please Aunt Emmy, please, please, please let me spend the summer at Calico Creek."

That night, Jonathan and Emmy discussed Callie's request.

"In a way, it might be best for Callie to stay here, dear. She would do nothing but fret the whole time she was in Europe that something has happened to Alex and she wouldn't know it."

"But who would take her to Calico Creek?" Emmy asked.

"That's simple. There won't be a need for Joshua here as a butler all summer; Jefferson can drive all of us out of town as though we're all headed to Europe. Then Emmy and Callie can transfer their belongings to the other carriage." Jonathan replied.

It was settled. Jonathan and Emmy would go to Europe for the summer; Callie, Angel and Joshua would spend the summer at Calico Creek.

Aunt Emmy held a candle in the window again that night. She gave the note to the man with specific instructions to only give the note to Captain Garrison.

"I love this place so, Angel," Callie said as she saw the cabin and the cleared area around the cabin at Calico Creek. Her eyes started to fill with tears. "I must go tell Mammy I'm here with her now."

Angel and Joshua started unloading the supplies from the wagon. The cabin was no worse for wear from having been vacant for so long. Angel put away the supplies in the kitchen and then began preparing the evening meal for them. Joshua took care of the horses, taking them to the stream for water and tying them in a nice grassy area for food. He had unhitched the wagon near the cabin and placed the canvas covering from the supplies onto the ground. This would be his sleeping quarters during the summer until he could build a more suitable place.

Callie sat on the ground beside Mammy's grave. Angel could see her place her head on the soil of the grave, stroke the grave, pick at the weeds now covering the site. Occasionally she could see Callie use the back of her hand to wipe tears from her face. She could not hear the conversation that Callie was having with Mammy. Finally, Callie rose and started walking towards the cabin. She stopped and looked in the direction where Rim had been tied near the cabin. She placed her cupped hand to her lips and blew a kiss in that direction.

"Oh Angel, I meant to help you and Joshua get the supplies off the wagon," Callie said as she entered the cabin.

"Dat's alrite Miz' Callie. Joshua knows jest how's he's put everthin' on da wagon. Makes it easy fo' da twos ov us ta git everthin' off. An' it wuz good fo' yo' ta spend sum time wuth Mammy."

"I had so much to tell her; all about Alex, Aunt Emmy and Uncle Jonathan, about the war. I've missed so talking to her. I'd love to hear her tell me to quit my 'traypinsen here and traypinsen there.' Mama would laugh and tell her there wasn't such a word but Mammy would say it was the only one she could think of to describe me flitting around everywhere like a butterfly." Callie laughed as she said that.

They carried river rock from Callie Creek and covered Mammy's grave with them. Joshua had stacked rock in a tube shape, filled it with sand from the creek and placed the wooden cross he had made at the head of the grave. The three of them stood holding hands as Callie said goodbye to Mammy and quoted words from the Book that she could remember her mother reading. Afterwards she had said to Joshua that she knew where there was the perfect mountain laurel in the woods they would dig and place behind the cross.

The vegetable garden so long neglected came to life once again through the efforts of the three of them. Callie had planted flowers around the outside so there was a profusion of colors with the tall green vegetables as a background. As they started blooming, she would pick some to put on Mammy's grave and some to take into the house for the table. I must have my Grandfathers green thumb she thought as she picked the flower and vegetables.

Joshua was an excellent hunter. The kitchen was filled with wonderful aromas that Callie and Angel prepared. They always made certain that there was enough cooked for four persons. Sometimes Alex would stop in unexpectedly to join them for lunch or supper.

"Oh Alex," Callie told him on one such visit, "I can not believe there is a more beautiful place in the whole wide world than right here."

"I'm going to make it even more beautiful for you after this war is over, dear. Just you wait and see." He hugged her. "Everything is being planned to make the war end soon. It's only another week until West Virginia will become a state on June 20th. You and I are going to help build this state to be a place that our children and grandchildren will be proud to call home."

June 20th, Callie, Angel and Joshua stood outside the cabin as Joshua fired his gun into the air in celebration of statehood. It echoed through the mountains and in the distance, a shot could be heard echoing back in celebration.

In Lewisburg, there were no shots to echo, only in the countryside surrounding it.

The Union forces were making plans to destroy the Confederate saltpeter works and gunpowder mills in West Virginia and capture the East Tennessee Railroad—Virginia Railroad to the south of Lewisburg. Union General William W. Averell left Virginia to accomplish this mission.

Colonel George S. Patton had 1,900 Confederate infantry force stationed near White Sulphur Springs. Their mission was to prevent the Union forces of General Averell from reaching White Sulphur Springs and the saltpeter mine in Organ Cave.

On August 26th, the two groups of soldiers met. The battle raged for two days. Colonel Patton's forces were able to repulse repeated Union attacks against their line. By noon the second day, General Averell withdrew his troops and returned to Virginia.

Brigadier General John Echols, Commander of the Confederate Army of Western Virginia, had given up his command in the summer of 1863. In civilian life, he was a lawyer. That summer he served on a three man court in Richmond investigating the fall of Vicksburg. When the investigation was completed, he assumed command of the Army of Western Virginia and returned to West Augusta.

Confederate Brigadier General John Echols had been sent to the White Sulphur Springs area and Confederate Coronal William L. Jackson had troops to the north near Mill Point in Pocahontas County. He was a cousin of "Stonewall" Jackson. His nickname was "Mudwall."

"Mudwall" Jackson and his troops had as their objective capturing and securing the Virginia State Law library in Lewisburg, retrieving the books for the Commonwealth of Virginia. This library had long been used by lawyers when preparing for trials at this western most point of civilized Virginia.

In the middle of September, Emmy and Jonathan returned from their European shopping trip. Callie and Angel were in the same carriage returning from Calico Creek. The women's tea group the previous week had learned of their impending arrival and looked forward to learning what Emmy had purchased, where they had traveled, if the group could get more than one word answers from Emmy.

"Paris and London mainly." Another short answer from Emmy that always drove Sarah crazy.

"You must tell us of all the beautiful furniture and other items you're having shipped back to the states, dear." Sarah commented sweetly.

The command was wasted on Emmy.

"I don't think I can recall everything. It was such a whirl wind of shopping."

This line of conversation is going no where, thought Sarah. She changed the subject.

"You must tell Callie that George is now with Brigadier General John Echols' forces in West Augusta." No one in Sarah's circle of acquaintance referred to the area as West Virginia. "George always asks about Callie when we hear from him. Please give her his regards."

"I will," Emmy replied then asked, "and is George well?"

Sarah leaped at the chance to brag on her son. "My heavens YES! He has been promoted twice while you were in Europe. General Echols values his knowledge of the area. He has been sent to help "Mudwall" Jackson plan for the defense of Droop Mountain to make certain none of those 'damm Yankees' can come down the Lewisburg-Huttonsville Pike and surprise our boys or attack Lewisburg. George is the most important part of the planning.

"THAT President of the 'Blue Coats' may think he's created a state but in Virginia's heart, this is still West Augusta. It intends to take it back from those turn coats once it defeats those "damm Yankees'."

Alex had been sent to scout the troop strength on Droop Mountain, general terrain and possible routes to advance up the mountain. He was to report his findings to General Averell who had moved his troops into West Virginia north of Mill Point. On his way to Droop Mountain, he had stopped in Lewisburg.

The seriousness in his eyes reminded her of the time Uncle Jim had told her how she must react to anything she heard when they arrived at the Garman Inn on their way to take Mama to Jackson River; that she must take Liza to Grandmother Hill.

"Callie, you will not be hearing from me for a while, but know my love, the last vision I see in my heart before I fall asleep at night will be your beautiful face. As soon as I can I will race to hold you in my arms once again."

It was a battle fought on the top of a mountain. Droop Mountain stands three thousand feet tall from its base in the valleys below. In the fall, fog fills these valleys. Standing on top of the mountain one can see only a carpet of white below.

On November 5th, General Averell attacked "Mudwall" and his 1,500 man force at Mill Point. His mission was to find out the strength of the Confederate force. Badly out numbered, "Mudwall" retreated to Droop Mountain. He immediately sent George to notify General Echols that he needed additional troops to defend this mountain position. With 1,800 soldiers, General Echols joined "Mudwall."

Even with this additional force, the Confederates continued to be out numbered. General Averell advanced toward the mountain with 5,000 men.

SOMETHING TO LIVE FOR

On the morning of November 6th, General Averell had part of his troops advance from the north side of the turnpike. He then sent a small group of men to zig zag along ditches and fences to avoid detection on the western side. Alex had discovered an obscure road leading to the top.

General Echols concentrated his troops on the east side of the mountain. He placed artillery aimed at the turnpike at strategic locations to bombard it if the Union forces tried to move on it from the north. George was sent with a small group to the western side of the mountain.

"Halt! Drop to your knees and place your gun on the ground!" George yelled at the man in the blue uniform. He had been startled to see a man suddenly appear out of the woods.

Alex looked into the face of the man who had given the order. Instantly there was recognition by both of them.

"You sneakin' Yankee, you! You stole my Callie from me. As God as my witness I will shoot you dead where you stand!" He raised his rifle to fire.

Instinctively Alex fell to the ground and fired as he was falling. His aim was true and it struck George in the upper part of his right arm near the shoulder. Bones shattered. George screamed in agony. This time, it was George who fell to the ground.

That shot and George's screams, brought Union troops out of the woods firing their rifles. This alerted the Confederate troops that the Union forces were attacking from the western side of the mountain. Rushing to defend that position left the eastern side open for Union forces to advance up the mountain. By afternoon, the Union forces crushed Generals Echols, "Mudwall" and their troops.

The battle on top of the mountain hadn't even lasted a day. It marked the last significant Civil War battle in West Virginia.

General Echols ordered a retreat towards Lewisburg through the Renick Valley. George was loaded on a wagon, screaming and drifting in and out of consciousness, for the twenty-four mile march south.

Word spread quickly through Greenbrier County that the Confederates had been defeated on Droop Mountain. Farmers and their families lined the route of the retreating soldiers. There were different sentiments expressed. Some cheered as the Confederates retreated; others yelled the Rebel yell and shouted, "We'll get 'em next time boys!"

In Lewisburg women began gathering their valuables to hide in safe places; men made certain that their rifles were ready to use to protect their homes.

All expected General Echols forces to stop there and wait for the Yankees that would be following. The Battle of Lewisburg had not lasted long; the Battle of Droop Mountain less then a day. The next battle in Lewisburg everyone predicted would be long and bloody.

18

A bedraggled, blood spattered young man in Confederate grey knocked on the door of the McKinney house in Lewisburg. Moans could be heard coming from the wagon parked in the driveway.

"Ken I hep yo', sir?"

"General Echols said I was to bring George McKinney home. Is this where the McKinney's live?" the young man inquired.

"Yes sir it is. I'se go gets the McKinney's fo' yo'." With that, the butler turned and walked into the house.

Mr. McKinney came to the door followed by Sarah. He looked beyond the young man at the wagon parked in the driveway. His heart leaped. He sensed its cargo.

"Sir, General Echols said I was to bring George home and extend to you both his regrets…"

Sarah screamed, rushed past her husband, the young man and to the wagon. She stood frozen looking into the wagon bed, turned to look at her husband and fainted.

"…for the injuries he has received and that you are to know that George fought bravely for the South in the battle on Droop Mountain." Mr. McKinney or Sarah did not hear these words spoken by the young man.

As he looked into the wagon, Mr. McKinney saw George in his blood drenched uniform. His right hand, covered in dried blood, was almost brown. He lay still with eyes closed.

"OH MY GOD! Is he alive?" Mr. McKinney shouted to the driver of the wagon.

George opened his eyes, stared briefly at his father and let out a blood-curdling scream.

This roused Sarah from her faint. "George, George, what have they done to you!"

She was on her feet staring into the wagon. Mr. McKinney caught her this time when she fainted.

"Get the men and come quickly to the wagon," Mr. McKinney shouted at the butler.

He picked up Sarah and carried her up the steps. Stopping at the door, he turned to the young soldier, "Please tell General Echols we are eternally in his debt for sending our boy back to us."

Entering the foyer, he turned with Sarah still in his arms to the soldier again. "Where are my manners, son. Can we get you a tall glass of tea or something to eat?"

"No sir, General Echols has already gone ahead to Union south of here and we're to catch up with him as soon as possible."

The men had entered the foyer holding George between them.

"Where's we puts him, sir?" they asked.

"On the sofa over there." He nodded his head toward the cut velvet sofa in the drawing room that was covered with white sheets. For an instance, they looked at each other with shocked expressions. Sarah allowed the ladies coming to tea to set on the uncovered sofa. They were the only persons to do so.

"NOW!" Mr. McKinney yelled. He placed Sarah in the captain's chair and motion for one of the women who had assembled in the foyer to attend to her.

Rushing to George, he took out his pocketknife and began cutting off the right sleeve of his uniform. He almost fainted when he saw the arm with bones protruding through the skin; an arm held only at places by skin to his upper body.

General Echols and his retreating troops narrowly missed by two hours Union forces coming from the west. Union forces once again occupied Lewisburg.

News rapidly spread through Lewisburg of the condition of George. Every kitchen, living room and bar was filled with the latest word on George's condition. First there had been the news that his right arm was amputated leaving only a stub at the shoulder. Always there were the stories of him wavering between being conscious, raving like a mad man or screaming like a wild animal caught in a trap.

"Sho as I'se a standin' heah, Masser George gonna end up in dat Weston." That was the prediction the servants were making among themselves.

The Virginia Legislature had approved building the Weston Insane Asylum in 1858. It was to be built in the north central part of the West Augusta. This large cut stone building was almost completed in 1863 and ready for the first patients.

"Now if that don't beat all!" people said about the new asylum when they learned it was to be built in West Augusta. "That Virginia Legislature tells us they're gonna build schools, roads and railroads in this part of Virginia. What do they vote to build? An insane asylum!"

"Goes to show how good they are at keepin' their word."

"Guess they figure they can dump all their crazies up here in the mountains for us to take care of and get them out of their sight. If war comes, I'm joinin' the Union and gonna get them crazies out of there; send them packin' over the hills back to that flat land country!"

Emmy was like a kid in a candy shop with a hand full of pennies. Callie and Angel could feel the great excitement in her as she showed them which corner she would place a certain piece of furniture she'd found on her trip; how she planned to have the drapes fitted to the windows; told them what colors the walls would be painted. They were touring the new home being built for her and Jonathan.

"I've bought a lot of bulbs we can plant this fall. Also there are some of the plants around the Smithson house I want to take starts off or transplant here."

Callie spoke up immediately, "I will love helping you with the flowers, Aunt Emmy. I bet I can find some wild azaleas, rhododendron, maybe a pink dogwood tree that we can transplant too."

"I bet you can too, dear. And I've been meaning to tell you that this Friday we are going to Rebecca Henry's house to start planning the upcoming Christmas Grand Ball at The Old White."

"Why would I be going with you to Miss Henry's house?" Callie asked.

"Rebecca asked specifically that you come. She wants input from some of the young people in Lewisburg on the Christmas Grand Ball; wants to make it a more enjoyable event for them this year. Heavens knows the youth of this town could use a little cheering up after this year."

Afternoon tea that Wednesday had been awkward. Sarah sent her regrets that she would be unable to attend because she was too busy caring for

George. Actually, no one outside the Smithson house had seen her since the day George came home wounded.

It was almost shocking to the women to realize how much Sarah had dominated the group. She picked the topics of conversation; organized all the social events. Sarah appointed, picked, those she wanted to work with her.

Betty and Josephine tried to get the conversation started by talking about the latest news they'd heard of George's condition.

"My understanding," Betty said, "is that after the arm was amputated at the shoulder, George developed a tremendous infection."

"That's true," Josephine verified. "He became even more delirious and screamed until his throat was so raw he could no longer scream. His bed linens were constantly changed because they became soaking wet from sweat."

"Poor Sarah, she must be beside herself." Betty added.

Then there was silence.

Finally, one of the ladies inquired, "What on earth are we going to do about the baskets for the needy? the Christmas Dance?"

"We should definitely make the baskets for the poor. And everyone in this town needs something to cheer them up from all the suffering that has been happening lately," another said.

Betty spoke then. "Josephine and I have talked about being in charge of the baskets for the poor because we have helped Sarah with that before. We are hoping that one or several of you will volunteer to start working on the dance plans."

Again, there was silence for a while.

Rebecca spoke. "I will be in charge of the dance under one condition. I would like Emmy to co-chair the event with me and hope that she will accept. And I want to involve the young people in the community in the event."

The other women looked at each other in total shock. Rebecca Henry was the young wife of Mr. Henry twenty years her senior. He owned the prosperous general store. As much as the "gossip squad" had tried to learn about her background or other information about her, they had been unsuccessful. Mr. Henry had simply appeared with her on his arm at church one Sunday morning after an extended shopping trip to New York and Philadelphia and introduced her as his wife.

What they did know was that she dressed well, had impeccable manners and kept a lovely home. It was tastefully decorated; she was a gracious hostess when the ladies tea group met there. She was almost as bad as Emmy in the use of one word answers.

Emmy was taken back at Rebecca's request.

"You two would be perfect to chair the Christmas Dance," Betty and Josephine chimed in together. "Please, pretty please Emmy."

Emmy thought for a while and realized that her "real" job in Lewisburg was completed if it was true what she had heard. The Confederate forces had almost totally left the mountains. More and more people were talking to Jonathan about getting into politics and running for office. It is time I start thinking about this new career move of my husband and become more actively involved in community social events she thought. "I'd be delighted to assist you in planning the Christmas Dance, Rebecca."

It was after the tea that Rebecca had asked that she and Callie come to her home Friday afternoon.

Rebecca met them at the foot of the porch steps holding her daughter as the carriage pulled up.

"I'm so happy to see you two. I wanted you to meet my daughter, Elizabeth, before the girls put her down for her afternoon nap." Rebecca held in her arms a chubby little red haired girl who was almost two. "And you must come see what Mr. Henry has had built for her in the backyard."

With that said, she turned and led them to the back yard. There was the most beautiful white doll house with a picket fence and rose trellis over the gate, shuttered windows with lace curtains.

"I don't know who will have more fun playing in the house, Elizabeth, or me. I can hardly wait until she's old enough to start enjoying it." She turned looking in all directions.

"Did you say her name is Elizabeth?" Emmy asked.

Rebecca smiled sheepishly and handed Elizabeth to Emmy. "I named her after your mother." Turning to Callie she said, "She is your cousin, actually your third cousin. Your Uncle Jim was your mother's cousin. That made him your second cousin. Elizabeth is your cousin but three times removed as they say here."

Emmy and Callie were speechless.

"I asked the two of you to come today because I want you both to know the truth. Your brother and I were very much in love, Emmy. He would stop by the house on the pretense of ordering supplies for Mr. Henry but he actually had come to see me. We were making plans that I would leave Mr. Henry after the war and join you and your mother, Callie, on Calico Creek."

Sadness filled her eyes and she hugged Callie. "I thought my heart would break in two when I learned what had happened. I wanted to die too. But knowing that little Elizabeth was coming, helped me get through his death. I was so sorry to hear of your Mother's death, Callie."

Then she looked at them both with that same seriousness that Aunt Emmy had shown on her face when she told Callie about her role as a Union spy. "Mr. Henry will never know the truth. He believes Elizabeth is his daughter and is making certain she will be the most spoiled girl in all of the Greenbrier Valley. I wanted you two to know the truth. I wanted you to know that a part of Jim lives on."

On the ride back to their house, Emmy asked Callie why she seemed so quite. "Aren't you excited about Jim's daughter?"

"I am. But what am I going to do about going to the Christmas dance? You know I'm in love with Alex."

Emmy gave her a big hug. "Now don't you worry your pretty little head about that. Your Uncle Jonathan and I will figure out something."

It is remarkable how well Rebecca and Emmy get along," Betty said to Josephine after the next Wednesday tea group meeting.

"And the plans they are making for the dance sound wonderful. I was so afraid we won't have a dance at all this year." Josephine replied.

Sarah was losing weight. She had a single bed moved to the bottom of George's bed. All night long she listened for any movement, any sound. Day and night she stayed in the room with him getting very little sleep.

She tired to feed him broth from the kitchen with a spoon. There were times when he would angrily hit her hand throwing the broth onto her face and refusing to eat at all. Other times she was able to get him to take a few sips. What he wanted most was the warm sweet tea. Secretly she had started adding laudanum to it. It calmed him, but she was aware that to keep him calm, she needed to add more and more. Mr. McKinney would not have allowed her to give his son laudanum; even the servants could not know for fear that one of them would tell Mr. McKinney. When she saw one drop of sweat on his forehead, she immediately wiped it off. She would ring for someone to bring cool water and a washcloth. Washing his face, arms and chest with cool water seemed to calm him as well.

What she was not doing was taking care of her self. There were times when she did not eat at all and the tray of food that had been sent up for her from the kitchen was returned untouched. She wore the same clothes for days; her hair became matted. Her eyes were sunken and had a blank look in them.

"I'se tells ya da truth. Dat Miss McKinney gonna end up in dat Weston rite side her son she don't starts takin' care herself." The maid was talking to the butler. "She's looks hav' mad now."

The butler was nodding his head. "Yo's rite. Best I tells da Master he betta do somethin' pretty quick fo' day both go ta da Weston."

"Honestly, Betty and Josephine, I think the baskets you all made this year for the poor were the nicest we've ever done. And delivering them for Thanksgiving and not just Christmas was wonderful too."

"That's right." another lady spoke up at the Wednesday afternoon tea. "And I heard the baskets really put a smile on the face of those who received them."

"Thank you." Betty said. "We decided we make them a little different this year."

"We're thinking of making the Christmas dance a little different as well. We'd like to discuss a couple of ideas with you all." Rebecca spoke up. "First, we'd like to call it a Christmas Grand Ball instead of a dance. Then what do you think of the idea that at ball we honor a member of the afternoon tea group for all the work they've done for the community? They would be crowned the queen of the ball; her escort the king."

Josephine responded immediately. "That's a wonderful idea. People like Sarah who have done so much through the years should be honored. It would be the community's way of thanking them."

"I agree." A chorus of voices answered.

Rebecca continued. "Emmy and I had thought that Sarah should be the first queen of the ball. After all, it was Sarah, I believe, who first started the idea of the Christmas dance and the Christmas food baskets."

"That's right." Betty informed the group. "But do you think she would come? No one has seen her leave the house since George came home. And from what I hear, she doesn't even leave his room."

Emmy spoke up this time. "We thought perhaps Mr. Henson could talk with Mr. McKinney about what we would like to do. Perhaps Mr. McKinney could persuade Sarah to come."

"That's a great idea." The voices in the room answered.

"This is really good news, Jonathan," George McKinney told him later that week.

He continued. "Please don't let this information leave this room but I am becoming quite concerned about Sarah. The butler has told me that she is not taking care of herself as she should. She is not eating or sleeping; spends every hour of the day watching George and taking care of him. I had planned to put my foot down with her soon, get her out of his room. This gives me a reason to do so. She must be presentable for the ball."

He was talking to Sarah that afternoon about moving out of George's room. She immediately burst into tears.

"But George needs me! There are things that only a mother can do for her son." She wailed.

"That may be true, dear. But unless you take care of yourself as well, George may not have a mother at all. Look in the mirror." He had raised her to her feet and turned her toward the full-length mirror in the room.

At first, Sarah closed her eyes and turned her head to her shoulder. Mr. McKinney continued to hold her facing the mirror until she finally looked into it.

Sarah was shocked at what she saw. She had always taken such pride in her appearance but the woman she saw staring back at her was someone she did not even recognize. Turning into her husband's shoulder, she started sobbing uncontrollably.

Mr. McKinney held her in his arms and stroked her hair. "There there, dear, everything will be alright."

George spoke up from his bed. He had been listening to the entire conversation. "Mama bring me tea."

They both looked at George in surprise.

"Of course, son. Your mother will bring you tea whenever you want it." His father responded.

And so it was settled. Mr. McKinney took control of George's care except for the tea. He instructed the man who would be in George's room that he was to get him up first thing each morning, sit him in a chair until he became too tired. Gradually he was to stand him up and have him take a few steps until George could eventually walk around the room by himself.

Secretly George was pleased that his father was taking charge. Now that the tea seemed to ease his pain, he was beginning to think more clearly. The wound where his arm had been amputated was healing nicely. When he had even tried to sit up in bed, his mother would rush to him and stop him. She was over protective of him for fear he would injure the remaining stub of his arm. What he had needed all along was someone to allow him to try to gain back his strength so that he could carry out a plan that was beginning to formulate in his head, and he needed the tea. George had watched his mother put laudanum in it. He had watched the same being put in the drinks of the wounded men on the battlefield. Someone had explained to him exactly what it was. They gave it to him when he was injured on Droop Mountain.

At the next afternoon tea, Emmy informed the group of her husband's conversation with Sarah's husband. Then she explained that later in the week, he had persuaded Sarah to attend the Christmas Ball.

"Then it's decided." Rebecca said. "All of you who agree Sarah should be the first queen of the ball say yes."

She didn't have to ask for no votes.

On the 8th day of December, General Averill left New Creek to once again destroy the East Tennessee and Virginia Railroad. This time he was successful.

He moved his troops in the direction of Salem through mountain passes believed to be impassable. Surprising the Confederate forces by taking this route, he was able to destroy some of the railroad tracks and small bridges. Also he burned Confederate commissary stores. Movement of men and supplies by the Rebels on the East Tennessee and Virginia Railroad was stopped.

Both sides of the war retreated to their winter camps and started making plans for the battles to come in 1864.

"And we discussed with the young people about performing a special Virginia reel for the queen and king at the Christmas Grand Ball." Rebecca told the group. "They are excited and practicing now."

"Also Mr. McKinney said that he has told her there will be some surprises. He thinks all this is all helping her get back on her feet again."

"Wonderful" the women exclaimed.

Callie's partner, when the young people practiced the Virginia reel, was Tommy Baxter, the son of Jonathan's law clerk. That's what the town thought he was. In reality, not only did Callie and Emmy have a secret, but also Mr. Baxter and Tommy had a secret. They were Union soldiers.

Mr. Baxter had been a lawyer before the war started. There were times when he had to catch himself from answering legal questions. Supposedly, his wife had died and he was raising Tommy, their only child.

His "son" Tommy had been a college student who just happened to have a young face and body. He easily passed as Mr. Baxter's seventeen-year son.

All the girls thought he was cute but he was standoffish. Try as they might flirting with him, he just didn't seem interested in any girl. It was quite a surprise when Callie announced that he was going to be her escort to the Christmas Grand Ball this year.

Not only was Sarah getting back on her feet again, but George was also. Samuel, the man who been selected to take care of him, was as hard a task master as Mr. McKinney had hoped and instructed him to be. George realized early on that he would not be able to manipulate Samuel as he had his mother.

"I'se not ringin' fo' yo' tea 'tils yo' clean ever scrap ov food ofen dat plate. Yo' needs mo' meat on dem skinny bones ov yo's. Tea don't put no meat on dem bones." Samuel suspected that Sarah was lacing George's tea with laudanum because of the calming effect it had on him. It made his job a lot easier with the young Master so he ignored his suspicions. "An' yo'se gonna be up sittin' in da chair when Miss McKinney brings it."

One evening after dinner, Sarah and Mr. McKinney had come up to George's room to tell him good night. Sarah was sitting in one chair on one side of his bed; Mr. McKinney in another on the other side.

"George, I am so pleased with how much you have improved recently. Samuel seems to be taking very good care of you," Mr. Mc Kinney said. "And don't you think your Mother is also looking much better now that she is getting more rest and eating better?"

He didn't give George time to answer the question. "And I have a wonderful surprise for you Sarah, actually two surprises. The dress maker is coming this Saturday to show you swatches of fabric, take your measurements and work with you to design a special ball gown to wear to the Christmas Grand Ball this year."

"The what?" Sarah asked.

"Well that is my second surprise, dear. The women have reorganized the Christmas dance to make it more fun for the young people and they've decided to change the name of it. They all insist you must come."

"But I can't leave, George" she protested.

"Indeed you can, my dear. Samuel spends every night with him now and there's absolutely no reason he can't spend the night of the ball with him. I will not take no for an answer."

George spoke up then. "You must go mother. How am I going to know who all the boys escorted if you don't go so you can tell me?"

They both knew he was really only interested in who was escorting Callie.

"There's just one thing though, you must bring me my tea before you leave when you're all dressed and ready to go. I want to see how pretty I know you'll look.

"And another thing Mother, I don't care how late it is when you all get home you must bring me some tea and tell me all about the ball."

George's wishes were Sarah's commands. It was decided. She would attend.

The Christmas Grand Ball was a huge success. Mr. Henry had been able to order two crowns from one his suppliers with whom he dealt. One was in the shape of a tiara with sparkly stones; the other was a simple crown in a gold type metal.

On one side of the ballroom, two chairs had been lavishly decorated to resemble thrones. When Sarah and Mr. McKinney entered the ballroom, the chamber quartette immediately stopped playing; the dancers separated and made an aisle leading to the thrones. Rebecca rushed to greet them.

On either side of the throne chairs stood Emmy and Jonathan holding the tiara and crown. Rebecca whispered to Sarah that she and Mr. McKinney were to take a seat, Sarah in Emmy's chair, Mr. McKinney in Jonathan's chair.

After they were seated, she made the official announcement.

"Ladies and gentlemen, I have the pleasure of presenting to you, the first queen and king of the Christmas Grand Ball, Mr. and Mrs. McKinney." The crowns were placed on their heads.

"Sarah this is a small token of appreciation that the town of Lewisburg wishes to bestow on you for all the kind work and deeds you have done for the citizens of this town. This ball is in your honor.

She continued. "The young people of Lewisburg have prepared a special dance for you."

The young people entered the ball room, approached the throne and either curtsied or bowed; then took their positions on the dance floor. When the last couple was in place, the quartette started playing. The dance was performed with perfection.

Sarah rushed to George's bedroom with his tea wearing her crown. He could see the delight on her face as she told him of being crowned the queen of the ball; how the young folks had performed a special dance for her, how she and Mr. McKinney were served drinks and delicious finger foods of every imaginable kind the entire night.

"And Callie, Mother?" George asked.

"That was very interesting. Mr. Baxter's son, Tommy, escorted her. She only seemed to dance the first and last dance with him. She danced all the other times with someone else."

Huh, he thought. Maybe I was wrong about that "damm Yankee" up on Droop Mountain. Maybe he hasn't stolen my Callie away from me. Maybe I still have a chance with her. He was holding onto those thoughts as he drifted off to sleep that night.

19

Alex had managed to send a letter to Callie in January of 1864 from Brandy Station in Virginia. He explained the success of Union forces during battles in the central part of the Shenandoah Valley after the retreat of General Lee from the Battle of Gettysburg in the fall. The Union forces had been camped in Brandy Station since General Lee's retreat. They were expecting and planning for battles to start once again as soon as spring arrived. As always, he told her how much he wanted to hold her in his arms again.

Early in January, Sarah was shocked when George informed her that he intended to have dinner with the family in the dining room the next evening. Her immediate fear was how he would safely navigate the stairs from the second floor with only one arm.

"Before you start worrying, Mother, Sammy and I have been practicing on the first few steps of the stair well. I have learned to balance myself using Sammy as my missing arm."

"But…"

"Now Sarah," Mr. McKinney spoke. "We both have seen the remarkable recovery George has made in recent weeks. Sammy has certainly seemed to understand how to encourage him to become active again. We must accept that George is a grown man, has his old fight back and knows what he can or cannot do. I'll hear no more protests from you. Sammy, please tell Martha to set a place at the table for George at dinner tomorrow and to set one for you in the kitchen."

Sammy had made extra effort in helping George dress for his first meal in the dining room. George had selected the clothes he wished to wear but it was Sammy who carefully tucked the extra material of the shirt in back to fit into slacks that had been gathered in back to eliminate as much as possible the "baggy" look of the outfit in front. He had practiced how to tuck the extra fabric on the missing arm sleeve to form around the now healed stub. With George's hair carefully brushed, shoes shined to a high polish, Sammy and George descended the stairs. Mr. McKinney had insisted that he and Sarah be sitting at the table when George entered the room. Also, he had warned Sarah she was not to leave her chair to assist George in any manner. George was to accomplish this feat by himself with the assistance of Sammy.

"It is certainly a pleasure to see you dressed, son, and sitting at your place at this table. Sammy, you are to be commended on the fine job you have done for our son. Both Mrs. McKinney and I are extremely grateful to you."

With that said, Sammy was dismissed to eat in the kitchen. Sarah rang the small brass bell on the table signaling that the soup was to be brought from the kitchen and served.

Mr. McKinney had moved Sarah's chair closer to his this evening. Each time she started to rise to help George in any way, he reached over; patted her knee and slightly shook his head "No."

George actually did not have too much trouble eating the various courses served. He and Sammy and been practicing on exactly how to use the various silverware that would be on the table. The kitchen servants were told to be certain, when preparing George's plate that the portions of meats or larger vegetables were cut into bite size portions.

Gradually Sarah relaxed and stopped watching every movement George made.

"I am going to contact my tailor in Richmond next week, George; have him come to take new measurements for your clothes. You have lost a lot of weight through this ordeal. We need to get you some clothes made that now fit your more lean muscular body."

"Oh yes dear, and we need to have the cobbler make you some new shoes to match your new clothes." Sarah could not resist the urge to leave her chair to hug him.

"Would you like some of your tea, dear, with dessert?"

"Actually Mother, I have not been drinking tea lately. I think I would like a cup of coffee. I think I've now proven that I'm grown up enough to enjoy it and a cigar with Father after dinner in the library."

SOMETHING TO LIVE FOR

The meeting of the Wednesday afternoon tea group was canceled in January due to heavy snowfall. However, in sending her regrets that she would be unable to attend when invited, Sarah had made a special request. She had sent the request to all who attended the gathering. To their delight, she had asked that the she be allowed to be the hostess for the February meeting. It meant that Sarah had finally come out of her deep depression and concern for George, was once again going to be involved in the community.

In February, Sarah stood proudly next to her son, George, as they greeted each woman upon arrival. He was neatly dressed in the new clothes that fit his now lean body minus the "belly that shook like a bowl full of jelly." The tailor had skillfully disguised the stump of the missing arm by gradually tapering the sleeve to fit into the belt as though a hand were holding it in place.

The women were ushered into the dining room where the table was festively decorated in red and white; an array of cookies and candies were stacked high on plates. Each lady was asked to select a plate of the cookies and candies that caught their eye, a very difficult choice with the variety before them. George or a servant then escorted each to the drawing room where they were served tea.

"I want to thank all of you for selecting Mr. Mc Kinney and me as the first queen and king of the Christmas Grand Ball. Neither of us can remember a time when we have enjoyed ourselves more. The honor you bestowed on us will be cherished forever. I truly believe that what you did and our son George's remarkable recovery from his war injury, has given me the strength to recover from the shock of it." Sarah was speaking to the group with great sincerity.

She continued, "Rebecca and Emmy, you are to be commended on the excellent planning of the dance and particularly for the involvement of the young people in the proceedings. When I told George of their special dance, I think it encouraged him also in his recovery; gave him a reason to want to be well enough to join in such activities of the young people again."

Rebecca spoke, "On behalf of the entire group, Sarah, there is no one else in Lewisburg who has done so much for this community to be chosen as our first queen. Thank you for attending."

President Abraham Lincoln appointed Ulysses S. Grant General-in-Chief of all Union forces in March of 1864. Ironically, Ulysses was not the name given to him at birth. His name was Hiram Ulysses Grant. When he was appointed to West Point, the Congressman making the appointment thought his first name was Ulysses because he had always been called by the nickname, "Lyss." The "S" was added for his mother maiden name, a custom of the time.

General Grant had come to the attention of President Lincoln at the Battles of Shiloh and Vicksburg. His defeat of the Confederates at Vicksburg had cut the Confederacy in two with the troops in the west no longer able to contribute to the south's efforts. It became Grant's plan to end the Civil War depriving the Confederate troops in Virginia and the south of reinforcement and additional troops from other areas such as the west to replace heavy casualty losses. The plan also included curtailing the availability of supplies for Confederate troops by blockade-runners in Northern Virginia and the south. It was a three-prong plan. He ordered General William T. Sherman to drive through the south, torch buildings, destroy or confiscate supplies that could be used by the South to trade for supplies with sources in other countries. The second prong had General Grant, with the Army of the Potomac, weakening the strength of and pinning down General Lee's Army of Northern Virginia. Finally, the Confederate Capitol in Richmond, Virginia would be captured.

It was into the Army of the Potomac that units from the newly created state of West Virginia were merged. A private with the 1st West Virginia Cavalry received the Medal of Honor for being one of only two men who were able to get through Confederate lines with dispatches for General Grant in the winters of 1864 and 1865.

The first robin seen in Lewisburg was a very welcomed sight. It signaled that spring was not far behind. Winter had been a bad one with ice storms in December and heavy snows in January. Emma had managed to oversee the completion of her new home west of Lewisburg however. By March, the carpenters and painters were putting the finishing touches on the walls and in the house. Angel had made the drapes for the windows. Callie was busy drawing sketches of just how new plants should be placed in the gardens surrounding the house with the bulbs planted in the fall. Already the bulbs were beginning to break the ground with their lime green shoots.

Word came that the furniture Emmy had ordered overseas would arrive in April. The women began to pack the items from the Smithson house that were

SOMETHING TO LIVE FOR

to go to the new house. There was much excitement as spring approached. Callie wrote long letters to Alex telling him of all the plans they were making. Occasionally a new recruit would be traveling through Lewisburg on his way to the Shenandoah Valley. He had been instructed to stop by the Smithson house to receive letters going to Alex. As for Jonathan, he was more than happy to leave all the plans for the move into the new house, the packing, and all decisions to Emmy, Callie and Angel. He was busy concentrating on the politics of the new state of West Virginia and had become one of the leaders among the men of Lewisburg and in the Greenbrier Valley.

George was also eagerly awaiting the arrival of spring. He had conquered the maneuvering of the stairs without the assistance of Sammy. When the weather permitted, he would take walks downtown to his father's store and spend time learning the business. Mr. Mc Kinney was very pleased with George's quick understanding of business matters. To a one, the customers would remark on how well George was looking, how his missing limb was barely noticeable and praising him on his remarkable recovery. George was gaining more confidence each day and enjoyed being away from his Mother.

On Sunday's he had started attending services at the Old Stone Church with his Mother and Father. To his amazement, it seems as though the young women of Lewisburg were even more attentive that they had previously seemed to be. George only had eyes for the arrival and departure of Callie. He took great pains to avoid letting others realize his object of affection. When Callie and he spoke, it was in a very casual and polite manner.

In hindsight, May was the turning point of the Civil War between the Union Forces led by Gen. Ulysses S. Grant and the Army of the Potomac; General Robert E. Lee, commander of the Confederate Army of Northern Virginia. Two weeks of battles fought in Spotsylvania County and Orange County in central Virginia inflicted large losses on both sides of men killed, wounded, captured or missing.

The Battle of the Wilderness was fought May 5th-7th. The Union army had crossed the Rapidan River at three separate locations to prepare for an attack on the Wilderness Tavern. This would allow the Union forces to avoid fighting in the Wilderness where they had been defeated the year before. It was a mass of tangled briers, fallen trees and thick woods curtailing the use of the Union's artillery.

General Lee's forces were out numbered almost two Union soldiers to one Confederate. Fighting in the Wilderness gave the Confederate forces more of an advantage against overwhelming odds. Although there was no clear winner in the battle, Lee's army suffered heavy casualties which he could not replenish.

On May 5, the Confederate soldiers engaged Union forces. The day ended with a standoff and neither side victorious. General Lee was anxiously awaiting the arrival of Lt. Gen. James Longstreet and two divisions from the west. Union forces were exhausted from by fighting in the morning when General Longstreet arrived at noon. Ironically, one of his own men shot Gen. Longstreet in the fighting. He was badly wounded. The shooting happened only four miles from where General Stonewall Jackson had died from friendly fire a year earlier.

That night a fire broke out in the thick underbrush. Hundreds of soldiers on both sides left the battlefield of burn wounds or died in the fire. General Grant had told President Lincoln, "Whatever happens, there will be no turning back."

General Lee won the battle when tactical maneuvers are considered. However, although both sides suffered heavy casualties, Grant's loss was a smaller percentage of loss than General Lee who had very little opportunity to replace his fallen troops. General Grant's strategy was gradually reducing the number of Confederate soldiers and in so doing wear down their morale as well. Instead of retreating north and to safety as one would expect, Grant marched around Lee's forces in the night placing the Union forces closer to Richmond.

It was an exciting time for all in the Smithson house. The furniture from Europe arrived and was uncrated in the new house. The warming rays of the sun had thawed the frozen ground. Flowerbeds surrounding the new house had been planted with an abundance of flowers and shrubs. Pink dogwood trees, mountain laurel, red bud bushes, other trees had been transplanted from the surrounding area woods. All of the items were almost packed that would be moved from the Smithson House.

"It is so good to see George attending church services and attending activities of the young people again, Sarah," Betty said at the meeting of the Wednesday tea group.

"He certainly has become a handsome young man who is amazing with all he has been through," another added.

"Mr. McKinney and I are so proud of him. He has been joining Mr. McKinney at the business and has a very quick mind for business my husband tells me."

"I've also noticed that the young women are paying a lot of attention to him too." another added.

One of the bloodiest battles of the war occurred at Spotsylvania Court House May 8th-21st. After the Battle in the Wilderness, a race was on to capture the strategic area around Spotsylvania. General Lee won. On the 10th, Grant tried to penetrate the Confederate defenses and although the line was broken at one point, the Union was driven back. General Grant began planning advances using the same strategy that allowed union forces to penetrate the Confederate lines the previous day. General Lee thought that General Grant's inactivity that day meant he was planning a retreat. He pulled the Confederate artillery from critical places in the line. It was a big mistake. Early in the morning the next day, Grant attacked the weaken spot and was victorious. He was also victorious because it had rained during the night. Many Confederate guns would not fire because their gunpowder had become wet during the night.

General Lee was so concerned with the situation that he announced he would personally lead 800 men in a charge against the enemy. The men refused to move fearing for his safety. Shouts of "Lee to the rear" forced him to abandon his plan to lead the charge.

Grant had vowed to "fight it out on this line if it takes all summer." By May 19th, he realized Lee's men could not be defeated on the line. Both armies left the area May 20th-21st to move closer to Richmond. The Confederate forces had suffered irrecoverable losses, more importantly, heavy losses among its best officers and veteran units. It would not regain its initiative after those two weeks in May.

One of those hot summers filled the Greenbrier Valley. Weathering the heat, sudden rain and booming thunderstorms, Aunt Emmy moved into her new home in spite of the weather. In September, people in Lewisburg and the surrounding area received the following invitation:

> *Mr. and Mrs. Jonathan Henson*
> *and*
> *their niece, Callie Morris*
> *request your presence*
> *at an open house at their new home in*
> *Richlands, west of Lewisburg,*
> *September 4th, 1:00 PM—5:00 PM*
> *PLEASE no gifts. Please contribution to*
> *the Thanksgiving and Christmas basket fund*
> *in lieu of a gift.*

Rebecca spoke first at the Wednesday tea group. "Emmy it was wonderful of you and Mr. Henson to suggest the contribution to the baskets in lieu of a present. I declare if we continue with the success of those contributions and the money raised by the Christmas Grand Ball, we will be able to deliver Easter baskets as well."

"How are the plans coming for the Grand Ball?" one was asked.

"Extremely well. The young people's dance rehearsals have been well attended. This year we are going to have the voting for king and queen by ballot. At our September meeting, you will be asked to nominate three women. At our October meeting, you will be given a ballot with the names of those nominated. Bring the ballots to the November meeting after you have voted. I am hoping our first queen, Sarah, will assist me in the counting."

Sarah had stopped dominating the meetings after George's injury and recuperation. She had realized that others in the community were perfectly capable of organizing and planning events. Today she had been particularly quite.

She had felt Georg's pain once again, when he told her that Callie had refused to be his partner at the dance and to attend it with him. She had said that Mr. Baxter's son had asked her earlier and she had accepted. George then invited Janie, Callie's best friend.

"I'll be delighted to assist you Rebecca." she responded.

In November, there was great happiness at the new home in Richlands. Jonathan was elected to the state legislature. Alex was able to visit Callie.

20

The final blow for the Confederate forces being able to receive supplies from blockade-runners from outside the country happened in North Carolina January 1865. Fort Fisher guarded the entrance to the port at Wilmington, NC. On the 8th Union land forces arrived near the fort. An armada of Union ships arrived on the 12th. On the 13th, the guns of the ships covered the landing of 6000 Union troops. By the 15th, the Confederate garrison surrendered. That surrender allowed the Union land forces to join General Sherman moving north from Georgia through South Carolina. Wilmington was left unprotected except for small Confederate forces stations in or near the city. Other Union forces started the attack on Wilmington. Realizing the city could no longer be defended, Wilmington was abandoned by Confederate troops on the 22nd. The port had been the last major one located in Confederate states on the Atlantic Ocean providing supplies.

Emmy and Jonathan had found a home to rent in Wheeling while he was serving in the legislature. That group wasted no time in passing legislation that alienated Confederate sympathizers in the state. On February 3rd, the governor signed an act abolishing slavery and providing for the emancipation of all slaves.

Callie, Angel and Jefferson, with the help of Big Man when needed, kept Emmy's home open in Richlands. The new law did not affect Angel, Jefferson or Big Man. Their "owners" had emancipated them years before the law was passed by the legislature.

The law created havoc in some homes in Lewisburg. The owners of these homes would awaken one morning to find that every slave they owned had disappeared in the dark of night. Panic came into their lives. Many of the wives had no idea how to cope with household chores; no idea how to prepare a simple meal.

"Po" white trash teenage daughters and sons filled the gap of missing slaves. They were employees given room and board and a stipend for their work. The money help supplement the meager earnings of their large families working small farms in the Greenbrier Valley. Quickly their employers learned that these employees could not be treated as some had treated their slaves. They became civil in their attitudes and more willing to help with some of the chores.

An opportunity to end the war happened in February. If the Union would recognize the South's independence, Confederate President Jefferson sent word to President Lincoln he would send a delegation to Washington to meet with President Lincoln and Secretary of State William Seward. President Lincoln refused to agree to recognize the South's independence and the meeting never occurred.

General Sherman's troops arrived in the Shenandoah Valley in late February. Moving towards Petersburg, he encountered Lieutenant General Jubal Early's troops in the valley near Waynesboro. General Early's troops surrendered leaving the Shenandoah Valley in the hands of Union Forces. General Sherman continued across the Blue Ridge to Charlottesville and destroyed the James River Canal locks. On March 26th, he arrived in Petersburg. The City of Petersburg surrendered on March 3rd.

March 4th President Abraham Lincoln was sworn in for his second term. He promised, "malice toward none and charity for all."

After escorting Janie to the Christmas Grand Ball at The Greenbrier, George became more certain that the dammed Yankee had not stolen his Callie. She danced with all the young men at the ball, including George. His dance lessons had certainly been worth the effort and his more lean muscular body minus the bowl of jelly helped. Even with only one arm, he was one of the better dancers at the Ball. Janie was thrilled that George had invited her. He had insisted that she place his name not only on the first and last spaces but on two others as well.

Janie asked Callie after the dance, "Do you remember when I asked you a long time ago if you knew what love was? The way I was beginning to feel about George at that time, I was sure I was falling in love with him. I am definitely sure now." She was beaming with happiness.

George attended every function of the young people, paid special attention to Janie and watched out of the corner of his eye for Callie's reactions.

Alex sent Callie a message that he had left the area of Petersburg, VA. He was optimist the war would be over soon. Confederate soldiers had started deserting; some were even surrendering to Union forces in order to get something to eat. Morale among the Rebel forces was low.

The first public school opened in Charleston, West Virginia. The legislation creating public schools stipulated that if there were thirty Negros in an area wishing to attend school, a school would be built for them as well as white children schools.

After the surrender of Petersburg, the Confederacy's President Davis and his entire Cabinet fled Richmond on the last available railroad and headed south. General Lee started pulling his troops out of the area on April 2nd. Confederate troops set fire to bridges and other buildings in their retreat. Fires burned uncontrolled and were about to engulf the entire city. The Mayor with other citizens went to the Union forces; surrendered the City of Richmond. Union forces eventually extinguished all the fires.

George spoke to his mother and father at dinner one night about a new plan to win Callie as his wife. He had become a partner in his fathers business; had financial resources to implement the plan. Aunt Emmy had placed the Smithson house on the market after moving to Richlands. Callie had always loved it. With his parents support, he would buy the house and have a place to move a bride. The Mc Kinney's were pleased that George was thinking about his future and making plans to marry, although he did not indicate to whom, to stay in Lewisburg and raise a family. They eagerly agreed to help him with the purchase of the Smithson house. Sarah knew his intended bride was Callie.

The end for General Lee's forces came quickly after he abandoned the Richmond area. General Grant realized that the Confederate troops were in big trouble. He sent word to General Lee that it might be time to consider the surrender of the Army of Northern Virginia. General Lee responded that he was not willing to surrender at the time but would be interested in discussing the terms of surrender; how the Confederacy would be affected.

General Lee's supplies had been destroyed at Appomattox. He decided to move west to Lynchburg for supplies. He received word from one of his officers on the route to Lynchburg that the officer's men were worn out from fighting the Union forces; unless he received additional support they could no longer fight. Hearing this, General Lee is quoted as having said, "Then there is nothing left for me to do but to go and see General Grant and I would rather die a thousand deaths."

General Grant received General's Lee's note requesting a meeting on April 9th. Responding, General Grant asked General Lee to pick a time and place. After one of Lee's men looked for suitable places for the meeting, it was decided that it would be at a brick farmhouse built in 1848 owned by Wilmer McLean.

General Grant's terms for surrender were that he would receive a roll listing all officers and men. Each Confederate officer would give their soldiers a pledge and have them swear to never take up arms against the Government of the United States again. Those officers would sign the same pledge notice, which would include the statement that each man under his command had sworn to the pledge. All guns, artillery and public property of the Army of Northern Virginia was to be turned over to Union forces. However, officers could keep their side arms, luggage and horses. All Confederate forces would be allowed to return home. As long as they kept their pledge to not bare arms again against the United States, obeyed the laws where they lived, they would not be bothered by any United States authority. The men in the rank and file could take home also their personal horses or mules.

April 12th the surrender document was signed. As the Confederate soldiers filed between two lines of Union Forces to give up their arms after the signing, the Union forces saluted them. Realizing the respect they were being given, the Confederate forces pointed their guns to the ground. General Grant had said earlier that the Confederates were now fellow citizens. The Union army would not celebrate their defeat.

April 14th President Abraham Lincoln was assassinated.

April 18th, the last Confederate unit surrendered in North Carolina. The Civil War had ended.

By June, all West Virginia forces had been mustered out of their units. In total, an almost equal number of West Virginias had served either with the Union forces or with Confederate forces, 22,000-25,000 men. In order to keep control of the new West Virginia government, the legislature passed a law that Confederate soldiers living in the state were not allowed to vote.

Callie saw a rider coming up the lane towards the house. His horse broke into a trot as he neared the house and saw her standing on the porch. Dismounting, he ran towards Callie as she ran into his arm. She didn't care that he was completely covered in dust, looked like he hadn't slept in days, it was Alex and he had returned to her as he had said he would after the war. He looked into her eyes and said, "I'm home to hold you to your promise that you will marry me, Callie. I love you with all my heart and want to spend the rest of my life with you."

Callie laughed and asked, "What took you so long to get here? Of course I'll marry you."

The next week they made plans for their future for their future together. Callie told Alex that she wanted to be married at the spot at Calico Creek where she, Mama, Mammy and Uncle Jim held church services. She wanted Aunt Emmy to be her matron of honor and Angel a bridesmaid. Instead of the usual white dress, she wanted to wear the dress she wore to her 16th birthday party at The Greenbrier where she first danced with him.

He told her how he had been making plans for the Calico Creek General Store. Knowing that he was going to need help, he had thought he'd ask Big Man, Jefferson and a couple of the other Union soldiers that worked for Aunt Emmy when she first moved to Lewisburg if they would be willing to move there and work for wages. There was enough space on the property that they could build cabins. Callie was thrilled that she would once again live on Calico Creek with the great love of her life, Alex.

All the men agreed to move to Calico Creek. When Callie asked Angel if she would also move, Angel was delighted. "I'se not knows how's ta liv' wiff outs mys Callie."

The men left for Calico Creek to check the property, determine what needed to be done, clear land for cabins and allow Alex to visit his family to tell them the good news. It was decided that the wedding would take place in the early fall; Callie and Angel would join them there.

On a bright fall day with robin egg blue skies, Miss Callie Morris became Mrs. Alex Garrison. Violets were out of season so Angel had put purple ironweed in her hair. She carried the purple purse that Angel had made her that still held the precious rock Alex had given her for her 16th birthday.

When the Wednesday afternoon tea group made plans for the Christmas Grand Ball, Emmy informed the group that Callie would be returning from Calico Creek to spend the winter and attend the Ball.

When Sarah told George that Callie would be coming to the ball, his heart started pounding.

"Mother, I must immediately send word to Callie to ask her if I can escort her to the Ball."

Callie's reply to his message once again was that she had promised to attend the ball with another. George again asked to escort Janie.

Callie and Alex entered the Ball with Aunt Emmy and Uncle Jonathan. Emmy immediately took the couple to introduce them to everyone as Mr. and Mrs. Alex Garrison. George felt this blood pressure reach stroke level when he recognized Alex, the Union soldier who had shot him on Droop Mountain. That night George asked Janie to marry him.

21

On Valentine's Day, George and Janie were wed at the Old Stone Presbyterian Church. It was a lavish wedding with all of the elite families of the Greenbrier Valley in attendance. Emmy and Jonathan had sent their regrets from Wheeling that they would be unable to attend. The West Virginia Legislature was in session and important votes were occurring which Jonathan could not miss. Callie had declined to be Janie's matron of honor. Weather was so unpredictable at that time of year for travel on the Kanawha-Staunton Turnpike, Callie did not want to commit and then be unable to attend because she could not get to Lewisburg. Snow did make it impossible for her to attend.

The Mc Kinney's gave George and Janie on a week, all expenses paid honeymoon to The Homestead in Virginia. After that week, they sent them for another week to Richmond with a blank check to buy furniture for the Smithson house George had bought before they were married.

The West Virginia State constitution denied citizenship and the right to vote to all persons who had supported the Confederacy. May 24, 1866 the voters of West Virginia ratified this decision.

"Poor George, after he fought so hard for the Confederacy and lost his arm, he will receive no pension for his efforts." Sarah told the afternoon tea group.

"I knew the Federal government is going to give pensions to Union veterans. But I thought Virginia was giving pensions to the gallant men who fought for the south." Betty stated.

"Oh no," Josephine answered. "Virginia is only giving pension to the Confederate veterans who are residents of Virginia."

"When you think about it, we're people without a state or a country because we supported the efforts of the Confederacy. It's just not right." another lady replied.

"I just don't know what this world is coming to since our brave boys were defeated by those damm Yankees," lamented another.

Clearing more land to build cabins and the general store was hard labor involving long hours. Callie and Angel made certain the men were well fed, tended the garden, put up winter supplies. The first couple of years Jefferson and Big Man slept in a tent. Angel had her own tent. When the weather turned severe, everyone slept in the little cabin that had been Callie's home as a child.

Building the Calico Creek General Store was the first priority. Callie and Angel gathered the sand from the creek bed, mixed in lime and clay to make the chinking used between the logs. Slowly the walls of the store were raised, rafters tied into the walls and the foundation for the shingles attached. Once it was under roof, on rainy or snowy nights, Jefferson and Big Man would sleep on the dirt floor inside.

Callie noticed that Jefferson and Angel seemed to work well together on various tasks as they had at the Smithson house and in Richlands.

One day while preparing lunch, she said to Angel, "I think Jefferson is in love."

"Callie, whys yo says thin' likes dat?"

"Haven't you noticed the way he always wants you to help him? How he watches you while you work? Seems to manage to sit beside you when we eat?"

"Table ain'ts big nuff fo him sits no wher's else."

"That's not it Angel, he makes sure he gets a seat next to you."

"Go on Callie! You'se seein' things ain't there." Secretly, Angel was hoping Callie was right.

What she remembered was him telling her after her first meeting with Big Man and she was crying because she was happy was that he was "never gonna understand women." As handsome, well mannered and polite as he was with a good sense of humor, she always thought he wasn't interested in women.

Janie was an excellent hostess. She had decorated the house beautifully, entertained the Wednesday afternoon tea group, joined in all the activities the wife of a prominent businessman ought to join. Mr. Mc Kinney was placing more and more responsibility on George anticipating the day when he would give the business to George.

George involved himself in work, learning to ride a horse, target shooting, joining other men after work at the local taverns, anything he could do to avoid being alone with Janie in the house. He always came up with some excuse as to why he couldn't join her for an afternoon trip to Pence Springs; visit her family. He dutifully took her to family dinners at his folk's home when invited; escorted her on his arm to church every Sunday. To the outside world, they appeared to be the happy, perfect couple. Behind closed doors was a different story. She saw less and less of him after Mr. McKinney gave him the store.

Beginning in Reconstruction, Virginia and West Virginia started arguing about the pre-war debt West Virginia owed for infrastructure, such as roads, railroads built by Virginia. West Virginia's Constitution provided for assumption of part of the debt. In 1871, Virginia decided it would assume two-thirds of the debt; West Virginia should pay the other third. It would take a Supreme Court ruling on the exact amount to settle the matter. West Virginia eventually paid the amount in full.

Time has a way of healing even political wounds. Is it time or is it that people gradually get on with their lives and the wounds are not as hurtful as when first experienced as time passes? In addition, there was an influx of new people into the mountain state. They did not carry with them the "baggage" of the bitterness of the years of political anger when the state was a territory of Virginia known as West Augusta. By 1870, the state's population had grown to almost 450,000. The political winds shifted. A new state constitution restored voting rights to all male citizens regardless of race and citizenship to all residents. This new constitution was ratified in 1872.

Alex had been correct in predicting that as settlers moved west and into West Virginia, they would need supplies from the Calico Creek General Store. The business had flourished. He built a two story white frame home for Callie and their five children.

Callie had also been right. The love bug had bitten Jefferson and Angel. They were married at the same spot Alex and Callie had been married. Callie was the matron of honor; Big Man was best man. As a wedding present, Callie gave them her childhood cabin. Their son Adam was born in the cabin.

Business was booming in West Virginia. Even more coalmines were opening and hiring more and more men. A timber industry was developing. Families were moving into the mountains seeking the same good life for their families that the early settlers had sought for theirs. A man could provide a good life for his family with hard work; even own his own land. There were still fish to be caught in the streams, animals to hunt in the woods for meat; the soil and climate was perfect for raising the vegetables to feed a family; fruit trees and berries grew profusely in the mountains. The color of ones skin did not matter. What mattered as men worked side by side was if they could "pull their own weight." It was a subsistence life style with the money needed to buy items necessary from the general store earned in the mines, lumber industry, even a beginning oil and gas industry. By 1880, only 10 years, the population had increased by over 175,000.

Some traditions never died in Lewisburg; just changed. The Wednesday afternoon tea group still met. Maybe the new constitution granting citizenship to sympathizers of the Confederacy, or maybe it was the younger women of the town assuming the responsibility of the charitable acts by the group that changed it. Political issues no longer were the hot topics at the meeting. Planning for charity events, raising children, talking about grandchildren were now the topics of conversation.

Unfortunately, Sarah could never join into the conversations about grandchildren.

22

George left Lewisburg early in the morning as the sun was breaking over the mountains in the east. He headed west along the Kanawha—Staunton Turnpike on a mission that he had planned for a long time. Sitting erect, teeth clinched, he kept his eyes focused straight ahead on the road ahead occasionally prodding his horse with spurs to move faster.

Janie awoke to an empty bed. She assumed George had gone to work at the store and busied her self with housework. When he did not come home for lunch, she assumed he had decided to have lunch with a customer.

Alex was working in the Calico Creek General Store restocking shelves with merchandise. Outside he heard his teenage sons, Alex Jr., Jim and Jonathan playing soldier; marching with sticks on their shoulders. The girls, Caroline and Emmy were playing hopscotch in the dirt road leading to the store. Pausing to watch his children play, he went to the front porch, sat in a ladder back chair. Big Man was working on his cabin nearby. He heard a horse neigh and looked in the direction of the sound coming from the direction of the road near the woods edge. There he saw a single rider outlined against the trees. Alex heard the neighing too. He got up and went back into the store to be ready to assist the customer that would be arriving. The rider dismounted his horse, tied it to the hitching rail and climbed the steps to the porch.

Janie became concerned when George did not arrive for dinner. She fixed a plate of the food she was serving for dinner and asked the driver of the family carriage to take her to the McKinney store in Lewisburg. If George planned to work late, he would have something to eat. The store was completely closed. She was driven to the McKinney home.

"Mother McKinney, is George here?"

"Why no dear, I have not seen him all day. Wait a minute and I'll talk to Mr. McKinney about it."

Sarah and Mr. McKinney returned to the drawing room. Her face was ashen.

Mr. McKinney said, "Yesterday before George left the store he told me he won't be in today; that there was something he needed to take care of today. I assumed he meant something around the house."

After a discussion of where George could possibly be, Janie decided that she was going home in case George had return. She told the McKinney that she would send someone to tell them when he arrived and asked them to send someone to tell her if he came to their house.

The shot that Big Man heard sent him running into the store. There he saw George standing over Alex reloading his pistol. Hearing Big Man enter the store, George turned and pointed the gun at him. Big Man lunged at George and grabbed his arm. The pistol discharged; the bullet lodged into Big Man's chest. He reached for the only object near him, an ax in a wooden barrel of axes, raised it high into the air. With all of his remaining strength and his last breath, he sent the ax crashing into George's head.

Angel and Callie ran to the store on hearing the first shot. Both women screamed a blood-curding scream.

Callie felt the start to of the black velvet curtain rising up to her.

"Angel!" She cried. "I'm going to …"

"NO'S YA AIN'T CALLIE!" Angel grabbed her by the shoulders and shook her. "You ain't gonna fall out. An' dat Old Devil's spell ain't gonna gets yo dis time! Yo ta strong. Yo done beat Old Devil at her game. STOP IT! Yo hears me. STOP IT!"

Callie stood up straight and shook her head as if to clear it of the smothering curtain thought. She sounds just like I sounded when I told Mammy she had to stop carrying on when Mama died. We had things we had to do then. Angel and I have things we have to do now.

"You're right Angel. No more black velvet smothering curtains or mind games. I will not go through those again nor will I allow my children to see me trapped by either." They held each other, sobbed uncontrollably drawing strength from each other.

SOMETHING TO LIVE FOR

A messenger arrived at the McKinney house. He handed Mr. McKinney an envelope from the undertaker in Gauley Bridge. Reading the letter, he yells, "Oh dear God, this can't be true!"

Sarah came running to the entry. "What can't be true?"

Mr. McKinney led her to the drawing room by the arm, had her sit on the settee and sat beside her with his arm around her shoulder.

"Look at me Sarah. Listen carefully. Our son, George, is dead."

The hired help came running when they heard Sarah scream like a wild animal caught in a trap.

Mr. Mc Kinney motioned for them to leave the area.

Through her sobbing, she asked him how George had died, all the details. Each time he answered one of her questions, that scream filled the house.

"He had two letters with him; one for us and one for Jamie."

Sarah stopped her sobbing. "Please, we must read ours."

Opening the bloodstained envelope, Mr. McKinney read,

"Dear Mother and Father, You were wonderful parents. You gave me everything a son could want but the one thing I wanted most, Callie. You couldn't give her to me because she was not yours to give.

My life started ending the day I met Callie. Events that followed, the Civil War, her marrying Alex, only hastened the timing of my death. I have always loved her; will always love her for eternity.

Know always that I will love you both for eternity. Your son, George."

Janie read the letter George sent to her alone setting on the fainting couch in their bedroom.

"Dear Janie,

You gave me all of your love and I appreciate that you did. If I had been a whole man, I would have returned the love you gave me. You were a good wife, good homemaker. I failed in our marriage. Part of me was missing, my heart.

Please go on with you life and find the happiness you deserve.

Your husband, George"

His funeral and burial was at the Old Stone Presbyterian Church in Lewisburg.

In the little graveyard near the woods edge at Calico Creek, Alex was buried with a plot left vacant between him and Mammy. That plot was reserved for Callie. Big man was buried in the third plot on the other side of Mammy.

Next to her, Jefferson would be buried. Between Jefferson and Big Man was the vacant plot for Angel. Aunt Emmy and Uncle Jonathan rested nearby.

Coal, the "black diamond" of West Virginia and railroads, changed this part of West Virginia rapidly and forever. The Virginia Central Railroad was built prior to the Civil War. Its lines stretched from Staunton through the Shenandoah Valley and on to the Jackson River Station at the foot of the Allegheny Mountains. During the Civil War, the Virginia Railroad was one of the Confederacy's most important rail transportation systems for troops, supplies and food. General Stonewall Jackson's "foot cavalry" moved rapidly from battle to battle on it. Union forces had destroyed all of it except about five miles of track by end of the war.

The Virginia Central Railroad and the Covington and Ohio Railroad (C & O) had been built by the Commonwealth of Virginia. Prior to the Civil War, the C & O had extended its lines all the way to Charleston on the Kanawha River. After the Civil War, the Virginia Central Railroad merged with the C & O Railroad. The new railroad was named the Chesapeake and Ohio Railway. Its planned route would cover 428-mile long line from Richmond, VA to the Ohio River. In 1873 at Hawk's Nest, the final spike ceremony was held at the railroad bridge there connecting it to Huntington on the banks of the Ohio River.

Alex Jr. grew up fast as his mother had as a young girl with the death of his father. At nineteen, with a quick mind, he immediately took on the responsibility of the "man of the house," learned the family business, gave guidance and love to his younger siblings. Callie, Angel, Jefferson and Alex Jr. continued the operation of the Calico Creek General Store.

When he was twenty-two, he told his Mother and Angel, "I think it is time we move the store to Gauley Bridge. If you have noticed, with the completion of the railroad, we no longer get the number of customers who stopped here to buy supplies to head west. I also think we should rethink the inventory of goods we sell in the store."

Callie beamed with pride as she heard Alex Jr. He is his father's son, she thought, thinking through a situation and developing a plan.

"It would mean that we all too, would have to move to Gauley Bridge. I know how much you love it here at Calico Creek. Mother, I promise you both, I will make sure that you and Angel come at least once a week when the weather permits to Calico Creek, we will hold all our family reunions here, your grandchildren can come with you and you can show them all the wonders of Calico Creek."

A lump formed in her throat but she dismissed it. She reached for Angel's hand, "This will be a change for us dear friend. But you and I have been through many changes together. Change is something we can handle together."

Turning to Alex, Jr., she asked, "But how would we move the store?"

"Once a new building is completed, we will move all the store furnishing that are appropriate into the new store. We will tear down the old store; sell off the lumber to new settlers moving into the area or one of the coal companies to build coal company houses."

Callie and Angel sat on the bank of Calico Creek at Callie's favorite spot where the swiftly flowing water dashed madly against the rocks and burst into countless crystal balls on one of their trips there. Sunshine highlighted occasional streaks of fading auburn in her grey hair. Angel's hair was completely grey.

Only the fireplace stood where her childhood cabin had stood. Gradually through the years the other cabins built on the property had fallen and been burned. Grass or trees now grew where once they and the Calico Creek General Store once stood.

"I guess we're the keepers of our family's histories now, Angel." Callie said as she reached for Angel's hand.

"Dat's we's are Callie. Dat's we's are. An' we's shoo beens through bunches ov it."

"I'm so thankful to have the memories of some of the history of this country we've witnessed, sad when I think of some parts, happy about some and thankful that some of the troubles of the past have been corrected.

"Did you know they erected a statute on the state capitol grounds in Charleston of a mourning President Abraham Lincoln with head bowed embracing General Stonewall Jackson, who grew up in West Virginia, on one side and a Union soldier on the other? Looking back on it that is the way it really was in the Civil War time. It was a time of mourning for this nation; mourning for our nation torn apart between the north and the south; mourning for all the men killed; mourning for all the family lives destroyed in such a short time. It was the reason…" a lump caught in Callie's throat.

Angel squeezed Callie's hand. "Yes 'em, it shoos wuz a mourin' time. However' goods come out it ta. Eve' wuths da hurts it cause, yo's free frum da clutches of da Old Devil; yo's kid nevah gets it an' deys 'n deys kids. Old Devil ken nevah tetch no bidy 'gin."

Callie reached over and gave Angel a big hug. "You are so right. We can be thankful for a lot in our lives. Look at the way our children turned out; our grandchildren are turning out. Think how lucky we've been, Angel. I married one of the finest men who ever walked on the face of this earth. So many women have lived their entire life and never had a great love. You too, Angel, married a great man and had the same great love. Think of how this beautiful state has developed through the years. We and our children have been a part of helping with that and our grandchildren and their grandchildren will continue helping with the development of it."

"An's yo knows whut's I'se hears dat Gran'dau'ter's names fo' yo tellin' her's lit'le sistah when's dey playin' schools oth'a day? Lit'el Mis Callie she say, 'Yo jest 'members Sissy, if'in yo's gots sumthin ta live fo', yo's gonna hav' 'nuff ta lives on.'"

They both broke out laughing with happiness as tears formed in their eyes.

EPILOGUE

Four generations of my family are in the picture located on page 111. My mother, Reba, is standing on the left of the seated lady. My grandmother, Velma, is on her right. Seated is my great-grandmother, Nancy. I am the baby she is holding. She was the daughter of a Union soldier captured at Cloud's Mountain. He died in Andersonville prison.

She and her husband owned a general store on Smither's Creek, the Calico Creek of this book. Her husband called her "Darly One."

My mother, Reba, and I are standing in front of the Old Stone Presbyterian Church in Lewisburg in 1985 in the second picture, located on page 112.

Happily, I can say, Callie's grandmother, Old Devil, is not based on anyone in my family. Callie mimics my mother and I in her great love of this state, the beauty she sees in it, her thirst for knowledge about it, and its history. She was raised by a loving family, who took the time to answer her endless questions, share with her the wonders of the cloud pictures in the sky, enjoy a sunrise over the mountains, the love of reading, the enjoyment and respect for all creatures large and small. So was I. My father Hayden's love of all history of this country added greatly to my knowledge of the Civil War.

My ancestral lineage in West Virginia has been traced to 1767 on my father's side when a Quaker minister settled with his flock in Braxton County. To my ancestors who chose this beautiful place where I was raised and call home once again, thank you.

LaVergne, TN USA
27 October 2010

202261LV00004B/7/P

9 781448 943579